PRODIGAL

J. V. SPEYER

For information contact:

Jessica Voloudakis
Writing as J. V. Speyer
138 Franklin Street, Braintree, MA 02184
857-212-6355
jvspeyer@gmail.com

Book and Cover design by Bad Doggie Designs
Edited by Quiethouse Editing
ISBN: 978-1-7355156-1-8

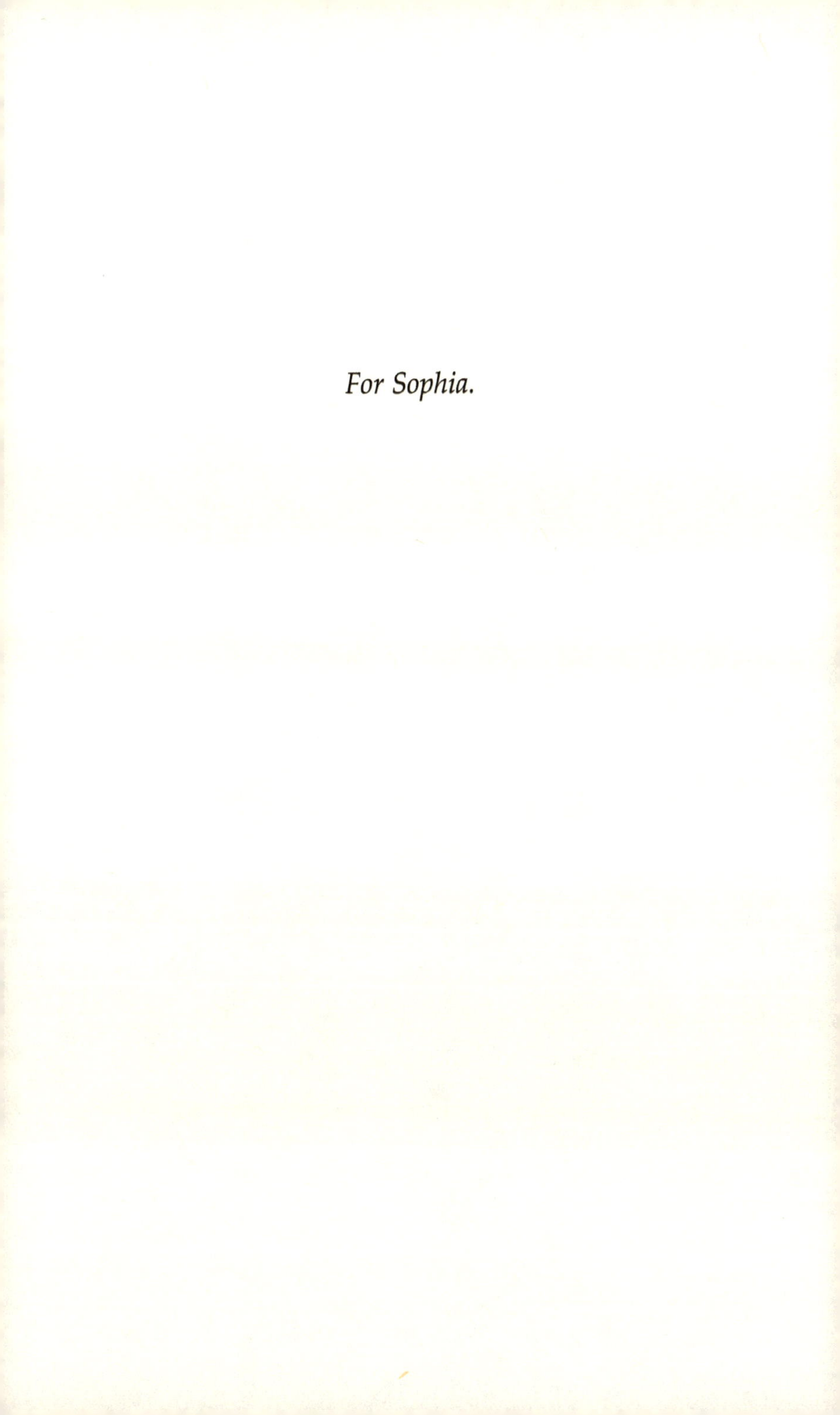

For Sophia.

CHAPTER ONE

Luis stretched his back as best he could in the cramped confines of the SUV's passenger seat. Sure, it was larger than a sedan would be. Anything would be cramped after four hours down mountain roads. "So. A killer who ties people to trees and waits for nature to take its course. I have to admit it's a new one on me." He and Kevin hadn't spoken since leaving Jay, Vermont, summer population five hundred and twenty-one whole people. Well, five hundred twenty now that Luis and Kevin had arrested Bob Rivard, forty-two, and sent him off to Newport to face trial.

Not that there was any doubt about the outcome. Luis and Kevin had caught Rivard watching some poor soul die, while masturbating. If Luis and Kevin's testimony wasn't enough, Rivard had been courteous enough to videotape himself in the act.

"Yeah." Kevin gripped the wheel a little tighter as they hurtled toward Chelsea.

It wouldn't be far now. They were almost there, so close to the finish line they could almost taste it. Of course, they both had long drives back to their respective homes. Kevin was probably thinking about that now. Traffic usually clogged up the road to Arlington no matter what time of day or night it might be. They could have gotten a hotel room for the night, but neither of them had wanted to stop.

"I don't suppose your fancy degrees have anything to offer on what's behind all that?"

Luis chuckled, but there wasn't any humor in it. "I wish. Yeah, no. My education did help figure out how to catch him, but not so much with the motivation. Other than sexual sadism and a deep sense of his own inferiority, I've got nothing. Which—he was the kind of guy who'd tie someone to a tree and record them dying, so I guess that sense of his own inferiority was justified."

"I just . . ." Kevin sucked in his cheeks for a second. "I don't understand how someone turns out like that. How someone goes from being an infant like any other to doing *that*. Stopping him, I get. It's our job, and we're fucking good at it, and I don't have any questions about that part at all. What I don't get is how Rivard went from point A to point B."

"If we knew, we could probably do

something to stop it." Luis shifted again, trying to alleviate some of the pressure on his ass. "Maybe. I mean we know people who were sexually abused as children are more likely to abuse others as adults, but most survivors *don't* go on to abuse and plenty of abusers weren't victims. We know head injuries in childhood may play a role, but plenty of people who've suffered head injuries don't go on to hurt others. Blah blah trauma, blah blah chemicals, blah blah whatever. There are tons of theories, but every last one of them can be debunked pretty quickly."

"There has to be a reason though." Kevin swerved to get around a Prius doing twenty miles below the speed limit. "It can't just be random."

Luis had passed beyond the stage where he thought there had to be a reason for some of the bizarre behaviors they found. "With some of them you can trace the specific influences—the combination of drugs, isolation, the exact ideology that guided their thinking and when they came in contact with it. With some, we never find out. And with some, I don't think I want to know."

Rivard was one of those suspects Luis didn't want to know the answers to. He could speculate. Rivard had grown up isolated in the Northeast Kingdom, the child of impoverished parents who made a virtue of necessity and went "back to the land." The land took care of everything for them. It was hardly a stretch to see where Rivard would expect the land to take care of people he saw as problems. Rivard could just as easily have been offering the land sacrifices in recompense.

"I guess at the end of the day, it's just a good thing we found him. Think they'll try an insanity defense?" Kevin took the Fourth Street exit faster than Luis would have ever considered trying. Somehow, the SUV stayed on the ground.

"They might. I can't wait to refute it. Dude knew right from wrong and went to great lengths to cover up his crimes. I think he's sick, and I don't think he'll get any better in prison, but he's a danger to anyone he meets and putting him into anything but the most secure setting risks him hurting everyone around him." Luis closed his eyes. He was no prison abolitionist—far from it. He knew prison wasn't even remotely rehabilitative for 90 percent of the people who went in, but that didn't mean killers and the like should be out doing their thing.

"Have you heard from your father?"

"No. But the warden at Cedar Junction called to tell me he got a little bit cut up. Apparently, he mouthed off to the wrong inmate. He gave almost as good as he got, and they both wound up in solitary for having shivs in the first place." Luis didn't bother to hide his disgust. "Donovan stopped me from putting money into the other guy's commissary account. They say it would look bad or something."

Kevin shook his head, but the corners of his mouth twitched with the beginnings of a smile. "Donovan's a good egg." He pulled into the parking lot at the FBI office and turned off the SUV. "Should we go inside and fill out our final reports?"

Luis shook his head. "It's late, it's been a long week, and I want to go home. We did preliminary reports before we left. They'll be enough until we get in tomorrow."

"You just want to see your guy and your cat." Kevin grinned. "I'll see you tomorrow."

Luis grabbed his laptop bag and suitcase from the back. "Bright and early," he agreed, and slipped into his waiting Honda. It was covered in a fine yellow film.

Wasn't pollen season supposed to be over already?

He shook his head and washed the windshield and back window. He'd forgotten about last summer, how the pollen seemed to spread until July. Everything in New England was weird and he still wasn't used to it, but it looked like he was going to have to deal with it. He owned a home here and everything. There was even a cat in it.

The thought of his town house, with his boyfriend and his cat, made him speed up as he headed back toward Burlington. He'd managed to focus while he was in Vermont, but now that the case was off his plate, they were all he could think about. This late at night, he only had a couple of traffic jams to deal with as he hurtled toward Burlington and the townhome development he and Donovan called home.

Who the hell was out driving around at eleven thirty at night, anyway, to make traffic jams in the first place? And why in the name of all that was holy did anyone think honking their horns was going to do anything about it?

The traffic jam doubled his commute. Fortunately, Donovan was still up when he got there, waiting for him. Tria sat in Luis' spot on the couch. She turned her back toward him, pretending to be mad at him for leaving. She'd get over it soon enough, but for now, she needed to demonstrate her disapprobation. Luis wouldn't have it any other way.

Donovan was more than happy to make up for any lack of warmth from Tria, anyway. He kissed Luis hard and deep, wrapping his arms around Luis' waist and holding tight. "Welcome home," he said as they both came up for air.

All the tension, all the horror Luis had carried since the first crime scene he'd been forced to see up in Jay, melted away. He rested his head on Donovan's broad shoulders. "You have no idea how glad I am to be here."

Donovan kissed the top of his head. "I can make an educated guess. The arrest made the national news. You hungry?"

"Nah, we got takeout before we left. Road food isn't the healthiest thing, but it sits on your stomach so you won't be hungry for the next ten days, so it all kind of evens out." Luis laughed and sat down on the couch.

Tria didn't quite climb into his lap, but she sat down close enough to touch his leg.

She still kept her back to him though.

"How you guys keep those physiques with that road food is beyond me." Donovan laughed and headed into the kitchen. He returned with two mugs of tea. He must have started the kettle when he heard Luis' car. "Must be nice. Your case is good?"

"Airtight." Luis nodded once and scratched Tria where she liked, right behind her ears. "The thing about guys in his category is that they always seem to want to keep a record of what they do, you know? It's part of the pathology. I understand why they do it, but it's actively detrimental—"

Donovan held up a hand. "Textbook says what?"

Luis blushed. "It just hurts them in the end. And they have to know it."

"We rarely meet the smart criminals." Donovan sat beside him and slung an arm around his shoulders. "She missed you, you know. I couldn't do your laundry. She was nesting in it. I didn't have the heart to take it away from her."

"Yeah, well, she's a sweetheart." Luis' heart swelled as he spoke. "I wish I could get away with bringing her along with me. Think I could pass her off as a forensic analyst?"

"I think she'd bite your suspects and open you up to a whole world of lawsuits. But hey, your choice."

Luis relaxed into Donovan's hold. "Clearly, you haven't seen Maxwell when he's in a mood. So you already know what I was working on all week. What can you tell me about your fun and games, Detective?"

Donovan groaned. "Oh, it's been super. Speaking of not meeting the smart criminals. We had an armed robber steal a delivery truck full of frozen chickens as a getaway vehicle. That was fun. You wouldn't think it would be state police jurisdiction, but then this guy goes screaming down the Pike and hurling frozen chickens at people's windshields as he tries to get away. I'm serious. Causes a fifteen-car pileup, and then he gets away somewhere around Lynn."

"And meanwhile, people are sitting there thinking, *How hard can it be to find the guy with the chicken truck?*" Luis knew the Boston media already.

"Right?" Donovan waved his free hand. "Meanwhile, everyone in his home neighborhood is cheering him on because, hey, screw the man or whatever, and causing a fifteen-car pileup on the Mass Pike is freaking *hilarious* when it's not *your* insurance going up, and now we've got to find a carjacker and armed robber named Sully in a town full of guys named Sully . . ."

Luis cringed in sympathy. Tria didn't care, just kneaded on the couch happily. "Have you caught him yet?"

"Oh yeah. Got him yesterday. There's already a hashtag for it. Free Sully. Can you believe it? There was a GoFundMe for his bail before we finished booking the bastard." He shook his head. "What can you do? It's Boston."

"It is." Luis managed a little grin. "And Boston's always going to be Boston, but at least you're here and part of it. You'll always be the best part of Boston. Even Sully can't take that away."

Donovan's pale cheeks turned a dusky pink. "Don't you say the sweetest things?"

Tria got up and plopped herself down in Luis' lap, as if reminding him she was part of Boston now too. He gave her the pets and cuddles she demanded as he soothed his boyfriend.

There had been other cases for Donovan. He hadn't spent a whole week working on a chicken thrower named Sully. No law enforcement unit could afford that kind of dedication to one case, especially without a body count. Donovan couldn't talk about most of his cases before they wrapped up, any more than Luis could talk about his. It was part of the downside of dating a detective, part of the reason so many cop relationships failed.

They put so much of themselves, their time, and their souls into their work, detectives more so than anyone else. They turned a case over in their minds even when they went home at night. Pressures of a case built up the longer a case went unsolved, and because they couldn't disclose any details, they couldn't get relief from that pressure. Luis had felt it a thousand times before, often enough that he'd stopped trying to have relationships and had settled for just sex.

Donovan was in the same boat, and while working for different agencies made some things more difficult, it eased the pressure in enough small ways to help. Donovan understood when Luis just needed a different perspective, and Luis could do the same thing for Donovan. Both of them knew all too well the horror of not getting there in time, all the people they couldn't save. They knew how to pull each other back from the brink, and it was enough.

Tonight, they finished their tea and went to bed together, laughing quietly at each other's jokes to distract from the shadows.

Donovan sent up a small prayer to any deities who might be listening. Whoever had invented the in-line water heater had clearly been a gift from heaven, to anyone who had to live with another human being. With the in-line water heater, Donovan didn't have to wait for the tank to fill and reheat before having his shower after Luis was done with his. He could admire Luis as he got dressed and then head into the bathroom and wash up while Luis headed to the office.

Showering with Luis would be more fun, but not something for a workday. And definitely not fun after Luis had been working out. Some guys had a sweat kink or whatever, but Donovan was definitely not among them.

He cleaned himself up, grabbed a quick breakfast and coffee, and then headed to his own office at headquarters in Framingham. He had a long day ahead of him, Friday or no, and it wasn't going to end any faster if he lallygagged.

Lallygagging. There was a Dad word if he ever heard one. Any time any one of the Carey kids didn't move fast enough for Fred, they were lallygagging. It didn't matter why they were slow. Sometimes, they really were dragging their heels or distracted. Sometimes they were sick or just too small to keep up with an athletic cop.

Negative associations aside, Donovan wanted to get through his work and get back home as soon as he could. Not that Luis had any particular reason to rush home. It was June, not any significant holiday or anything, and it was just a regular weekend. Donovan had been looking forward to spending some time alone together, maybe getting together with Alicia and Nicky. He understood the job would pull Luis away from home sometimes, often for gruesome reasons, and he was just glad to have him at home.

Major Crimes was, as always, a study in organized chaos. Some of the night shift detectives were finishing up for the day, while some of the day shift folks had gotten an early start. Everyone was on their phones, admin staff ran amok delivering paperwork, and every once in a while, uniformed officers would drag a suspect through to an interrogation room to add a little spice to the chaos. Someone from private industry walking in would probably wonder how anything ever got done in here.

Sometimes, Donovan had the same thought.

He found his way to his desk, which one of the night shift detectives had used to "temporarily" store files on, and put his coffee down. He relocated the files to a windowsill, logged into his workstation, and got to work.

Sully had made bail, a surprise to no one. Donovan wouldn't be shocked when he didn't show up for his next court appearance, but it was out of his hands now. The People had spoken, and now their favorite was out to rob and terrorize again. He called the teller and manager Sully had tied up and threatened, giving them the bad news. They weren't surprised either. They followed the news.

His other cases weren't in much better shape. At least no one could pretend Sully hadn't done it. He had a child rape case, worked with Abused Persons, in which the child's own family was pretending she was somehow at fault for her own victimization and Protective Services' hands were tied apparently. He had a murder on the verge of going cold, by virtue of the fact that no one cared enough about a homeless man in Cambridge to testify. And he had a serial arsonist in Maynard who seemed to be escalating without any clear motive or pattern to his crime.

He reached out to Protective Services. Surely, there must be something they could do to ensure this child's safety, if they all just thought outside the box a little bit. Yes, he knew the social workers were carrying a higher caseload than they were allowed to have. Yes, he knew foster care was an extreme option to be used only if there was no other way to keep the child safe. They had to have some way of helping this child who had been victimized, and saving other children.

The murder might be a lost cause. It burned at him because every human life had value. There was no way no one had seen a man killed in broad daylight. If it had been self-defense—unlikely, considering the victim's poor physical and mental condition—someone would have spoken up. The problem was, whoever had done it hadn't left any evidence behind. Maybe someday the killer would strike again and they'd find Donovan's victim's blood on this guy's clothes, but until then, Donovan was kind of stuck.

And that left the arsonist. There was absolutely no pattern to the person's crimes.

Donovan had to assume they were male because the vast majority of serial arsonists were. They struck occupied and abandoned buildings without differentiating between them. They hadn't killed anyone yet, but it was only a matter of time. They struck commercial buildings, residences, even churches. They'd struck St. Lucy's during Mass, and they'd torched an abandoned house with origins dating back to the War of 1812. They tended to use gasoline as an accelerant, but otherwise didn't seem to distinguish their crimes.

The only reason Donovan knew it was the same arsonist was the presence of the occasional security camera nearby. Every time, the camera had caught a fleeting glimpse of a medium-sized masculine figure in a threadbare brown coat. That was all. Forensics hadn't come away with much, thanks to the whole burning thing, and the fire investigator was on his ass to find the arsonist yesterday.

He massaged his temples. It would be *great* if the fire investigator would contribute to finding the arsonist instead of just complaining about it.

A shadow fell across Donovan's desk. He looked up to see Emerson Porras, another detective. Porras wasn't exactly a friend. He worked the night shift, and he and Donovan were friendly enough, but not more than that. Donovan hadn't had the opportunity to get to know him much better.

He wasn't a bad-looking guy. He stood about five eleven, white with a kind of light-tan note to his complexion, with brown hair in that messy hairstyle a lot of guys cultivated. Right now, Porras wore skinny dress pants with a dress shirt, almost like he was here to pick someone up and not solve cases. He could probably manage to do both at the same time if he put his mind to it.

"Hey, Carey. How's it going?" Porras plunked a cup of station coffee down on Donovan's desk. He had another one in his hand.

This was a friendly thing, then. Okay, Donovan supposed he could work with friendly.

"Not too bad, Porras. They got you putting in overtime, huh?" He sipped from the cup.

Porras had somehow figured out exactly how Donovan took his coffee. How odd.

"Yeah, well, you know. Killers don't care about shift changes, I guess. They found a body by the train tracks last night. We're waiting on the formal ID and cause of death, but it looks pretty clear-cut. Dude bled out from the legs after getting run over by the train. Not exactly homicide but . . ."

Donovan nodded in sympathy. "I've had a few of those. Gruesome stuff." Every suspicious or unattended death had to be investigated, even if the answer seemed obvious. "Hopefully, it'll be just what it looks like, and you can cross it off your board."

"Yeah. Didn't seem to be any other signs of foul play, but we'll see what Wong comes back with. Anyway, I saw you were here and figured I'd drop in and say hi." He glanced around and dropped his voice. "You know, this month is ten years since the riots in Government Center."

Donovan put his coffee down and blinked. "Is it? Christ, it doesn't seem like it's been that long at all." He rubbed at his jaw. "Who wants to celebrate that shit, you know? It was a mess all around."

"Oh, that's right, you were there." Porras half sat on Donovan's desk. "I don't know. I feel like we gave those folks what was coming to them. You throw shit at cops, we retaliate. That's all there is to it."

Donovan shrugged. He'd heard about people throwing things, even though projectiles hadn't made it into the official report. "No one was throwing anything where I was working. I had a couple of people trampled when folks started running, but that's it. I'm not saying it didn't happen, I just didn't see it where I was. Most of the folks around me were women and kids, you know?" He didn't want to think about it. The last image he needed in front of his eyes right now was a wall of people running, fleeing something he couldn't see while his radio squawked in the background.

"I remember hearing shots," he said quietly. "I didn't know where they even came from. I just focused on the job in front of me."

"Right." Porras nodded a couple of times. "I don't mind telling you, it was a real horror show. I was up near the guys from Boston PD back then. I was holding the line down near Faneuil Hall. A lot of brave cops out there that day. Of course, the media's all over it now. Screaming and yelling about racism and police brutality and all that nonsense."

Donovan pressed his lips together. The protesters out there that day had been protesting police brutality, and some of them had died for it. He didn't know what had sparked the riots. He'd been willing to give his brothers in blue the benefit of the doubt for a long time, but over the past few years, he'd learned not all of them deserved it.

After all, his dad was one of the most racist people he knew, and Fred had been a cop too.

Porras reached for his phone. "Check this out." He pulled up an article and passed the phone to Donovan. "Can you believe this shit?"

Donovan scanned the screen. " 'Ten Years

18

On, the Government Center Riot Leaves a Bitter Legacy of Brutality and Racism.' Yeah, okay. Everyone's questioning the cops right now because some cops got caught doing some super shady stuff. I wish it could be different, and it sure as hell makes our jobs harder, but I can't blame anyone for looking at us a little more critically, you know? I mean they caught cops planting drugs and guns on people they killed, man. In more than one town." He sighed and shook his head. "It only makes sense to ask questions, and sometimes, we're going to look bad when the answers come back." He passed the phone back. "All we can do is try to be as clean as we can be going forward. I don't see any other way, you know?"

Porras rolled his eyes. "Come on, bro. One or two bad apples doesn't mean we're all a bunch of racist cowards."

"No, it doesn't. But we do need to stop covering for the ones who are." Donovan grinned. "Hey, I know I'm clean. Isn't that what we tell suspects all the time? If you're innocent, you've got nothing to hide?"

Porras smirked. "Yeah, you're right. It is. And I know I'm cleaner than a hospital OR."

"That's good." Donovan didn't take a whole lot of time to reflect on what a bizarre statement that had been to make. He had an arsonist to catch.

"I know it was a tough day for a lot of people, both us and them, you know?"

"That it was. I just hope the anniversary doesn't bring up a lot of shit that should have stayed buried." Porras checked his phone. "Hey, that's Wong. I've got an ID on Train Guy. Now for the fun part—family notification."

Donovan winced in sympathy. "Good luck."

"See ya." Porras disappeared.

Donovan sipped from the coffee Porras had brought him and contemplated the arsonist file again. Then he brought up a map of Maynard. Maybe if he plotted out the arson sites on the map, he'd find a pattern.

Two hours and a lot of swearing later, he had a pattern. All the fires had taken place within a one-and-a-half-mile radius of one house, and that house held a young man who fit the profile of a serial arsonist to a *T*. Donovan knew that because Luis had explained the profile of the "typical" serial arsonist to him one evening while they'd made dinner together.

First, Donovan was going to go out to Maynard and talk to this young man. Then, with any luck, he could go home to Luis with a win under his belt.

CHAPTER TWO

Luis stared at his computer screen. Paperwork didn't bother him, most of the time. He didn't necessarily like it, but he understood why it had to be done. It was part of the job and created a paper trail in case of disputes later on. Hell, anything could happen. If Luis got killed or fired or suffered a head injury and forgot pretty much everything, it should be possible to recreate everything he'd done to close the case.

This case from Vermont though—it defied forms, and it defied description. He couldn't divorce his disgust in the killer, or in his methods, from his words. He stretched his fingers and erased the vitriol he'd just typed into Form 87-B. Then he tried again.

Agent Rourke and I traced the suspect back to a remote cabin. We found the suspect engaged in a solo sex act while viewing the looped video we'd patched in of Victim Johann Doe (see evidence video 3643-1). We donned nitrile gloves before making the arrest to avoid

He stared at the words on the screen. They didn't convey the full horror of what he'd seen in that cabin. Was that cheating? Was that letting Rivard off easy somehow?

He turned his gaze back to the screen.

PROFILER SECTION: Explain the suspect's pathology.

Jesus Christ, how was he supposed to explain this guy's pathology? It wasn't like he'd sat down to interview Rivard. Maybe someday he would have the opportunity. Maybe someday, years from now, he'd even want to.

He took a deep breath and started typing. *With the limitations imposed by circumstance, it's difficult to arrive at an accurate diagnosis for Rivard. He has never received even cursory mental health care and his physical health records are scant at best. He is the product of extreme poverty and, like many in the Northeast Kingdom region, prides himself on his self-reliance. He resents any display of wealth. His victims all come from higher socioeconomic statuses, but this does not narrow down the victim pool.*

He stared at the screen again.

There are some indications of butchery, but they

are old. Rivard did not kill from hunger. Rivard killed for entertainment. Again, within the limitations of circumstances, he is a sexual sadist who doesn't need to be physically near his victims to achieve his release. He is aware that what he does is wrong. He simply does not care.

He checked quickly for typographical errors and hit send. Then he fled to the men's room so he could wash his hands. Even remembering that case, the scene he'd walked into, made him feel filthy. He never wanted to think about it again.

No one said anything. They'd all had cases like that.

When he got back, Brick Fontana was dropping a copy of the local tabloid paper onto Kevin's desk. The cover had a photo of some kind of riot; Luis didn't recognize it. He thought he recognized Government Center though. The headline, in giant screaming bold letters, proclaimed the riot to have been "TEN YEARS AGO."

"You remember this, Kev?" Fontana slurped from his coffee. "What a clusterfuck."

Kevin sighed and picked up the paper with the barest tips of his fingers, like it was a dead mouse. "Yeah, I remember. *Clusterfuck* doesn't even begin to describe it. Hey, Luis, did this make the news down in Miami or no?"

Ten years ago, Luis had been finishing up his master's degree and working Vice. Riots in Boston had been the furthest thing from his problem. "They all kind of ran together. Refresh my memory. Was this the one when your team won the Super Bowl, or when they lost it, or was this the baseball one?"

Borchard and Wragge, the other two members of the team, had taken an interest.

"Cute." Wragge flipped him off, but without heat. "I'll have you know sports riots are an important part of Boston's cultural tradition."

"Riots in general are an important part of Boston tradition." Kevin snorted. "We get a little grumpy and immediately start throwing bricks. It's like Southerners saying y'all. This one was about police brutality though. Guards at one of the prisons had beaten a man to death, and people protested. Like you do."

Luis nodded. "Okay. There was a lot of that going around for a while. I'm not going to pretend it didn't draw some attention to some shady practices."

"It did," Kevin said after a second, while Borchard looked away and toyed with a pen on Kevin's desk. "You're not wrong. Anyway, this was a planned protest with a permit and everything. I'm not sure what went wrong. Cops blamed Antifa, who weren't a prominent force at the time but were still running around. Protesters blamed cops, media blamed protesters and 'outside agitators.' Whatever. It got messy in a hurry and a bunch of people got killed. Like, five."

Luis frowned. That was a special number in Bostonian riot history. "Let me guess, they started calling it the next Boston Massacre?"

"How could they not?" Wragge snorted and shook his head. "I was in New York at the time. I wasn't here. Boston had a thing where they called in the state troopers and the National Guard, it was a real mess. At least that's how it looked from outside."

Luis nodded slowly. He didn't care about a riot ten years ago. He cared about police brutality, and most of these police brutality protests had their roots in race issues. Luis knew more about those than he wanted to think about right now, but it had been ten years ago. He doubted his colleagues wanted his professional opinion, or his opinion as a person of color. They just wanted to remember.

The door to SSA Holcombe's office swung open. The agents' boss had a small wrinkle in the middle of her forehead, one that hadn't been there this morning. Luis almost cheered when he saw her because she was breaking up an awkward moment, but the wrinkle stopped him. Whatever she was coming to say or do couldn't be good.

"Gomes, Rourke, in here please."

Luis ignored the pit in his stomach. It was just anxiety, trying to make itself heard. He was doing a thousand times better with his issues now that his father would never see the light of day again, but anxiety was a chronic disorder. It wouldn't ever go away. Luis had to accept that, but he was a professional. He could differentiate between anxiety's lies and reality. At least, he could make that distinction most of the time.

Kevin closed the door behind himself, and they sat down in front of Holcombe's desk.

She closed her eyes for a long moment and slumped. "I know the two of you just got back from a challenging trip."

Kevin managed a quirky little grin. "I don't know. Vermont's not so bad this time of year. Even Luis here didn't complain too much, since there wasn't snow or ice."

Luis huffed out a little laugh. "You realize it was basically as cold as our winters back in Florida."

"Still, not the—what was it you called it back in January? Cursed wasteland of slush and pain?"

Holcombe's grin almost looked genuine. "I'm glad things are looking up. Agent Gomes, how much do you know about the Government

Center Riot of ten years ago?"

Hair on the back of Luis' neck stood up. "Only what I've been told, ma'am. And that not two minutes ago. I have the feeling I'm going to be learning a lot more about it though."

"Everyone tells me you're a genius." Holcombe's grin disappeared. "Lawsuits have been winding their way through courts for a decade—and well they should. There was no concrete plan. Police panicked. There was no reason for anyone to die that day. I completely understand when we have to kill dangerous suspects in the heat of an actual confrontation, but this was a peaceful protest.

"The FBI has been waiting, ready to provide assistance if asked in finding out what started things off ten years ago. Up until now, no one's asked because nongovernment agencies can't really make the request and police agencies aren't going to invite us in to make them look bad. That changed today."

Luis glanced at Kevin, who glanced at Luis. At least Luis wasn't alone in his trepidation here.

"What exactly changed?" Kevin leaned forward. "As I recall, the staties and Boston PD have been passing blame back and forth quite happily for years."

"They have. Yesterday, Boston PD arrested

a man by the name of Jason Harper for felony possession of heroin with intent to distribute. Harper's lawyer dropped a bombshell today. In exchange for reduced charges, to include no jail time, Harper will reveal the name of the person who fired the first shot."

She passed a file folder across the table to both of them. Kevin flipped through it, wrinkled his nose, and passed it to Luis.

Luis understood Kevin's facial expression right away. "Any lawyer worth their degree would challenge this witness' credibility in a heartbeat. *I'm* challenging this guy's credibility. He's doing it to avoid jail, he's got a rap sheet longer than my leg, and that rap sheet includes convictions for impersonating an officer and aggravated assault." He shook his head. "Why are we giving this guy the time of day?"

Holcombe sighed and massaged her temples. "One, because he's offering something up at a time when people are already coming to Boston to stir things up in 'honor' of the victims of the riot. We've got a whole host of nationally prominent activists coming here to lead marches, rallies, and whatever in the name of justice. So this was already on our radar.

"Two, the lawyer went to the media with the offer. This ties everyone's hands. If they don't take the offer, they're denying justice to the victims. If they take it, they're letting a drug dealer back out onto the streets.

"Three, the person he's naming is Donovan Carey."

The whole world went far away. Luis heard Kevin the way he heard people from underwater. He made himself laugh. "You're joking. You can't be taking him seriously."

Kevin put a hand between Luis' shoulder blades, and the room came back into focus again. "Well, I know Donovan *now* is pretty cool. But ten years ago, who knows? And he does come from a family with certain . . . er, quirks. Especially the dad."

"Donovan lived with *me* for four years." Luis glowered at Kevin, as if he could cut through Kevin's arguments. "He's not going to go taking potshots at protesters."

"It doesn't have to mean he was doing it for racial reasons. He wasn't ever trained for crowd control." Holcombe sat up a little straighter. "It's not uncommon for young officers in his position to panic. It wouldn't take away from all the good that he's done since then."

"Except for the fact that we have nothing but some jackass gang member's word to go on." Luis set his jaw.

"That's why I called the two of you in. We've been formally asked to become involved by the Department of Justice Hate Crimes Division. Ordinarily, I'd want you as far away from the case as possible, Luis. You're dating the suspect—you're living with him. But the Hate Crimes Division was very specific about including you, and I honestly think you're the best one for the job. You'll be able to handle the evidence with respect and with a truly neutral eye. I trust you two to get this done."

Luis bit down on the inside of his cheek. He wouldn't lash out, even though he knew exactly why he'd been *specifically requested*. Putting a brown guy—one of the few in the FBI, never mind the Boston office—made everything look nice and tidy. No one could accuse law enforcement of bias if they had a cop of color on the case, no matter who was really calling the shots.

He had to get himself removed, before he set fire to his career and possibly the office. "You know I can't hide it from him. He's going to know. If nothing else, I'll be poking around in his stuff and asking his friends and family a lot of weird questions."

"I'm not asking you to. He'll know he's under investigation, and he's too smart to go after Harper." Holcombe looked away, and for a second, she looked impossibly old. Then she straightened up. "It's not fair to you to expect you to be part of this investigation, Luis. Nevertheless, the request came from above me, so here we are. I trust you to do the job and do it well, wherever it leads. For what it's worth, I hope Harper's lying."

Kevin rose, and Luis followed suit without thinking. "We'll keep you updated."

"Please do."

Luis' mind spun out of control as he followed his partner back down into the bull pen. As he staggered back to his desk, his phone buzzed with an incoming message.

He hadn't seen the number in a while, but that didn't make it unwelcome. Dwayne Mason had been a partner back in graduate school. They'd parted as friends, and Luis could use one of those right about now.

Hey, L. Just got into Boston. Stuff is up and we need to talk.

Luis rubbed at his jaw. *It'll be good to see you. I might need to bend your ear about something work-related, even though I know it gives you hives. You free this afternoon?*

Donovan warred between rage and disbelief as he sped home toward Burlington. He couldn't bring himself to believe what Lt. Power had just told him. Some pissant little con—convicted drug dealer, among other things—had accused Donovan of firing the first shots during the Government Center Riots. He couldn't understand how anyone could possibly believe Jason Harper—who'd impersonated a police officer in order to get access to an apartment and beat eighteen kinds of shit out of someone who owed him drug money—over him.

Oh, and the FBI was investigating. Joy.

He hadn't been suspended—yet. It was that *yet* that was eating at him. Donovan knew exactly what he'd done that day. He'd defended injured people from being trampled. He'd provided first aid. He had done nothing else, and he certainly hadn't raised a hand to anyone.

The FBI could investigate all they wanted. The people wanted a scapegoat, and someone had given them Donovan.

He threw the car into its parking space with more force than necessary and slammed on the brakes. Cars weren't living things, but he thought he heard a sigh of relief when he killed the ignition and slammed the door before heading into the town house.

Luis, shock of all shocks, was home already. Donovan would have been happier about that if Luis were home alone. He needed the comfort of his partner right now, not company.

Instead, he had to see his boyfriend sitting in their living room across from a tall, handsome Black man in skinny jeans and a loose white henley. Donovan thought he might have seen the man before, something about his wide, intense eyes looked familiar, but he couldn't quite place him.

"Luis," he said, putting a jovial face on. "You didn't tell me we were having company."

Both Luis and the other guy stood up.

Luis stepped forward and gave Donovan a hug. "Hey. It's good to see you." He kissed Donovan's cheek. "Donovan, this is Dr. Dwayne Mason. He teaches history at William and Mary. Dwayne, this is my partner, Donovan Carey."

Dwayne held out a hand and smiled, but the smile didn't reach his eyes. They seemed to be evaluating Donovan, weighing something. "The man of the hour. I'm pleased to meet you. I never did think Luis would settle down."

Donovan held back a groan. *Another ex.*

It didn't make sense to be jealous, and he knew it was just a symptom of his personal insecurity. Still, he didn't need to face his own shortcomings on top of everything else today. "It was kind of a surprise to us too. Can I get you anything?"

"I'm good, thanks. Luis invited me over for professional reasons actually." Dwayne's smile retreated a little, still professional and polite, but not as big.

Donovan glanced at Luis. "Serial killers based on history again?"

"Again?" Dwayne did a double take. "You're going to have to fill me in on that one. It sounds like a trip."

Luis made a face. "Oh, it was a trip all right. This guy was fixated on a serial killer from the early nineteenth century and decided to go and try to one-up him." He waved his hand. "I should've called you once it was over just because you'd have gotten a kick out of the historical aspect of it, but I was a little out of it after the arrest."

"Because you were shot." Donovan nudged Luis with his shoulder.

Dwayne shook his head. "Now see, if you'd gone into academia like a sensible person it probably wouldn't have happened like that. We almost never get shot."

"True. But the killer would still be out there, so." Luis grinned at him, like it was an old dispute between them.

The penny dropped for Donovan. "Dr.

Mason—you're that guy from TV, the one who hates cops." He blushed as he realized how he sounded, but he couldn't un-say the words.

It didn't seem to bother Dwayne at all. "I'll admit I'm not exactly the Police Benevolent Association's top fundraiser. I'm not going to try to convince you of my reasons though—not in your own home." He chuckled. "So Luis tells me someone's made an accusation about the Government Center Riots."

Donovan turned to Luis. "Do FBI agents gossip like high schoolers or something?"

Luis grimaced. "Well, yes, but you knew that. That's not why the subject came up." He swallowed hard, his Adam's apple bobbing. "Kevin and I got the case."

Donovan fell down onto the couch. Maybe it rose up to meet him as the rest of the world collapsed away. "That's a huge conflict of interest."

"I said the same thing." Dwayne smirked. "So did he. And his boss. But apparently, the orders came from pretty high up, so it is what it is. We do what we can with what we have. Luis tells me the man who made the accusation has some credibility issues."

"Dude's a convicted piece of crap. Impersonated a cop to beat someone almost to death." Donovan shuddered. "I get that people have perfectly valid reasons not to trust us. I come at some of those reasons from the other side sometimes, but I understand where people are coming from."

Dwayne snorted. "Do you really? I mean you're a lifelong cop, your family is cops for multiple generations on both sides. Do you really understand why some folks can never feel comfortable around you?"

Donovan rolled his eyes. "Not on a visceral level, no. But I'm also not going to sit here and pretend I don't see what's happening. I'm not going to tell people to ignore their own lived experience. Can we get back to this Harper guy? I don't blame people for not trusting us for valid reasons. Guys like Harper make people not trust us for some pretty bullshit reasons, and that pisses me off. Hate us for the things we do, not the things other people do."

Luis blinked. "That was kind of convoluted, but I guess it made sense."

Dwayne shrugged. "Fair enough. But here's the thing. Even people who do bad things have rights, and even people who do bad things can see things and tell the truth."

Sweat broke out on Donovan's scalp. "I wasn't anywhere near the shooting. I heard shots, sure. I was farther away from the gunfire, between

Government Center and the State House. When shots were fired, I pulled some people out of the stampede because they were hurt and being trampled. That's about all I did."

"What does Harper get from lying?" Dwayne tapped his fingers on the coffee table.

"Other than a get-out-of-jail-free card?" Donovan scoffed, not bothering to hide his bitterness.

"Yeah, other than that." Luis sighed. "The thing is, he didn't just claim *some cop* shot people. He claimed *you* shot people, by name. What does he get from that, and why would he name you if it weren't true?"

Donovan rounded on Luis. "You can't actually believe I'd do something like this."

"The Donovan I know wouldn't shoot someone unless he had to." Luis met his eyes, without flinching. His dark eyes were wide and sincere. "I have to consider all of the evidence with an open mind. One possibility is that you actually did it. Another possibility is that Harper is lying. If he's lying, there's a reason. What's the reason, and why *you*? Have you ever encountered this guy before, either on a case or in a traffic stop?"

Donovan rubbed his face with his hands. His head understood why Luis was responding this way. His heart proclaimed it to be bullshit.

"No. The name isn't familiar. It's kind of generic, but when I looked through his record, it didn't come up with my name associated anywhere near it. We never encountered each other."

He closed his eyes for a second, and then looked back at Luis. "Look, there's cameras all over that area. You must be able to see some proof I didn't even pull my gun that day."

"Hours of footage proved inconclusive at the time." Luis grimaced. "We've got techs in Quantico looking through it now, but I don't have a lot of hope for video. If we can find photographic evidence—say from a journalist—putting you where you say you were, that would be helpful."

"Because that's not like looking for a needle in a haystack." Donovan stalked off toward the kitchen. He needed a beer. "Hey, Dwayne, you want a beer?"

Dwayne blinked in surprise. "Sure, if you're offering."

"Luis isn't a drinker, but this is quite possibly one of the worst two days of my life. The other one being the day this guy got shot. So—yeah, I'm going to have a beer. If you'll have one with me, that would be great." He brought back two open bottles and passed one to Dwayne.

Dwayne still looked surprised, but accepted the offering. "You have to know, I'm still not a hundred percent sold on your innocence. I'm not convinced you're guilty, but—well, the jury's out."

"That's fine." Donovan took a long swig of his beer. "I can't hold that against you. We don't really know each other."

"And I can't work out a motivation for Harper to lie. Not about someone specific." Dwayne toyed with his bottle. "I can understand why he'd lie to stay out of jail. That's a normal impulse. But bringing in a specific cop, when that cop has a lot of cop family and cop friends who could make life extremely difficult for him—that's dumb if it's not true."

"We never meet the smart criminals." Donovan studied Dwayne's face. "Luis does, sometimes. Not guys on my watch."

Dwayne chuckled. "No, I suppose the smartest don't get caught. If you can't convince me, you're not going to convince a jury. Not that juries care if a cop is guilty or not. It's almost unheard of for a cop to get sent up for murder."

Luis winced. "It is, but there's a lot of pressure to close this case. It makes everyone look bad, and Massachusetts likes to think of itself as not like those other states. If they can show they held someone accountable for what happened, they can prove they're better."

Dwayne rolled his eyes up to the ceiling. "As

if. No, I get it. And I'll admit that gives me some cause for concern. The way his lawyer went straight to the media looks like accountability, but in reality, it can also be just setting someone up for a fall. That someone being you, Donovan."

Donovan didn't need to be reminded. "So why did Luis bring you in, again?"

Luis put a hand on Donovan's back, and some of Donovan's jealousy faded. It would always be a little bit of an issue for him, just because he'd missed out on so much.

"I found out he was in Boston, and since police brutality is kind of a specialty for Dwayne, I asked if we could get together and talk after I got assigned to the case. As it turns out, he was here for the protest ten years ago, and he's here for the anniversary now. So he's got some good insight I couldn't have had because I wasn't here and wouldn't have known any of the players."

"I'm not selling anyone out." Dwayne's eyes bored into Donovan's. "I'm concerned about a lot of this. I'm not going to be part of a cover-up, and I'm not going to be part of railroading anyone either. That said, if I hear anything or if I come up with any relevant information in either direction, I'm happy to pass it on."

"It's all I can ask for." Luis smiled. "I appreciate it."

"No problem." Dwayne drained his beer and stood up. "I'll give you two some privacy. I'm sure you have a lot to talk about with that bombshell you got today. Give me a call, Luis. We'll grab lunch."

Luis escorted Dwayne out and returned after only a few moments. Then he pulled Donovan in close and held him, without words.

"You don't really believe I killed people back then, do you?" Donovan asked after a long few moments.

Luis was quiet for a second. "I have to be open to new information. I'd sure as hell be surprised to find out you'd done it. It's not like you, even in a crisis situation, but anything's possible." He licked his lips. "I didn't ask for this assignment."

"I know you didn't." Donovan sighed. "And I know you'll follow wherever the evidence leads you. I guess I'm just worried about where that evidence comes from. I mean, if this jackass Harper pulled my name from somewhere, and people will believe it enough to sic you on me, what else will they find and believe?"

CHAPTER THREE

Luis jumped when someone dropped a book onto his desk. He looked up to see Kevin smirking down at him.

"Long night?" Kevin raised an eyebrow at him.

Luis couldn't tell if Kevin was trying to imply something, or was joking about trying to imply something, and ultimately, he was too tired to figure it out.

Luis ran a hand over his face and picked up the book. *Boston Riots.* Apparently, this town was just a powder keg, always ready to go off. They even wrote books about it. "Not in the fun way. This is a mess. I'm one hundred percent the last person to be poking into this, and everyone knows it."

Kevin shrugged and pulled his chair over. "You're not wrong. Apparently, some decision maker had strong feelings to the contrary. Not sure what to say about that, except we do the job in front of us. I know you're capable. You probably started work before you left the office last night."

"I did. I heard from an old friend and pulled him in to ask questions about the protest that started it all. He's trustworthy. Anyway, the big sticking point is the accuser. He's got plenty of incentive to lie, but why lie about Donovan specifically? I mean, why choose him, out of everyone? Was this guy even there, and can we prove it?"

"Or disprove it." Kevin rested his chin on his hand. "We need to head down to the site, I think."

Luis turned his chair to look more fully at Kevin. "For real?"

"Yeah. You've been there before, but not in this context. We've got statements from officers on the ground at the time. We've got ballistic evidence, or at least some of it. The police union intervened and wouldn't allow testing of the bullets to individual officers' guns."

Luis rolled his eyes. "Of course not." He sighed. "You're right. I kind of know the area because we used to have offices near there, but I haven't looked at it like a crime scene. It's hardly the first cold case I've worked. I need to step outside of this and work it like any other."

"Good man." Kevin clapped him on the shoulder, and they headed out toward the fleet of government SUVs.

Kevin waited until they were in the car before checking in about Donovan. "So how's he taking it?"

"About as well as can be expected. He insists he was never near any of the shooting. I mostly believe him, but Dwayne's right—why would this Harper guy pull his name out of a hat? It doesn't make sense. Either Donovan's lying, for whatever reason, or there's something else going on that goes beyond what we're seeing. Either way, we're going to have to dig deep to find it out." He rested his head against the window. He should believe Donovan, but he had a job to do.

"And, either way, it's probably going to be a disaster for Donovan." Kevin grimaced. "Yeah, I don't see it going well either way, I guess. Have you heard from the family?"

"Not yet. It's going to be a fun conversation no matter how it plays out, I'm sure. Maybe Fred will resurface, won't that be a delight?" Luis sat up a little straighter.

Kevin winced. "I'm sure Donovan knows better than to give his father the time of day. It's not like Fred showed up when little Pat was born."

"No, he didn't. He couldn't. The mom took out a restraining order after Fred got aggressive. That . . . well, it takes a lot. But we'll see where the investigation takes us. We might not be able to get detailed ballistics reports, but we should be able to get deployment records." He closed his eyes. "I can't be the one to arrest him if he is the one who started it all."

Kevin squirmed. "They're not going to actually arrest him. They might fire him, but they wouldn't arrest him. The union wouldn't stand for it, not under those circumstances. A young cop in a panic situation? Sure, it's not good for him to panic but it's not illegal either."

Luis bit his tongue. A cop who panicked at the sight of people protesting injustice shouldn't have a badge or a gun. This was Donovan though. Donovan wouldn't panic in that kind of situation, so if he'd been the one to start things off, it wouldn't have been from panic. They'd been apart for a few years by that point, but he was still the same man Luis had loved.

Government Center, which lay between Beacon Hill and Faneuil Hall, was an ugly place. It was a masterpiece of brutalist architecture, a little piece of Stalin's Russia dropped into the middle of all the colonial and Victorian buildings of Boston like a syphilitic pustule. "This place makes the eyes burn every time I see it." Luis shuddered.

Kevin chuckled. "It's supposed to. It's intended to symbolize the strong fist of the government smashing parts of the city it doesn't like. Once upon a time, this wasn't Government Center. It was Scollay Square—Boston's red-light district."

Luis could follow the logic. It was grotesque, but he understood. "We don't like what's going on here, so we're just going to tear everything down and drop something hideous on top of it. Fair enough." He shook his head and tried not to watch as a partially skeletal man in colonial attire walked through the glass wall of a modern bank, tugging at his belt. "I guess it was like that for a while."

"Yeah, you could say that. Kind of scandalous, considering that's Beacon Hill right up there." Kevin pointed. "Beacon Hill with the State House, churches, etcetera. Finish up with a day of legislating, help yourself to a few beers, and enjoy yourself with the locals." He shook his head. "It was probably worse before they built the State House and actually held legislative sessions in taverns, but whatever."

Luis didn't know what to say to that. "Fucking Boston. I've never been in a drunker city."

"And don't you forget it." Kevin grinned at him. "Okay. So the march started on the Common and cut through the park over to the State House. Up to this point, everything is peaceful, if somewhat loud."

Luis nodded, although Kevin only had part of his attention. A pair of ghosts loitered against modern brick walls as Kevin spoke, listening with apparent interest. Both had probably been white, and they looked to be on the young side. If Luis had to guess, they'd probably died sometime around a century ago, although he wasn't exactly a costumer and couldn't be sure.

"After they shouted at an empty State House for a while, they turned down Beacon and marched toward Tremont and Government Center. This is where stories differ. According to official Boston Police accounts, a protester threw a bottle of unidentified liquid at an officer assigned to crowd control. According to accounts from protesters, a cop accused a protester of giving him 'lip' and hit him with his nightstick. Either way, the ensuing panic was very real, and now the marchers started running." Kevin kept speaking, because he couldn't see the ghosts.

"The first fatality, Dorcas Flannigan, was shot right where you're standing." Kevin pointed to the ground under Luis' feet. Someone had placed a fresh memorial there, if a temporary one. "She was sixty-two and witnesses say she was trying to stop a riot cop from shooting a young teen."

Luis sucked in his cheeks. *What a way to go.* "Donovan claims he was several blocks away, on Somerset by the Garden of Peace Memorial." He glanced over at the ghosts again, who seemed indifferent. Their discussion was entertainment for the dead. "A young, fit guy could run, I suppose. It's not likely, but it's not unheard of either. We need to find witnesses and confirm his alibi."

"Which, of course, no one thought to do at the time because it wasn't important." Kevin sighed. "There should be hospital or EMS records of people treated for trampling injuries in that area though. It's a place to start."

"Right. Hey, Kev, Bostonians do the riot thing a lot, right?"

"Yeah, kind of. It's the weather. It makes us cranky. Why?"

Luis glanced back at the ghosts. "Were there other riots . . . er, right here?"

"I did just give you a book."

"Right, but you *just* gave me the book. You didn't give me time to read it."

Kevin widened his eyes. "And we have company?" He frowned. "Usually don't they smell kind of bad?"

"This whole area kind of smells bad." He wrinkled his nose.

"Valid. Um, yeah. In 1919, the whole Boston

Police Department went on strike. It was a whole thing. They pushed the State Guard—which was like the National Guard—into service, they gave guns and badges to a bunch of Harvard kids and told them they were *even more* special and important—it was a mess." Kevin curled his lip, a gesture that was mirrored by one of the ghosts.

Which was difficult to do when half the lip was rotted away, but the ghost managed.

"There were a bunch of fatalities all over town, but mostly right here. Only one person *wasn't* killed by the State Guard, and that was a striking police officer who disarmed two state guardsmen with his bare hands before being shot by an auto parts dealer." Kevin sighed. "Like I said, it was an unholy mess. A lot of people saw the strike as a reason to ignore laws, and a lot of guardsmen saw the strike as an excuse to make every offense a capital offense. One guy was killed for refusing to leave a craps game."

One of the ghosts wheezed out a laugh and held out a pair of dice in his skeletal hands. The rattle as he shook them echoed from the buildings, loud enough for even a couple of passersby to pause.

"I think we might have found a couple of special witnesses." Luis didn't want to deal with ghosts right now, and he definitely didn't feel up to trying to explain *special witnesses* to SSA Holcombe. He'd had enough trouble trying to explain his injuries after a ghost tried to drown him on a human trafficking case. "I'm going to duck down this alley."

Kevin paled but otherwise took Luis' announcement in stride. "Try not to die."

"Thanks." Luis slipped into a narrow alley behind one of the less ghastly, modern buildings. He didn't have to look to know the dead were following him. Their scent gave them away, even with the protective cover of the general odor of the area.

The alley revealed the modern brick to be either a replacement for something that had come before or a mere facade. The paving back here was nothing more than cobblestones, and those indifferently maintained at best. The stink from a dumpster, which seemed to hold mostly old dairy products, partially masked the corpse stench.

The two ghosts exchanged glances, and then the one with the dice nodded at Luis. "Henry Groat."

"Luis Gomes. FBI." He steeled himself and shook the dead man's hand. Then he reached for the other's.

It seemed to surprise him, but the ghost introduced himself anyway. "Robert Lallie.

What're you doing poking around here, anyway? There ain't been a killing around here in a good while. Ten years, anyway."

"I know." Luis wondered if he'd ever get his hand warm again. "I'm looking into that one. Someone's lying about it, and we're trying to figure out who."

"Ten years on, why would anyone lie about it?" Groat scoffed and toyed with his dice. "Don't they got anything better to do?"

Luis chuckled. "Apparently not. You both were killed in a riot too, weren't you?"

"Yeah, a bunch of bloodthirsty Huns." Lallie shook his fist toward Beacon Hill. "I got no love for the police, but when they send soldiers out to do police work nothing good can ever come from it."

"Got that right." Luis let out a breath and tried to breathe through his mouth. "Were you around to see what happened ten years ago?"

"Some of it." Groat shrugged. "It didn't make any real impressions. I'm sure it makes us sound like bad people to you, but the way things are for us it just kind of all runs together. There's always people around, and you don't know to pay attention until things are already happening. It's like you're just kind of drifting along, watching some new automobile drive itself down the street wondering what they'll think of next, and then

52

bam! There's gunfire. You didn't know to be looking for it."

Luis managed a little grin. "Yeah, not much different from being among the living, I guess."

"Exactly." Lallie huffed out a little laugh. "Those state guardsmen are the ones lying though. I don't need to have seen anything to know that. They lie just as easy as breathing."

Luis' heart sank. The ghosts weren't going to be able to help at all. Maybe they could help at some point down the road, but for now Luis didn't know enough to ask the right questions. "Thanks for your time, gentlemen."

He returned to Kevin. "We're on our own."

Donovan gagged and pulled away from the vehicle. The stench of overcooked pork filled the air. The death looked self-inflicted. The victim had left a note, sent via email not long before his car was spotted on fire in the parking lot of the abandoned nightclub in a no-man's-land along Route 2. Personally, Donovan doubted Wong would be able to get much from the remains, but he wasn't about to say so. Maybe there was some evidence that could survive this kind of inferno or the means firefighters had to use to put it out.

In the meantime, Donovan would have to treat it like any other homicide, until proven otherwise. Lord knew it wouldn't be the first time a death had been staged to look like something it wasn't.

"I hope you didn't contaminate anything." Wong sniffed down at him as Donovan doubled over, walking away from the car. "I won't have my results being called into question because of you."

Donovan counted to ten. "Wouldn't dream of it, Doctor. I understand the remains are extremely delicate under these circumstances?"

Wong blinked at him, like Donovan had just spoken another language. "Well, yes, of course. You have ash, and the bones—"

"Thank you, Doctor. I know you'll get me the results just as soon as you're finished." Donovan gave him a bland smile and walked away as quickly as he could.

He was trying a new tactic with the nasty doctor. He knew it could easily backfire, but for now, confusing his enemy seemed to be the order of the day. *Kill him with kindness, that's it.*

As he walked, he passed a burned spot on the pavement just a few feet away from the car. It could have been nothing. After all, firebugs had been attracted to places like this derelict nightclub for decades. At the same time, it looked fresh, and it had the same shape as a gas can.

He gestured to a crime scene tech. "Get a picture of this, would you? And see what you can get for trace. I know it won't be easy."

The tech just nodded. She didn't need to be told what the implications were. If the fire had caused burns to the gas can, the chances that this man had killed himself had just plummeted. Sure, he could have doused the car in gas, gotten out, put the gas can somewhere, and then set the thing off—but people didn't usually do that. It didn't fit typical behavior in a suicide.

Plus, the gas can wasn't here anymore. *Someone* had removed it, and it wasn't the guy in the car.

He sent a message to the office to have people check hospitals for anyone coming in with burn injuries. He expected to see them coming in, not to the closest hospital, but to one of those in the next tier around. The burn from the exploding gas can would be painful, but they wouldn't want to tip anyone off.

By the time he got back to Framingham, officers had tracked down the dead man's brother at a hospital two towns away with third-degree burns on his arms and second-degree burns on his face.

Donovan got right back into his car and

drove out to the hospital. He didn't even have to ask any questions. The brother admitted to everything. Apparently, the brother had had his "eye on" the dead man's wife first, but she'd preferred the deceased, and then something about a joint business that went bust—Donovan just didn't care. The case was closed, the killer would be going to jail just as soon as he got out of the hospital burn unit, and Donovan had done his damn job.

Funny how it all felt so hollow.

He filled out the report, unable to shake the feeling that somehow everyone in the bull pen had their eyes on him. The case had been in the news yesterday, and not the fake suicide either. No, someone had brought up the anniversary of that stupid riot and, of course, the accusation that he'd been involved with killing people.

No, murdering people.

Donovan had been forced to pull his gun in the line of duty, but he knew the difference between a justified shooting and murder. He'd tried to avoid fatal shootings. He'd been successful so far, but he knew that was more luck than anything else. He wasn't a sharpshooter by any stretch of the imagination. When it came right down to the heat of the moment, and a cop had to make a decision between taking one life or letting someone take other lives, there wasn't a real choice to be made and there wasn't room for error. The torso was the biggest target. You aimed, you pulled the trigger, done.

What had happened at that riot, at least to start it off, had been murder. Even if a protester had chucked a bottle of something at a riot cop—so what? Yeah, it was gross. Yeah, it was an arrestable offense. Yeah, it was fine to put the person into cuffs for it. With the amount of gear a riot cop wore, there was no way he was going to be harmed with anything that had been thrown, and given that none of them had their guns drawn (or weren't supposed to, Donovan had gotten the same instructions as everyone else), the choice had been deliberate.

So, murder. Donovan knew the difference, and he dealt with it every day.

He wasn't capable of murder, but somehow all these people thought he was.

Lt. Power emerged from his office. "Come on, Carey. We've got a quick presser about the Rt. 2 murder."

Donovan meant to get up, but he found his feet rooted to the floor. "Is that a great idea right now, sir?"

Power faced him, head tilted to the side. "Well, yeah. You solved it in two hours. It's a huge win for the department—and for you, personally. The best thing for you is to get out in front of this thing and show what a competent state trooper you really are."

Donovan took a deep breath. He wasn't going to challenge Power again, not in front of everyone, but somehow, he didn't see any of it playing out that way. He focused on moving one foot forward, and then the other, until they made it to the elevator.

It got easier after that. Fewer people stared at him. He could keep his eyes between Power's shoulders and follow him into the pressroom, not thinking about anyone who might or might not be watching. He trailed his boss into the room and stood to his left, just beside the podium, and let his eyes unfocus. He knew there were a few bodies, reporters from various local media outlets, but he couldn't differentiate and he liked it that way.

Power cleared his throat and began. "As you already know, at eleven thirty this morning, we received a call about a burning vehicle at the site of the old Inferno nightclub. While signs pointed to suicide, we dispatched a detective as is required for all unattended deaths. Detective Carey found a major clue that led to the apprehension of a suspect within two hours of finding the body. Detective Carey will take it from here."

Donovan cleared his throat as he stepped forward. "Before we get started, I'd like to ask that people remember a man's life was taken today. He leaves behind a wife and a small child—and the murderer has a family too, who are likely just as confused and heartbroken. I'd like to be as sensitive to their needs as we can, given that any of them may come across what we discuss."

A few people shuffled. Then a reporter spoke. "Detective, what was the motive for this crime?"

Donovan cleared his throat. "I know the suspect cited family issues and some money issues in his confession. I can't speak to whether or not that's the full story."

Someone else, a male reporter this time, asked, "Did the killer act alone, and is there any danger to the general public at this time."

"At this time there is no evidence that the killer had any accomplice, and we do not anticipate any danger to the general public."

A third reporter stood. "Detective Carey, what was *your* motive in shooting those protesters ten years ago?"

The room fell silent. Donovan gripped the podium, more to keep himself from falling over than for any other reason. "Excuse me?"

"I said, 'What was your motive in shooting

those protesters ten years ago?' It's a very simple question." The voice came from a male reporter near the middle of the room, young and white with a bushy beard. Donovan had to force himself to focus on the pale-blue eyes of the person who had asked.

"I didn't shoot anyone ten years ago. Next question."

"Why would the accuser lie, Detective Carey?" The same reporter spoke, a little sneer crossing his face.

"You'd have to ask him. Any questions about the Inferno case?" Donovan's mouth had gone completely dry, but there was no water. Even if there were, he couldn't drink it on camera. It would make him look too guilty.

"All right, we're done here." Power gently nudged Donovan away from the podium. "Let's go, Carey."

Power hustled Carey right back to his office, where he closed and locked the door. There, he reached into his desk drawer and pulled out a bottle of bourbon. Two tumblers followed, and he poured out generous portions into each. "Well," he said, pushing one toward Donovan. "That was exciting."

Donovan hesitated, and then he accepted the glass. "Who even was that guy? I don't think

I've seen him at any of the pressers before." His heart thudded against his rib cage, but it slowed a little as he sipped from the bourbon.

"I have no idea. I'm going to find out. That was some damn fine work you did today, and you deserved to get recognized for it, not ambushed by some . . .some blogger with an axe to grind." Power ground his teeth for a moment. "Thanks for sparing me the I-told-you-sos."

"Not a problem." Donovan bowed his head for a moment. "You know I didn't do it, right?"

Power hesitated. "I can't picture you doing it," he said after a second. "It's not consistent with the cop and detective I've known for years. I think anything can happen when we panic in a riot situation, but again—I wasn't there, so I can't say. I'd be surprised to find out you *had* done it.

"My concern is that I'm not sure it matters."

Donovan almost choked on his drink. "What do you mean?"

"After ten years, someone turns up and suddenly remembers you were there—a random young face in a crowd of riot cops?" He snorted. "I don't trust it. It smells, Carey, and it smells *bad*. I don't know if it's because you're hanging around with the FBI or if it's because you're gay or if it's because you've had a lot of success lately—but it seems oddly targeted. And I don't like that one little bit."

Donovan's world lurched. "There's nothing I can do about it, is there?"

Power's eyes focused on something far away, something Donovan couldn't see. "I don't know. I don't think there is. I hate to say it because I've never been the kind of guy who likes to just trust in things to go his way. But this is one of those situations where a guy getting too active in his own defense can backfire in the worst way possible, if you know what I mean."

Donovan shuddered. "I do."

"Good. That smart-ass FBI guy of yours is on the case, isn't he?"

"Yes, sir." Donovan squirmed. "I know it's a conflict of interest there."

"It is. And between us, we both know they just put him on the case for show—tokenism is what it is. I've been there myself. But he's still smart as hell. He'll figure out what's going on, Donovan. You just have to trust that he can see past what some people want him to see."

Donovan pressed his lips together. Luis saw more than anyone would ever know. That wasn't the issue. It was making other people see what Luis saw that was going to be the problem.

CHAPTER FOUR

Luis stared at the screen in front of him, willing it to rearrange itself into something that made sense. It failed to comply because it was made of whatever screens were made of and not flesh and bone. Luis could force something living to obey him. He could sometimes even compel obedience from the dead. Machines were a different story, and it was pissing him off.

"If you break that mug, I'm not buying you another one." Kevin pushed his chair over into Luis' space and nudged him. "You broke two already."

Luis put the mug down and took a deep breath. "I can't work this case. This is ridiculous." He glanced over at the little graveyard of coffee mugs with shattered handles, sitting on the corner of his workspace. "Can't I sue for hostile work environment or something?"

"Let's be real. If anyone else were trying to work this case you'd never be out of their faces, not even for a second. You're the only one who can work it, for the health and safety of every other agent in the Bureau." Kevin snorted and glanced at Luis' screen. "What's this—Harper's record?"

"Yeah. According to this, Harper was arrested the day after the riot for an assault that took place in Portland, Maine, the day of the riot." Luis used a pencil to point to the relevant section in the wall of text that was Harper's record.

"Okay, but Portland's maybe two hours from here on a bad day." Kevin shrugged. "It doesn't mean anything."

"Right. But when he decided to go after Bartholomew Mitchell's shins with a baseball bat and a fire extinguisher and whatever the hell else, he did it in front of a security camera. The whole thing is on video, with a time and date stamp. It took place ten minutes after the shootings happened. Now, we know the shootings took place. That's not something he could have made up, and we have absolute time values for them. They're not in dispute. So if this Harper guy is up in Maine hitting some guy in the head with a fire extinguisher until his eyes bleed, why does anyone believe a goddamn word he's saying about Donovan?"

Kevin opened his mouth. He closed it again. Despite Luis' confusion and anger, he couldn't help but get a chuckle out of the image. Kevin's gift of gab had finally met its match. "I'll . . . I don't know." Then he scratched his head. "I thought he went after the guy's shins with a bat."

"Things escalated."

"Have you run this past Holcombe?"

"I've documented it." Luis closed his eyes and pushed his laptop away. "Unfortunately, I think it's gotten bigger than Harper now. Some blogger, probably with good or at least not evil intentions, picked up the story and thought he'd be cute about confronting Donovan yesterday at a press conference. Hijacked a conference about a family murder—which, by the way, had happened that same day—and made it all about Donovan and these fake accusations." He clenched his fists.

Kevin shuddered. "And let me guess. People are running with it."

"Right. Everything bad the state police have ever done is coming to rest on his shoulders alone. And since his family has been in law enforcement for generations, anything that's ever had *any* Carey's name attached to it is coming back to bite him in the ass. When we went to bed last night, we just had to see clips from that press conference looped on every station, every news website, every blog. Also, you do not want to hear the voice-over when they dub Donovan into Portuguese or

Spanish."

"Er, you're right, I don't." Kevin blinked slowly. "But by this morning, it had gotten out of control."

"I didn't even know that Kate wound up having to get a restraining order against Fred, but here we are. And somehow, that's being held against *Donovan* in the press." Luis threw his hands up. It doesn't matter that he's helping Kate and the baby, it doesn't matter that Donovan doesn't speak to his father, it just matters that some guy who lies—and lies a lot—pretended to see him at the riot."

Kevin put a hand on his shoulder. "Maybe we should head downtown and have a chat with Mr. Harper."

"His lawyer already got him sprung from jail." Luis found himself laughing, bitter as could be. "Jail is an unsafe place for one in his position, you see."

"I think I'm going to be sick." Kevin rubbed his temples. "And let me guess—he won't be talking to us."

"I did reach out. I wanted to bathe in bleach after talking to the lawyer for ten seconds, but I reached out. And as much as I resent the guy, the lawyer isn't stupid. He's not going to let Harper talk to us because he knows Harper's full of shit."

Luis ground his teeth. "We can't get to the bottom of this crap until we talk to Harper, but we can't talk to Harper until we get to the bottom of this crap."

Kevin bit down on the inside of his cheek. "It definitely sounds like a grudge thing. And just about anyone could be nursing a grudge against your guy. It could be anyone he's arrested or anyone who came up in an investigation who felt wronged even if they were cleared. We've definitely seen that happen a time or two."

Luis bit back a sharp retort. He'd already gone through all these possibilities, but he knew he shouldn't get mad at Kevin. Kevin was being helpful, and Luis' temper was short because Donovan was under attack. "We have. It could be someone from that trafficking case we worked too. It does strike me as the kind of thing mobsters do. Look at Abe Reles."

Kevin nodded and scratched at his chin. "Yeah. That's a possibility. I've been poring through documentation from the riot, trying to figure out if we can figure out what actually happened. There wasn't a whole lot of accountability at the time, you know? There was a half-hearted attempt to put together a timeline, and then it all got brushed under the carpet. Which, frankly, isn't a great look on any local agencies, but what are we going to do?"

Luis reserved comment. It happened all the time, and accountability was rare. As soon as someone in power had the chance to label something a riot, no one cared much about who did what. As long as someone put down the scary rioters, it was fine—as long as the rioters weren't drunken white sports fans, of course. That put a whole different face on things.

But they had a chance to change things now, for *this* riot in *this* time and place. Luis and Kevin could put things right.

"Do you think he might have done it?" Kevin leaned back in his chair. "I mean just in the heat of the moment. Maybe his life was in danger or something."

"Nope." Luis met his eyes. "I think he's capable of doing whatever he needs to do to survive. I don't think he'd have hidden it for ten years. He wouldn't be proud of doing it, necessarily, but he'd be just fine with being accountable when it happened."

Kevin seemed to consider that, tilting his head to the side. "Yeah ... yeah, I can see that. Makes sense. I don't disagree with your assessment, let's put it that way. If you'd said something along the lines of 'Oh, he wouldn't hurt a fly,' I'd think you'd lost your touch."

Luis snorted. "We're both pros, Kev. We're both capable of things that should scare us." His phone buzzed, and he glanced down at it.

The incoming text had come from Dwayne. *You free for lunch? We should talk.*

Luis showed the text to Kevin, who raised an eyebrow. "Are you seriously considering this? Donovan's got a jealousy problem, he's already going through something stressful, and you're getting together with a hot activist who hates cops?"

Luis laughed, but he couldn't hide his blush. "He and Dwayne already met. If Dwayne says we should talk, it's because he's got information. And Dwayne always knew what I was. I already had a badge when he met me, remember?"

"Sure." Kevin rolled his eyes and pushed away slightly. "I also know he wants every law enforcement officer to stop carrying a gun, like they do in England. Can you imagine?"

Luis shrugged. "I'd feel naked without mine, but notice how we're not together anymore. Believe it or not, I can be friends with folks with different views." Luis raised his eyebrows. "And if he's got information that can help Donovan, I'd talk to the ghost of Bin Laden himself. At least Dwayne is a good guy who wants the right things, even if we disagree on how to get them."

Luis texted back and told Dwayne he'd meet up, and lunch was on him. After all, they were meeting for official Bureau business. He could get reimbursed for this one.

They agreed to meet up in Cambridge, in Central Square at a little Indian restaurant. Dwayne wrinkled his nose at the neighborhood when Luis arrived, but passed him a menu anyway. "This neighborhood has changed so much since I was last here. Gentrification is the actual devil. At least this place is still here." He shrugged. "I have to admit I never figured you for a Boston kind of guy, Luis."

Luis laughed and ducked his head. "I never figured myself for a Boston kind of guy either. You should have seen me this past winter. I was *miserable*. I'm surprised no one shot me, whether to put me out of my misery or to shut me up. Donovan threatened to try to teach me to ski—once."

"Christ. Whose bright idea was it to put boards on your feet and aim yourself downhill again?" Dwayne recoiled. "Hard pass, thanks. I take it the residence isn't exactly voluntary?"

"Yeah, the Bureau decided they needed to split the profilers up and send us around the country. Lucky me—I got sent to the tundra. Although I guess it worked out because I reunited with Donovan."

A waiter came by to take their orders and

disappeared again.

"Yeah, that . . . well, it was a bit of a surprise, to be honest. He seemed a little pale for your usual type." Dwayne smirked and took a sip from his water. "Not that I've been checking up on you or anything, but you know how it is."

"Yeah, I do." Luis took a deep breath. "I didn't think I'd ever see him again, but we were thrown together for a case. And I guess there was a lot of stuff still between us." He swallowed. *A lot of stuff* covered a multitude of things. "It's been weird and good and just bizarre at the same time."

Dwayne smiled, warm and genuine. "I'm glad. You seem happy. You deserve it. For your sake, if nothing else, I hope your guy didn't do what Harper says he did."

"Harper was up in Portland ten minutes after the shooting." Luis glanced around. There weren't many people in the restaurant, but he couldn't be too careful. "Some people drive fast, but no one drives that fast."

"Fair enough. I've spoken to him."

"Harper?" Luis only kept his reaction minimal through years of careful practice.

"Yeah. His lawyer won't let him talk to you guys, which shouldn't shock you, but had nothing to say about talking to me." Dwayne put a hand on his chest. "Now, I'm not soft on cops. Not at all."

"No one's accusing you." Luis toyed with his water glass.

"There've been a lot of unfamiliar faces around Harper's place. A lot of white faces, and believe me when I tell you, in his neighborhood, they stand out." Dwayne pressed his lips together. "So do those haircuts."

Luis knew exactly what he meant. Cops, especially white cops, tended to favor certain hairstyles. Luis didn't understand it because it made them so easy to spot and it was only a flattering cut on one face type, but they hadn't asked him. "It's Boston. Neighborhoods still tend to be pretty segregated here, even if it doesn't have force in law anymore. I don't know . . ." He let himself trail off. "It's not us."

"Is it him though? Because I can definitely see where it would be good to get rid of a guy who was making those kinds of accusations, false or not. Maybe especially if they were false, who knows?" Dwayne looked up and paused as the waiter brought their meals to the table. "I saw on *Interceptor* that your guy's whole family is in law enforcement."

"They are." Luis' head spun.

If Donovan's family were trying to intimidate a witness, they were definitely hurting more than they were helping. They should know better—but then again, some of them were pretty old-school. They'd done this kind of thing for decades and gotten away with it.

"But they're not all on speaking terms with each other. I'll see if I can get some of our guys to discreetly get some surveillance, get some pictures. I don't have time for people who make false accusations, but there's a reason for it and we can't find out why if the guy rabbits."

"And no one should be intimidated like that." Dwayne's shoulders slumped. "I saw some of these guys for myself. They wanted to be seen. They didn't care, Luis. They just . . . didn't."

"They wouldn't. The whole point is putting you in fear. It's terrorism." Luis sent a text to Kevin. The lack of discretion worried him. Maybe it wouldn't be a bad idea to check on Harper, and not just because of Donovan's family either. "I'm not letting them get away with it."

"Good." Dwayne covered Luis' hand with his own. "I still don't like the way policing is done in this country. I never will. But if we have to have cops, I'm glad at least a few of them are on our side."

Luis gave Dwayne his most reassuring smile. He couldn't say what was on his mind. He didn't have to. Dwayne had a PhD in this stuff. Dwayne already knew all about jurisdictional issues, the pissing contests between local and federal authorities, and the limits of one federal agent's power.

Donovan glanced at the time. Only four more hours until he could get home to Luis. He knew Luis was working hard to get to the bottom of whatever the hell was going on with his case. He trusted Luis to do the right thing here. He knew Luis was a damn fine investigator and a genius besides, never mind the whole thing where he could talk to dead people.

Wait, why couldn't he just go find the ghosts of the dead rioters and ask them who'd done it?

Donovan already knew the answer, so he didn't need to go embarrass himself in front of his beloved like that. Luis didn't get to pick and choose who came back as a ghost, and even if he could, he wouldn't do it. As far as Donovan understood it— and he freely admitted he didn't understand much—once people crossed over, they were gone and that was it.

Even if Luis were willing to grab someone from heaven and ask them a few questions, and even if he had the ability, it wouldn't do Donovan any good. Dead people couldn't testify. They couldn't give media interviews. *He* knew he was innocent; it was the rest of the world he needed to believe him.

A shadow fell across his desk, and Donovan jumped. He'd been so lost in his own self-defeat he'd lost any kind of situational awareness, and that kind of thing could get him killed.

"You look like a ghost walked over your grave, Carey." Porras sat down on the edge of Donovan's desk and put a cup of coffee in front of him, a little smirk playing across his face. "This whole mess must really be eating into your life, huh? I read in *Social Justice Daily* that you're being investigated by the FBI."

Donovan stared at the coffee for a second. "I mean, yeah, the feds are involved with investigating the riot. They should've been involved ten years ago, when the internal investigation went nowhere."

Porras scoffed and picked up a pen from Donovan's desk. He tossed it into the air, playing with it. "Oh, come on, think about where you'd be if that had happened. Everything you've done, everything accomplished. You wouldn't have pulled any of it off if they'd found out about you years ago, you know?"

Donovan hesitated. "You know I didn't actually shoot anyone that day, right? I wasn't near where the shots were fired."

"Sure you weren't, buddy. Sure you weren't." Porras patted him on the back. "Look, no one here is going to hold it against you. I mean rioters are rioters. They do their riot thing. They have to know the risk before they start, am I right? They deserve what they get, as far as I'm concerned. But now the feds are involved, and they've got all these weird-ass mandates. Gotta make sure no one got their feelings hurt or whatever." He rolled his eyes so dramatically Donovan wondered if he was going to hurt something.

"Look, no one's going to complain about a shooting that's actually justified." Donovan set his jaw. He'd known plenty of cops who had the same views. He had plenty of family members with the same ideas as Porras. "All I'm saying is it's hard to say whether or not this one is justified or not, since I wasn't there and didn't do it. I've never fired a fatal shot from my gun in my life, and if I had I wouldn't hide it. That's literally the worst thing you can do, okay? It makes everyone look bad."

"How so?" Porras went still.

Donovan sipped his coffee. "Look, ten years ago, there wasn't such a thing as accountability for an officer-involved shooting, right? Everyone, or everyone who had the power to do anything about it, always sided with the cop. Even now, the only time anyone gets called on it is when they try to freaking hide it or lie about it. When they went around planting evidence, or crap like that, those are the rare times a jury has convicted them.

"A situation like that riot? Nah. The cop has always gotten the benefit of the doubt. So there would be no reason for me to sit there and lie, and say I didn't do it, if I had. The fact is, it wasn't me." Donovan took another sip of his coffee, so he could settle his stomach and his thoughts. He never thought he'd have to rely on a lack of police accountability to prove his own innocence, but here he was.

Porras seemed to be listening, but he shook his head. "I don't know, bro. I mean you're talking a good game, I'm not going to lie. At the same time, what incentive does this clown have to pull your name out of a hat?" He patted Donovan's shoulder again. "Don't you worry though. No one's going to let this stop you. I mean you're one of the best detectives we've got, right? We're not going to let some dirtbag get the drop on your career."

Before Donovan could ask Porras what he meant, Porras slid off the table and walked away. Donovan watched him go. For a second, Donovan wondered why Porras was even in the office at one o'clock in the afternoon. Wasn't he on the night shift? Shouldn't he be at home, sleeping?

Then the enormity of what Porras had said sank in. He got out his phone and ran out to his car, just to get some privacy. As soon as the doors were locked, he sank in his seat and called Luis.

Luis picked up right away. "Hey, how's it going?" His voice was soft with concern.

"Er. It's going. Listen, I just had a conversation with one of my colleagues. I promise, I'm not trying to interfere with the investigation. I'm not. But he said something I thought you should hear about—private, you know." Donovan's car had been left out in the sun all morning, so he'd have been sweating anyway. He knew the sweat running down the back of his neck hadn't come from any kind of greenhouse effect.

"Are you absolutely sure you should be telling me this right now?" Luis' voice changed a little, became crisper and more professional.

"I don't think I can avoid it. He said 'we' aren't going to let 'some dirtbag' get the drop on my career." Donovan swallowed and tried not to hyperventilate. "I'm not being nuts here, am I? That sounds like a threat, right?"

"Yeah." Luis hesitated for a second. "I can't tell you much, but I might have gotten some information over lunch that corroborates what you just told me. Listen. I know you already know this, but it's different from the other side. Play cool. Don't let on that you're suspicious. Whoever told you that is not your friend, Donovan." Luis went silent for a second, probably because he muted his phone. "Sorry about that. You know how it is. Listen, I'm going to go. I think it's going to get pretty bad. Remember that I love you, okay? I'll see you when I get home."

The line went dead, and Donovan slumped lower in his seat. His mind spun. If he understood even a little bit of what Luis had just said, Luis had gotten a tip about a threat to Harper already— possibly only a few minutes ago.

But why would that be a problem for Donovan?

Well, there was the obvious reason. It would be a problem for Donovan because the guy accusing him of something had been threatened. Why would Porras be a threat to Donovan though? Wouldn't it just be a misplaced sense of loyalty, the thin blue line gone awry?

Luis was showing an incredible amount of trust in Donovan by believing him about his whereabouts that day. Donovan had to return the favor. If Luis said Porras didn't mean him well, Donovan had to trust him.

He took some deep breaths to calm himself, the way Father Geoffrey had taught him. Box breathing, they called it. In for four, hold it for four, out for four, hold for four. The idea was that focusing on the rhythm of the breaths would force him to get out of his sense of panic.

Donovan had been raised with certain ideas about masculinity. Real men did not let things spin outside their control. That applied to romantic relationships, family life, and definitely to their careers. He'd already had his relationship with Luis explode once—because Donovan had lost control of himself. Now the career he'd struggled for and devoted everything to was spinning the same way.

His breath, filling his lungs like fire, pulled him back. Those ideas about masculinity had come from a man who, as it turned out, couldn't control himself any better than the average feral tomcat. And whatever was going on with these charges now might be coming from somewhere outside of his control, but he could sure as hell control his responses.

He turned his car on and let the air-conditioning blow until he no longer looked like a boiled lobster. Then he headed back to his desk, head held high, and got back to work.

He zipped through the tasks on his desk with renewed focus for the next two hours. He was still himself, Detective Donovan Carey. He still solved crimes.

At 3:30, Lt. Power summoned Donovan into his office. He didn't do it vocally. Instead, he sent Donovan a text. Whatever Power might have to say, he didn't need for the whole team to hear it. The hairs on Donovan's arms stood up.

He headed silently toward his supervisor's office, conscious of eyes on him the whole time. Every footfall on the cheap carpet echoed. Donovan's knock on Power's door might have shaken the whole building down.

He entered when bidden and shut the door behind him. Now everything was silent, like the speakers had cut out in an empty movie theater. Donovan inched forward and sat down in the seat Power indicated.

"Detective Carey." Power spoke slowly and clearly, like a man speaking for the camera—or a hidden recorder. "Can you tell me where you were between eight thirty and nine thirty this morning?"

Donovan stared at him for a second. Power knew exactly where Donovan had been. Had Donovan stepped through the looking glass or something? Donovan had been right here in the office. "Yes, sir." Donovan had no knowledge of any recording devices, but he spoke in the same tones as Power anyway. "I clocked in at eight. Records from our database should show I accessed files for the Altobelli kidnapping at eight twenty-five and updated them sometime around eight forty, which means I was updating it—from my desk. Then I was in the morning meeting with you and everyone else from the day shift from eight forty-five to nine forty-five. You were there. You saw me. We talked about my cases, specifically about the Altobelli kidnapping."

"This is correct. Thank you, Detective Carey. The reason I'm asking you this question is because sometime between eight thirty and nine thirty this morning, someone shot Jason Harper in the back of the head in his apartment in Roxbury."

Donovan's mouth went dry. He'd known something was going on when he spoke to Luis, but he'd figured it was just threats. He had no idea it was anything this serious. "I'm sorry—I thought you just said someone murdered a witness in a federal investigation."

Power raised an eyebrow. "An investigation into you, and into both the state police and the Boston Police Department. But right now, the investigation does seem to center on you regardless." He closed his eyes and sighed. "His attorney had spoken to him at eight thirty, and Dr. Wong estimates the body lay where it was for approximately four hours. So that's our timeline."

"We're not investigating this one, are we?"

Donovan knew the answer before he spoke.

"We aren't. Under the circumstances, it would be inappropriate. The FBI is handling this one, which is ruffling more than a few feathers. I'm not sure if those feathers are justifiably ruffled." He moistened his lips. "Harper was supposed to be their witness. He should have been under their protection."

Donovan bit down on his tongue for a second. "Harper was a liar, sir."

"I know that. And you know that. But he was still their witness, and without his cooperation, we'll never find out why he shows up ten years later with a cup of coffee and a bag of lies—about *you.*" Power slammed his hand on his desk. "I should be kicking those agents' asses for this. They came in here and they seagulled all over yet another case, and now they're making one of my best detectives look guilty when a five-year-old could see he's not."

Donovan sucked in his cheeks. He didn't know why Harper hadn't been in protective custody, but he knew Luis must have had a reason. All he had to do was figure out what that reason might have been.

CHAPTER FIVE

Luis knew this was going to be a bad one before he got out of the car. The triple-decker listed to the right, because no one had bothered to keep it up in probably about fifty years. The paint had probably been brown once, but now the siding had that grayish look wood took on when the paint had peeled away and New England weather had done its job. If a house could be a ghost, this triple-decker was one. Even the satellite dish on the third floor seemed precarious, one good wind gust away from shattering on the pavement below.

The house was roped off with crime scene tape, which had caused some irritation for the families living below Jason Harper. Women, men, and children gathered just outside the perimeter and glowered at everyone in a suit or uniform, clearly put out about getting kicked out of their homes.

Part of Luis sympathized. Most of these folks wouldn't have had good interactions with the police, not down here. Luis had lived in a neighborhood just like this when he first came to the US, so he knew. And a situation like this, being rousted from their homes and kicked out onto the sidewalk, wasn't going to tip the scales toward amity. Who knew what they had going on in their lives, that this situation had interrupted?

A light-skinned Black man approached as Luis got out of the car. He seemed oblivious to the bloodstain on the sidewalk, and after a second, Luis realized he was the only one who could see it. *Awesome. Not the first murder here. Fabulous.*

"If I'm late to work, I'm going to lose my job and my family cannot afford this." The man's voice was tight, and his hands were clenched at his side. "The jerk in the crime scene uniform said I had to wait for the investigating agent. Is that you?"

Luis took a deep breath and made himself smile. "I'm Agent Gomes, this is Agent Rourke. What time does your shift start, Mr. . . . ."

The angry man blinked. "Garrison. And it starts at four. I work in Radiology at the Brigham."

"Fantastic." Luis checked his watch. Three thirty. If they used a siren, maybe he could make it. "How about this. Do you live on the first floor?"

"Yeah?"

"Perfect. Agent Rourke will escort you in to get your uniform. While he does that, he'll take your statement. Then he'll put the pedal to the metal and take you to work. If your supervisor gives you any grief, Kevin will be there to back you up."

Kevin side-eyed Luis. "Obviously, I'm happy to back Mr. Garrison up with his boss, but why me specifically? Do you think I have some kind of magic power over people's supervisors?"

"I'm a Southern boy. We don't drive on the sidewalks. You're from here, you're cool with it." Luis grinned and shook Garrison's hand. "Everyone else, I'm really sorry for the intrusion and inconvenience. I'm going to go in to take a look at the crime scene, and in the meantime, my colleagues will be around to take your statements. Thank you for your cooperation, and we'll try to get out of your hair as soon as we can."

The families grumbled, but they didn't have a lot of choice. Living in a dump like this, they probably hadn't had a choice about much. Luis had been there himself once. He wondered if calling Inspectional Services would help or hurt the situation.

He put the shoe covers on, to ensure he didn't contaminate any evidence, and climbed the rickety stairs to the third-floor apartment. Triple-deckers existed elsewhere, of course, but they were a Boston tradition Luis had come to despise. In some places, they were owned and inhabited by families who kept them for generations.

Down here, they were death traps.

He passed the ghost of a young woman—white, so she must have lived here more than fifty years ago—standing at the top of the stairs. She cradled her swollen abdomen with skeletal hands and her head hung at an impossible angle. "They'll get you too," she whispered, stroking her belly. "They'll get you too."

Luis ignored her. He had to. He wasn't alone. Crime scene techs were everywhere. The body of Jason Harper lay facedown on the living room floor, unmoved but fragrant already. Black powder indicated people had already dusted for prints, and the body had already been outlined in chalk.

Wong appeared behind Luis. "You haven't touched him, have you?"

Luis turned around to see the medical examiner and his assistants, waiting with a gurney and a body bag. "No, Dr. Wong, I haven't. They said you estimated time of death to be sometime between eight thirty and nine thirty?"

Wong sniffed and immediately looked like he'd regretted it. "We know it was after eight thirty based on his cell phone. Given the state of the body—barely beginning to get into pallor mortis—

and the conditions in which the body was left, four hours is a good approximation. Of course, I won't know for certain without a full autopsy—"

"Of course." Luis cut Wong off before he could go into full-lecture mode. "Thank you. I'm sure you want to get him back to the lab and into a drawer before he can decompose any further."

"Naturally. Photos have already been taken, so if you don't mind." He gestured for Luis to get out of the way.

Luis had no problem stepping back. Harper's bowels had released sometime between death and now. The more space he could put between the smell and himself, the better.

He stepped softly through the room. He didn't know what, exactly, he was looking for. Harper hadn't been a great housekeeper, so signs of a struggle could have been masked. A gun lay on the ratty coffee table, with an evidence marker beside it. Luis had no idea if it was the killer's or Harper's. It could go either way, not that a convicted felon like Harper was supposed to have a gun at all.

Harper didn't have any books. He had a large-screen TV, but not a new one, and a gaming system. Luis donned gloves to examine his few games, but most games could be downloaded these days and he didn't expect to find any clues in the cases. He was simply checking, being thorough.

The bedroom yielded a little more information, although not much. He found a handgun hidden under the bed, one the evidence techs had missed, and brought Maxwell in to tag and bag it. A discarded lace thong in the sheets had probably not belonged to Harper, but they'd get the sheets and the thong tested. Maybe whoever had been with him had some role in the murder. Luis didn't think that would be the case, but he'd seen more elaborate setups before.

He turned around when he heard footsteps. Brick Fontana was just now coming into the room, eyes darting around like he expected something to jump out at him at any minute. "Hey, Gomes? There's a neighbor downstairs who you should speak to, but she won't do it here. Says it's not safe." He tugged at his collar and narrowed his eyes. "And, uh, she'll only talk to you."

Luis took a last glance around the room. The dirty glass in the window, still original, seemed to twist as he looked at it. *Who needs LSD? You can just suddenly turn psychic and get all the psychedelic crap you want!*

He followed Fontana back outside. His frenemy brought him to meet the neighbor who lived immediately downstairs from Harper, a dark-skinned woman from Cabo Verde by the name of

Camila.

Camila was elderly, probably in her eighties, and her English was best described as hit-or-miss. "I'm old," she told Luis in Portuguese. "I've lived a long time. If I have to forget something, it can be my third language, instead of my family. I'll take that trade."

Luis privately agreed with her. "Why don't you want to talk here, ma'am? Why do you feel unsafe?"

She snorted. "There have been so many policemen coming and going around here—not your men. They don't look the same. They've all been white though. There's a church just up a couple of blocks. You take me up there, and I'll tell you what I know."

Luis' skin itched. He hadn't set foot in a church since his mother's funeral except for crime scenes, but if he wanted to find out what Camila wanted, he'd have to do it.

"Do you mind if I record you while we're there?" He offered her his arm. "Since I won't have any witnesses, it makes sense to be able to prove you said what you say."

She nodded. "Of course, of course." She made small talk as they strolled toward the little Pentecostal church she had in mind.

They entered, and Luis managed to keep his

skin on. He gripped a digital recorder and took rapid notes as he spoke. One method might fail, but not the other one. "All right, ma'am. Thank you for agreeing to speak with me. You said there've been a lot of white policemen around the house?"

Camila nodded. "That Jason—he was no good. He tried to sell some heroin to my grandson. I caught him, I threw the cooking water at him. Lost the rice that night, but it was worth it. I won't have my grandchildren getting hooked on that mess. We got little Abel into a good rehab, it wasn't cheap, but it worked and he's got a good job now."

"I'm glad to hear it." Luis made himself smile. He wouldn't have had to force himself if this case didn't center around Donovan. He had to take his heart out of it, or he was going to lose everything.

"Thank you. He's a good boy. So many are, but they get caught up in these things and their lives are ruined. I'm sure Jason was a good boy at some point. Anyway, I knew he was no good, so the first time I saw those cops coming around, I thought to myself, *Oh, they're coming to arrest him, maybe we can get a good young man up there*. We never do, of course, but a girl can dream." She eyed Luis. "I don't suppose you want to move to Mattapan?"

Luis held back a snicker. "I just bought a place out in Burlington, ma'am."

"It's a shame. Why do you want to live in Burlington anyway? Nobody out there speaks a real language, and they only want to talk about their lawns." She rolled her eyes. "Who thinks about grass that much? Anyway, the policemen didn't arrest him. They weren't just hanging around the house though. They were going up to visit him. Going up the stairs, giving me the eyeball every time they caught me looking at them—every time."

Luis almost dropped his pencil. "If I showed you pictures, do you think you'd recognize them again?"

"Maybe. I would try. They all have that same haircut, and they were all white. Otherwise, they didn't all seem to have a lot in common. Some were younger, some were older." She tapped her finger against her jaw. "They all had to be at least in their early thirties though. Some had to be nearly sixty, maybe more."

"All of them old enough to have been at the riot." Luis mused out loud without thinking. He'd suspected it might be one person with a grudge against Donovan, but this was sounding like a conspiracy.

"What, the one ten years ago? The one that everyone's all worked up about?" She shook her head. "Lord, that was a mess. My son was down there. I told him not to go, I told him it was nothing but trouble, but he said he had to. He got hurt when people panicked and ran. Said some state trooper grabbed him and pulled him into an alley, bandaged him up and kept him safe until they could get him to an ambulance."

Luis sat very still. "I don't suppose he remembers the name of the trooper who did that?"

She looked up toward the ceiling. "He mentioned it. Something strange, it sounded like a girls' name. Carrie, like the scary movie, I think it was."

Luis had to stop himself from hugging her. "I don't suppose he'd be willing to testify to that in court?"

Camila widened her eyes. "Well, I don't know. We'd have to ask him, wouldn't we? But I do know he thinks that trooper saved his life, so I'm sure he'd like to do right by him."

Donovan had a thousand questions for Luis when he got home that night, but he didn't ask them. He knew Luis couldn't answer them.

He also knew Luis well enough to recognize most of his tells. Luis had the fire in his big dark eyes that suggested he was onto something, but he didn't breathe even a hint of what that might be to Donovan. He had a grim set to his jaw too, that screamed rage and righteous fury. He still didn't say anything about it, just blew Donovan so sweetly and tenderly Donovan wondered if he were dying.

Donovan even resorted to checking Luis' notes while he was asleep, which was wrong of course. His notes were in Portuguese. The only thing Donovan could get out of them was that he was in a church and apparently expected to be struck by lightning, which Donovan only got from a little doodle in the corner.

"I understand why you're frustrated." Luis put a hand over his, when he caught him looking at his notes. "Just like I know you understand why I can't say anything."

"Okay, but why are your notes in Portuguese? You never take notes in Portuguese."

Luis chuckled and shook his head kind of sadly and went to work. Donovan noted the still-grim set to his jaw and felt bad for the heavy bag in the FBI gym.

He had to go to work too, although he found the front entrance to headquarters absolutely full of media. The case had already been getting national attention. Now that Harper had been murdered, it was even worse. The stupid vultures had filled every available flight to Boston yesterday. A buddy of his who worked at Logan commented on it.

Fortunately for Donovan, there was a back route into the parking lot that most folks didn't know about. He took the long way in and managed to sneak into the office undetected. At least he managed to get in there without anyone from the press noticing him.

Porras was another matter. "Hey, bro. It's pretty wild how big this thing has blown up, huh? It's not like anyone would have given a crap about a dirtbag like Harper if anyone else had killed him."

Donovan raised his eyebrows but accepted the coffee Porras held out to him. He remembered Luis' advice. *Play it cool. This man is not your friend.*

"Do you *know* who did it, Porras? Because based on what they're announcing as time of death, I've got a whole squad of Homicide detectives who'll tell you I was right here."

Porras laughed. He might have been a handsome man but his laugh made Donovan think of a hyena. "Oh, come on, bro. You wouldn't have had to lift a finger to off that dude, and we both know it. You'd have just had to blink to make it happen. Your entire family tree is either blue or French blue." He tugged at his shirt, indicating the gray state trooper uniform. "And who could blame

96

you, right? You're being targeted by some scumbag who's just basically causing trouble for his own entertainment."

Donovan shrugged. "Maybe. My family aren't assassins though. If I were doing something wrong, believe me, they'd let me know and be more likely to take me out for it than anyone else. Even a guy like Harper." He watched Porras carefully.

"Come on, the thin blue line is there for a reason." Porras nudged his shoulder.

"It is. But it's not supposed to be there to protect us when we go rogue, you know? Look, last year I screwed up, went off the deep end, and torpedoed my relationship with Luis. Believe me when I tell you, my family was more than happy to let me know who was in the wrong, and that it was not Luis. They're not going to sit there and kill a guy to keep him from testifying against me."

Porras looked doubtful, but before he could say anything, shouting erupted from behind Power's closed door. "It's deliberate sabotage!" Power's voice should have taken the whole building down. "Your incompetent men should have had that jackass in protective custody, and you know it. There is no reason he should be dead right now, except to try to make my detective look guilty."

Power's door flew open. After a stunned

second, Donovan realized it had been flung open by Luis' boss, SSA Holcombe.

"Lieutenant Power, Mr. Harper was not in protective custody because his agreement with the court precluded it—as you would know had you bothered to consult with his attorney. If you're concerned about apparent guilt, I suggest you convince your own union to turn over the records we requested and convince your own men to stop giving interviews that shoot Detective Carey in the foot. I will not have you maligning my men when this is your screwup, not mine. One more attempt to impugn the Bureau or its agents, Lieutenant, and I will make goddamn sure you have a jurisdictional battle over each and every case that crosses your desk from the tiniest robbery to the most open-and-shut barroom manslaughter. Are we absolutely, positively, one hundred percent clear?"

"You'd better be prepared to make good on that threat, sister." Power leaned over his desk, snarling.

"It's a promise, Lieutenant Power. And I am not your sister." Holcombe stormed out of the office.

"Carey, get in here." Power glowered after Holcombe as the rest of the office scurried to get back to any kind of work they might be able to pretend to do. "And, Porras, what the hell are you doing here? Your shift ended two hours ago. I'm not authorizing any overtime for you to gossip. Don't think I didn't see you talking with that girl from MSNBC."

Donovan rushed to obey. He wasn't going to think about why Porras had been talking to a reporter. Maybe the reporter had been cute. Donovan hadn't seen anything so he couldn't really say, but he couldn't blame Porras for trying to salvage something from this situation. Someone should get something out of it, at least.

He closed the door behind himself. "Yes, sir?"

"Have you taken a look at today's papers?"

Donovan had not, and said as much. "It was a little too much for me before coffee, sir."

"Can't blame you. Apparently, some of our own, under 'condition of anonymity,' have been opening their mouths to the press. Talking about how 'ridiculous it is to try to railroad a man ten years after the fact while he's got an exemplary record since then.' I think they think they're helping you." He curled his lip. "They can't be that stupid, but here we are."

Donovan bit back a scream. "I guess at least they're trying to do something?"

Power threw himself into his chair. "You're not that stupid either. You know damn well how that's going to play out. Whoever put Harper up to this nonsense is out for blood, and they knew what they were doing. They made sure things were arranged exactly the way they wanted. They won't be satisfied until your life is destroyed, utterly. You might not go to jail, but you'll lose your badge and never find work again. It doesn't matter that you didn't do it. It only matters that they *think* you did. Now tell me your pretty boy has something, anything, to work with."

"He's not going to tell me, sir. He can't." Donovan spread his hands wide. "It's bad enough he got assigned to this case. He even took his notes yesterday at the crime scene in Portuguese."

"What? That's so far outside of protocol it's ridiculous! I'm going to call up Holcombe and—"

"Sir—think about that for just a moment." Donovan took a chance and put his hand on Power's phone. "She can kill you and make it look like an accident, outside of everything she said."

Power took a deep breath. "I'm not going to pretend I'm not angry, very angry. There's no reason under God that man shouldn't be alive right now and confessing to who put him up to this."

"If his agreement with the lawyer meant he wasn't going into protective custody, I mean it was stupid but whatever. It was basically signing his own warrant." Donovan sighed. "Which means he didn't think he had anything to fear."

"Of course not. Because he had protection already."

"And Holcombe asked for information about cops, that the union wouldn't let her have."

Power's face went ashen, and he tilted his chair back. "You think he was working with a cop."

Donovan swallowed. "Luis doesn't tell me much because he can't, but he did tell me he got information yesterday during lunch. I called him with something someone said offhand to me, that I thought might be pertinent, and he hung up. They found the body after that." He hoped Power wouldn't ask who'd said something, or that Power would have remembered seeing him talking to Porras and made his own conclusions.

"And requested information about state troopers." Power took a deep, shuddering breath. "Carey, this is . . . this is a lot. The agency is already reeling from that overtime scandal. That's probably why the media is coming at you so hard."

"It's probably got something to do with it anyway. Cops all over the country have been getting away with some very shady behavior for a long time. Not all of us, but enough of us." Donovan rubbed at his face, like it could wake him up from this nightmare. "I don't know what Luis has found, or will find. And I don't know how he'll find a way to get at who killed Harper without the information. But he's going to find a way, because it's Luis. It's what he does and he knows it's me on the line."

Power managed a sad little smile. It was funny how Donovan hadn't realized just how old Power was until this moment. "It must be nice, to have someone love you that much."

"It is, sir. After all this is done, you'll have to come over to the house for a cookout and see just how nice it is." Donovan had to hope there would be an after. "But first, we have to figure out how we can best support this investigation."

"I'd guess he was trying to do a photo lineup." Power spoke after a moment, sitting up straighter. His moment of weakness and fragility had passed, and he was every inch the strong commander again. "I will happily bring men up to Chelsea for a lineup with whatever security measures he wants to have in place for his witness. You'll be in the lineup obviously. We can't make it obvious."

"Of course, sir. I wouldn't have it any other way." Donovan managed to smile. They were going to win this thing, somehow. He could feel it in his bones.

CHAPTER SIX

Luis glanced idly over at Kevin, who was driving. Kevin always drove. Luis had privately assumed it was a rank thing or maybe an age thing. Today though, SSA Holcombe was in the back seat as they drove out to Framingham. She outranked both of them by quite a wide margin, and Luis wasn't going to try to guess at her age.

He wished he could feel supported about having his boss follow him out to Framingham to conduct interviews about this case. He knew that was her intention. He'd heard about her "discussion" with Donovan's boss, directly from Donovan. His discomfort came from anxiety, and nothing more. Knowing the origin of the nagging voice insisting the boss who'd assigned him the job didn't think he could do it didn't make the voice any less real.

Fortunately, he didn't have to pretend to be comfortable. He just had to be a professional about this whole thing, and he'd been doing that for more than a decade. He could handle this without a problem.

"Agent Gomes, tell me what kind of person you think would be behind the murder." Holcombe's voice came crisp and clear from the back seat.

Luis didn't hesitate. "Our murderer is almost certainly in law enforcement. He's white and at least in his midthirties. He's got a Blue Lives Matter decal on his personal vehicle but probably doesn't have a flag hanging from his house or anything because that would be too much. He's conservative in his views but may not necessarily identify that way."

"That makes no sense." Kevin gripped the wheel a little harder.

Luis fought for the right words. "He doesn't think of himself as holding conservative views, but when asked about specifics, he reveals himself as holding distinctly 'traditionalist' views of American society and about law and order. If he has daughters, he will have vastly different expectations for them than he does for his sons. He will go light in cases of domestic abuse because clearly the woman provoked it and you know, a man has his limits.

"He doesn't think of himself as a racist, but if he ever worked in traffic enforcement, he stopped people of color at a higher rate than whites, and that difference will be hard to miss. He doesn't think women belong in law enforcement, and he'll insist it's because they can't handle the 'physical part' of the job. But he still won't describe himself as conservative."

Holcombe snorted. "Right. That just narrows it down to sixty percent of the men in that building."

"Are we sure it's a man?" Kevin shifted position as he aimed the giant black SUV toward the exit. "There are plenty of women cops who hold those views. Luis, didn't Patricia sound like that until recently?"

"Except for the part about women, yeah." Luis gripped the passenger-assist bar as a Honda Civic with a giant aftermarket muffler zipped around them on the right, in the shoulder. "But the witnesses were pretty firm about only seeing men. They went into Harper's apartment too. So we know this is something they set up with Harper."

"And we're sure about that." Holcombe's voice was so tight Luis could have strung a guitar with it, if he were a musical kind of guy.

"They were going in and out of Harper's apartment, both before he made the accusation and after." Kevin cleared his throat. "Plus, the nearest witness told Luis her son can put Donovan several blocks away from the scene of the shooting. This is one hundred percent a setup, and there's no other reason for them to be spending time with Harper."

"Sure there is." Luis rested his head against the cool glass of the window. Outside was a cesspit of humidity to rival any swamp in Florida, but the glass was smooth and cool. "They could have been trying to get him to become an informant in any other case. It's not what I believe, all things considered, but it's what they'll say and it's what a jury would believe. Plus, we're professionals. We do have to consider the possibility that it might be true. We use felons as informants all the time."

Kevin thumped the steering wheel. "I hate investigating cops."

"We all do." Holcombe tapped the seat. "Don't miss your turn."

Kevin only made the turn by driving on the lawn. He didn't seem to care, and neither did Holcombe. The ruts on the grass suggested he wasn't the first and probably wouldn't be the last.

"If I keep living around here, I'm going to rediscover religion." Luis muttered and shook his head as he unbuckled his seat belt. "You're all looking to decrease your lifespan by ten to fifteen years from the way you drive alone."

"Not our lifespans." Holcombe smiled at him, sweet as sugar. "Just . . . you know.

Outsiders'."

They walked into State Police Headquarters and presented their badges to the poor rookie assigned to the front desk that day. The guy had a sling on, so he clearly couldn't be out in the field. At least he could work, instead of being stuck at home with a mischievous ghost giving him shit all day. Luis was jealous, which didn't exactly improve his reaction when he saw the young trooper curl his lip at the sight of their credentials.

"We're expected by Lieutenant Power in Homicide." He met the young man's eyes and leaned a little closer. "I've been given to understand he doesn't like to wait, but it's your call."

The trooper swallowed and called Lt. Power.

Kevin nudged Luis with his elbow. "Well, you sure put the fear of God into that guy. Aren't we supposed to be playing nice?"

"I didn't punch him." Luis didn't smile.

"Keep that in reserve." Holcombe's lips thinned out, but Luis thought he saw the slightest hint of a smile teasing around the corners of her mouth. "We haven't gotten to the bottom of this yet."

A white guy about Luis' age in a cheap suit with a loose tie jogged into the lobby. He glanced around before his gaze landed on Luis, then Holcombe and Kevin. He jogged over to them. "You must be the feds."

Holcombe narrowed her eyes. "I'm Supervisory Special Agent Holcombe, these are Special Agents Gomes and Rourke."

The newcomer shook hands all around. "I'm Detective Porras. I work Major Crimes. Come on back."

Porras wasn't a bad-looking guy at all. He was on the tall side, maybe six one, with a slightly more stylish high-and-tight haircut than the typical cop. Big brown eyes and a generous mouth completed a picture Luis probably wouldn't kick out of bed, if he were being honest. He kept himself in good shape, and Luis could at least admire the view as he followed Porras back to the Major Crimes unit.

Luis had been here before, of course. He'd been here more than once. When he'd worked the Sudbury murders, and then the Freetown murders, they'd split time between here and FBI offices. He knew where to go, and he knew Lt. Power. The one person he didn't recognize was Porras.

The path to Power's office led past Donovan's desk. Donovan didn't look up. Luis didn't expect him to, under the circumstances. Luis couldn't exactly stop and give him the hug and kiss he wanted to. His heart still broke to see his lover sitting there at his desk, so stiff and alone. He managed to brush up against Donovan as they passed. The contact would look accidental, at least, and Luis could pass it off as innocent. Donovan would still know he was thinking of him.

Donovan didn't acknowledge his touch in any way, but Luis could still feel his muscles unclench as he passed by. It was enough.

Power stood up to shake their hands. "Agent Holcombe, I want to apologize for shouting at you the other day." Kevin closed the door behind them as Porras left them alone. "I was upset about Detective Carey being railroaded, and I hadn't considered the possibility of the lawyer not allowing protective custody. I was out of line."

"I understand. We can all get protective of our team, or at least we should. It's only right. Let's discuss where we stand." Holcombe sat in the middle chair. "I'm sure you can understand, per our emails, why we need to be as discreet as possible."

Power squirmed and glanced at the door. "You think state troopers are involved."

Holcombe glanced at Luis, who cleared his throat. "Yes, sir. Witnesses specifically stated they saw both 'gray' and blue."

"It's actually French blue." Power frowned

at him.

"I'm aware." Luis heroically refrained from rolling his eyes. "It's come up before. The average citizen isn't aware of the nuances, however, and simply sees a shade of gray. They don't differentiate."

Kevin stepped in, a little more quickly than he might have if there wasn't an entanglement between Luis and someone involved with the investigation. "Sir, can you think of any reason any state police officers might have been speaking with Harper at any point prior to his death? Was he an informant in any investigation, to the best of your knowledge?"

Power shook his head. "We're not above using informants, but a guy like that is death on the stand. I usually leave the lawyering to the lawyers, but nothing destroys morale like working your ass off and then seeing your guilty as fu—your guilty suspect walk because people didn't believe your evidence. A guy like that? No. I was willing to *listen* when he accused Carey of shooting people. I didn't necessarily believe him, and I wasn't going to take Carey's gun or badge because of it."

Holcombe nodded, and Luis found himself doing the same. He could learn to like Power.

"Has Detective Carey been having any trouble on the job?" Luis kept himself still,

110

unwilling to give away more than Power already knew. "Has he made enemies on the force, whether from professional jealousy to personality clashes, to other issues?"

Power steepled his fingers in front of himself. "That's . . . a little bit of a challenging question, I suppose. He's a damn fine detective with a great closure rate, and of course, his closure rate has only improved since the two of you got together."

Luis couldn't hide his startled reaction. "Excuse me?"

"It's not rocket science, Luis." Holcombe glanced at him. "You've got two great minds sharing space, bouncing things off of each other. Even when you're not discussing a specific case, you're exchanging ideas, talking about things happening around you, old cases, whatever. You're still learning from each other. Your game has improved since you two got together too."

Luis hadn't thought about it that way, although now that his boss mentioned it, he supposed his solve rate had improved. Donovan had given him confidence, assurance. He'd never lacked for reasons to fight. Now Luis had something to fight *for* and something to go home to.

"If anyone's resentful of that, they haven't

told me," Power continued as though no one had brought up Donovan and Luis' relationship. "They might have let a couple of other issues slip in passing. Some people are a little . . . er, resentful of the whole family business aspect. They think he got his position through nepotism instead of through being a hard worker and a damn good cop. And who knows, maybe he got into the academy because of some family legacy? I couldn't say. Everything since then has been all him, one hundred percent, and if it put Carey in a position to get into my squad, then I will cheer that nepotism until the day I die."

"You mentioned some other issues." Kevin leaned forward.

"Well." He cleared his throat. "I didn't want to make a thing of this because it's a relatively small minority of folks, and they don't deserve to have thoughts like this see the light of day. But there are some people on the force who feel that homosexual people have no place in law enforcement, never mind as detectives. Carey's been out for what, a year and change? A few people did ask for him to be fired. Said he couldn't be trusted anymore. Refuse to work with him." Power held his hands up. "Those people were all reassigned because we do have laws and no one's going to coddle that kind of nonsense. But since you asked, yes, they're

112

out there."

"Did you happen to keep a record of who they were?" Luis wasn't going to hunt them down and exact retribution, although the thought did occur to him.

"I did not, but I do remember who they were and I can give you their names." Power started typing.

"What about any other workplace issues?" Holcombe glanced over at the door again. "Is there anything else you can think of that might lead to him being targeted?"

"No. You could ask his cousin, who works in SWAT. People don't necessarily know they're related and so might be more open in front of her. Agent Gomes, I think you know her. Alicia Kennedy."

"I'll speak to her off-site." Luis made a note. "Probably more discreet for everyone."

Power nodded. "Listen, I know the union is opposed, but this is an active murder investigation and we're cops. This is what we do. My men, at the very least, will go down to Chelsea and participate in any lineup you want. I have two priorities—justice, and Detective Carey. That's it."

"Me too." Luis shook Power's hand.

Kevin and Holcombe stayed with Power for a moment, but Luis needed to step out. He knew where the restroom was, he didn't need an escort to find it, but when he started walking toward the exit, he found he had a shadow.

He let Porras follow him as far as the men's room because he was truly curious about why this guy would be following him, but stopped him once he was sure they were alone. "What's up, Detective?"

Porras gave him a sheepish grin. "That obvious, huh?"

Luis just gave him a smile and held back the snarky retort. This was, at least apparently, someone Donovan had to work with.

"I guess I've got a question. I . . . well, I applied for the FBI a handful of years ago, and they turned me down without an explanation."

Oh. Okay. "Sometimes they've just met their quota of recruits for the year, you know? It happens. It's not anything personal or anything you did wrong."

"Yeah, I know. I get that. I just—I was hoping you could maybe put in a good word for me or something? I've been padding my resume, working Major Crimes for the past three years on the night shift and everything. I'm not sure what else I can do to beef up my chances."

Luis hoped the red flags going off in his brain weren't visible on his face. Why would someone who worked the night shift be in the office at eleven o'clock in the morning? "Wow. You're certainly motivated, doing all the right things."

"I hope so. Not that I'm not happy to be doing Major Crimes. Solving crimes is the name of the game, right? I guess I'm just hoping to do something a little meatier, a little more challenging. And, you know. The Bureau's standards are something everyone wants to live up to, right?"

Luis nodded slowly. "Yeah. Absolutely. They're rigorous, all right. You got a card?"

"Definitely." Porras passed him a business card.

Luis took it carefully and put it into his jacket pocket. "Thanks, man. I'll be in touch, but right now, I really need to take care of something." He glanced at the door of the men's room.

Porras blushed. "Oh yeah. Sorry. I'll let you get back to your business. Talk to you later." He turned around and headed back to Major Crimes.

Luis watched him go, overflowing with questions.

Donovan had to be content with Luis brushing against him as he passed by to go meet with Donovan's commanding officer, about Donovan. It was infuriating, it was absurd, and it was still enough to let Donovan relax just a bit.

At least, he relaxed until the feds all left. Then he had the enviable opportunity to stare at his email for ten minutes, until Power summoned him to a meeting with Power's boss. Donovan had met Captain Killough once. It had been a brief interaction, consisting of a handshake and not much more.

Even Fred, Donovan's father, was afraid of Killough.

Donovan couldn't refuse the meeting. He had to go. He followed his boss through the halls of State Police Headquarters to the better-appointed offices where more senior brass worked. He knew the oak paneling was fake, but it still looked better than piss-yellow walls and fluorescent lighting.

It's good to be the king.

Killough's office, despite the fake-wood walls, didn't have a lot of frills to it. Killough himself was an old-school trooper, with close-cropped hair in an iron-gray color that matched his eyes. His skin was so pale as to be almost translucent. His face seemed to frown perpetually, even in his official portrait.

He gestured for Donovan and Power to be seated across from him and glanced over a paper file, in a folder. "So, Detective Carey. I see there's a mess of trouble with your name all over it."

Donovan swallowed hard. "Yes, sir."

Power rolled his eyes. "It's a little more complicated than that, sir. I've just met with federal investigators."

"Have you now? These would be the same feds who let John Connolly and Whitey Bulger get away with God knows what for God knows how long?"

Donovan winced. The whole Boston office all but spat at Connolly's name, but Killough wouldn't know that. Donovan didn't think he'd care either.

"Different division, sir." He sat up a little straighter. Killough might not care, but Donovan did, and he knew the feds did too. "These are the same folks who took down that Sudbury killer and who helped deal with the serial killer in Freetown and the human trafficking ring in Boston after the Organized Crime group screwed it up."

Killough turned those hard eyes of his onto Donovan again. "Ah. So friends of yours are investigating . . . you. How professional of them."

Power frowned. "Sir, I'll admit it's unorthodox. I questioned it when I found out. The decision came from higher up in Virginia, and while I suspected tokenism, I think it's probably one of the better ones they could have made. It took them all of five minutes to figure out the accuser—who's now deceased—could not physically have seen what he claimed. Sir, this whole thing is a setup of Detective Carey. He is innocent of these charges."

"I'm sure he is." Killough raked Donovan over with his gaze, and somehow Donovan's verbal acquittal at his hands didn't make him feel any better at all. "What does that have to do with anything?"

Power pulled his head back. "Excuse me, sir?"

"I'm your boss, but don't forget that I have bosses. And those bosses report to the people of this Commonwealth. The people of this Commonwealth, Power, don't want to hear that your guy Harper was a liar—especially not now that he can't defend himself." He put his folder down. "And my bosses have to think about the larger picture. They have a public safety issue. This agency has taken a bunch of hits over the past few years. We've had scandal after scandal."

Donovan ran his tongue against his teeth. He thought he could see where Killough was going with this, but he didn't want to believe it. "And this is another scandal."

"Either way it goes, it's another scandal."

Killough glared at him because he'd spoken out of turn. "Don't think I didn't hear about the feds' request for that photo lineup. Don't think the higher-ups didn't either. You tell me which one is going to make this agency look more competent in the public eye—an agency correcting a mistake from ten years ago or an agency with a massive conspiracy targeted against one detective?"

Power stared openly at Killough. "You're joking."

Killough didn't flinch. "I wish I were. I'm not saying it's right. I'm not saying it's good. I'm saying it's reality, and we'd better all start waking up to it.

"Right now, they're not asking anything be done about Detective Carey. Not yet. For one thing, the union is still protecting him. It seems the union is just fine with protecting someone who shot five protesters."

"But I didn't!"

Power elbowed Donovan.

"As other cops start to get investigated, that's going to change. Again, I believe you, Carey. All I'm saying is that you'd goddamn better have all your ducks in a row because you're dealing with an agency that desperately needs to restore public confidence. The best way to do this is to make it look like there's one bad cop, not however many of them there are."

Donovan bit down on the inside of his cheek. Outrage threatened to spill from his mouth, or maybe it was bile. Either way, letting it spill wouldn't get him anywhere.

Power spoke for him. "I would think, sir, that the best thing for the agency and for public safety would be for there to be *no* bad cops. Because the truth will come out. I'm not making any threats, mind you. But I've worked with these agents before. These aren't some buffoons sent by Quantico who don't give a crap and just want to move on to the next case. These are good people, smart people, who won't stop until the job is done. And when I tell you that they will take their findings public if they even think they sniff a cover-up, I am not joking. Again, this isn't a threat. These are just the facts. SSA Holcombe will make you cry, and that's a fact too."

"I'm not afraid of her. This is bigger than her. It's bigger than all of us." He glanced over at Donovan. "I'm sorry, Detective. But the needs of the Commonwealth outweigh everything else. We can't keep people safe if we don't have their trust and faith."

Donovan took a deep breath and forced his shoulders to relax. "I understand, sir." He understood, all right.

"You're dismissed."

Donovan rose with Power, and they both left the office. Donovan didn't realize until they'd left the executive area that his supervisor was shaking. Power didn't say a word until they were back in his office though, with the door safely closed.

Then, silently, he pulled a digital recorder from his pocket and turned it off. He handed it to Donovan. "This is illegal, unless you consent to it right the fuck now."

Donovan blinked. "Sure, okay. I give my full and enthusiastic consent." The enormity of what Power had just done slammed into him. "Holy shit." He slipped the recorder into his jacket pocket, where it was least likely to get accidentally erased. "Thank you, sir."

"It was absolutely necessary. Now you obviously have to be out of the office for the rest of the day, for that Altobelli kidnapping."

Donovan didn't have to guess at his meaning. He needed to get that recording out of the office and into Luis' hands, right away. He thanked his boss and headed out of the office.

Luis wasn't home when he got there, but Donovan didn't expect him to be. It was still early. Tria, the kitten, looked up at Donovan from a carefully constructed nest of Luis' dirty undershirts and hopped up to come demand cuddles though.

He supposed his distress must have shone through for the cat. She usually only bestirred herself when Luis was around. He took shameless advantage of the situation, pausing only to put the recorder in his sock drawer before picking Tria up and holding her close to his chest. What did he care about getting cat hair on his jacket? Pretty soon, he wasn't going to have to worry about the suits anymore no matter what.

He knew he needed to have a more positive outlook. Blah blah positive thinking, whatever. He'd make more of an effort later, but right now the whole thing looked bleak. His boss' boss had just told him, in no uncertain terms, the truth didn't matter. The agency to which he'd devoted his entire career had decided he would be a scapegoat, through no fault of his own, and there was essentially nothing he could do about it. His only hope was to put his faith in someone he'd wronged repeatedly in the past and hope Luis could somehow convince his *own* bosses Donovan was worth the trouble.

Yeah, because that was going to happen.

Luis found him like that when he came home, hours later. Tria unfurled herself from her position under Donovan's chin, gave Luis his evening greeting, and retreated to her nest in Luis' laundry. Luis seemed to understand the message. He got rid of his suit and climbed into the big bed with Donovan, taking him into his arms and holding him close for long enough Donovan lost track of time.

Donovan didn't say anything. He just lost himself in Luis—Luis' strength, his scent, just the heat Luis put out. "I'm sorry I didn't say anything when you stopped by," he said when he finally felt he could speak.

Luis kissed the top of Donovan's head. "I get it. After talking with Lieutenant Power, I get it a little bit better, I think. You work with some interesting people, love. Tell me about this Porras guy."

Donovan looked up at Luis. "Seriously? He's a detective, like me. Works the night shift. He's been friendly lately. Always brings me coffee." He swallowed. "He's the one who told me—you know, the 'we're not going to let some dirtbag' thing."

"I wondered about that. Has he been spending a lot of time hanging around during the day shift?"

Donovan considered. "Yeah, lately. I figured he was just being supportive, in his way."

"Maybe he is. I don't know. I can't say anything, you know I can't. But seriously, be very cautious with this guy." Luis ground his teeth for a second. "I hate having to hide things, or give you incomplete information."

"You're doing what you have to do." Donovan stroked Luis' chest. "And right now, I wouldn't have anyone else on this case. I don't trust anyone else." He sat up and went over to his sock drawer. "After you guys left, Power and I had an interesting meeting." He looked away. "I don't need to hear this twice, so maybe you could go into another room."

Luis fished in his bedside drawer for a pair of earbuds. "Way ahead of you, love." He plugged them into the digital recorder and listened.

Donovan fidgeted. He wasn't sure how to act, and Luis wasn't giving away anything on his face. He wouldn't—Donovan knew how he was when he got into his solve-the-case mode. Instead, Donovan toyed with the bedspread.

When Luis pulled the earbuds out, Donovan looked back at him. "It's a lot, isn't it?"

Luis had gone sallow. "It's more than a lot. It's a bombshell is what it is. I'm . . . I'm pretty shaken. I don't know how to respond. That's some wild shit. It's good to know your boss has that much faith in us, I don't mind saying so. And he's right. There's nothing we're not going to do to make sure the right person is brought to justice for these crimes.

"And if we're told to stand down, for any reason, or if the state police somehow manage to obstruct us badly enough that we can't do our jobs? Then Power is damn right we're going to make sure everyone knows about it. If they thought the thought of *you* killing the protesters brought a scandal down onto this department, wait until they find out you were deliberately set out there as a scapegoat to minimize the truth. I know Dwayne will help me get the word out."

"Would he? I'm just another white cop to him." Donovan rolled over.

Luis wrapped his arm around Donovan's waist and pressed their bodies together. "Yes, he will. One, because we're friends and he knows I'm not going to lie to him about something like this. And two, because he knows exposing this kind of setup only helps his cause in the long run. It helps all of us because getting rid of cops who pull shady shit like this makes our jobs easier and safer too. Which is why I call him about work stuff when it comes up."

Donovan rolled over again. Luis' gentle smile was so warming, so loving, Donovan could almost start to hope again. Almost didn't cut it though, not completely. "It's going to get worse before it gets better though. Isn't it?"

Luis took a deep breath and lowered his gaze. "Probably. Dirty cop cases always do. They hurt like burning. But we've got this. We're strong, and we'll get through this together."

CHAPTER SEVEN

Luis got out of the car and stretched his legs. "I miss having the office down here," he told Kevin, scanning the former red-light district. It looked different at night. It always had, but now that Luis could see things differently, he appreciated the emptiness more. "Chelsea's got its good points but you've got to admit, there's something to be said for being right down in the middle of things here."

Kevin locked the car and hurried over to the crosswalk. "You never stopped complaining about parking down here when we were here."

"I'll never stop complaining about Boston. Y'all give me fresh material every day, Kevin." Luis poured the Southern accent on extra thick.

"Just for that I'm dragging you to a game at Fenway. We're going to get seats on top of the Monstah—but I'm sticking you in a Yankees hat." Kevin jogged across the street in direct violation of several traffic laws.

Luis ran to catch up. "Excellent. I'm looking

forward to tossing someone off the side. That is the whole point of those seats, right?" Luis tried to look innocent. He knew he was probably failing.

"Why are we down here again?" Kevin couldn't seem to hide his grin.

Luis looked around. If he let himself go, he could see so much more than an ugly city hall and occasional splashes of tourist puke. "Something's still bugging me. We've got witnesses telling me there's Boston cops and state troopers at the Harper residence, but we're only getting pushback from the staties. The Boston patrolman's union isn't cooperating, but we're not having interaction with them at all."

Kevin raised an eyebrow. "Yeah, so? You've got an inside source at the state troopers, and it's a statie being targeted. We don't have a motive for BPD to be involved at all, and we don't have anyplace to get a foothold there. We don't have anywhere to start looking."

"True enough." Luis started walking west, toward the alley where Donovan had saved Camila's son. "That's why we're here. I need something to work with."

"Didn't the ghosts already tell you they didn't see anything?"

"How many witnesses do we see who don't even know what they saw until later? We have to ask the right questions. We didn't know the right questions then." Luis watched as the faded impression of a wall of people, mostly men, surged past him like an old movie. For a second, they seemed to pass through him—but this was residual energy, not real ghosts, and he only had a passing chill from the experience.

At least, that was all he felt right now.

He caught a glimpse of something a little more solid watching from the alley. It was Groat, the youth who'd been killed for playing craps. A car drove past and shone his light right through him, revealing a skeletal outline against a brick wall, but only Luis seemed to notice. He told Kevin to wait and approached the ghost.

"Mr. Groat. How are you this evening?"

Groat shrugged, although his grin seemed to suggest he found some amusement. Of course, half of his face was stuck in a permanent grin, since he only had bone on that side. Luis might have been projecting. "Same as ever, I guess. Some little kid got lost from his parents. I taught him how to play craps for an hour before they finally figured out he was lost and came and got him."

Luis didn't have to fake his grin. "You might have saved the kid's life. You kept him in one place, instead of letting him wander. Makes him easier to find."

"Exactly." Groat smirked. "I might be dead, but I ain't stupid. And hey, the kid will have a good life skill whenever he gets back to Muncie, Indiana."

"I don't meet a lot of stupid ghosts. And you never know when that kind of skill will come in handy." Luis scratched his chin. The kid's parents would probably have something to say about it, especially if they had strong views about gambling. It wasn't his problem though. "Listen. Ten years ago, during the riot, there was a cop who pulled some injured folks into this alley."

Groat's eyes lit up. "Yeah, sure. I remember that, now that you mention it. First time you came down here, it was like you were asking me to remember something vague in more than a hundred years of vague stuff, you know? This, this I remembered. It stuck out. This guy was in a state police uniform, which was weird, and he was helping people instead of hitting them or worse." He shook his head. "Maybe that one wasn't a useless sack of skin."

Luis snorted. "His colleagues aren't high on my list right now either. This one might be a little harder. Do you remember anyone who might have seen it—anyone living? If they had a camera that would be ideal, but whatever."

Groat rolled his eyes to the sky. At first, Luis

thought he was just looking upward, because with all the light pollution they couldn't see a single star from down here. Then Luis realized he could pick out one or two. The streetlights down here had dimmed back to what they'd been in 1919 while Groat wracked his brain.

"I remember a guy. He had some kind of thing around his neck, I don't know. He did have a big fancy camera, so he must've been with the paper or something. They don't wear uniforms, but he did get a picture of your guy dragging a Black man out of the crowd. The guy couldn't stand up, so your guy had to drag him. Had his hands under his shoulders while there was some tear gas in the background. I'm sure it was a very dramatic picture."

Luis could hardly contain himself. If he could find the photographer, he could completely exonerate Donovan. "Do you remember what this photographer looked like?"

"Short fellow, long beard like one of them Russian priests. Like Rasputin. Blond. Dressed like a slob, but everyone dresses like a slob these days." Groat wheezed out a laugh. "Is that helpful?"

"It is. Thank you, Mr. Groat. Is there anything I can do for you? Anything you need?"

Groat seemed to think about it. "Not that I can think of. I've got a pretty sweet deal here right now, you know? I go where I want, I do what I want. I kind of like it."

"Are you a drinking man?"

"Well yeah, but who ain't?" Groat paused. "Wait, don't tell me the stupid teetotalers got that amendment passed."

Luis chuckled. "They did, but it got overturned. I'll bring you a bottle of rum soon."

Luis had just been guessing at the rum. A tank of molasses had ruptured in Boston the same year Groat had died, drowning several residents. If there was that much molasses on hand at the time, rum must have been part of the Boston scene too. When Groat's eye sockets lit up, Luis knew he'd said the right thing.

"Thanks, Agent. You're all right."

Luis returned to Kevin. "I didn't get a lot of background for why there would be Boston cops involved with trying to frame Donovan. But I did get a lead on where we might be able to get some photographic evidence for Donovan." He described the photographer for him.

Kevin, because he'd been around since time began, pursed his lips and nodded. "I think I might know who you're talking about. I'll make some calls. What if we were to go farther up the route, closer to where the deaths took place? Maybe we could get some more closure there."

Luis doubted they'd find closure until they got to the bottom of this elaborate conspiracy against Donovan, but they'd try. Kevin's idea was still a good one, just a stop on the way to the closure they needed. They retraced the march route back up toward the Common, following a path Kevin had laid out in his phone with the murder locations plotted on a map.

"Kevan Powell, victim number five, died here." Kevin stopped on Tremont, in front of the Granary Burying Ground. "So did our fourth victim, Shawn French. Both shot in the back."

Luis caught a glimpse of two Black male bodies, one collapsed on top of the other. Both were young, no more than twenty. He didn't see them for long; the images faded back into the sidewalk and left only a stain on the concrete to remember them by. Even Kevin seemed unable to see the stain.

When Luis looked into the graveyard, he found dozens looking back at him. Some were no more than skeletons in ancient rags, but five stood out. They wore colonial clothing, maybe from around the Revolutionary War, and stared at him with undisguised contempt. Four of them were white. One was Black, and all clustered around one particular marker.

"You think you can avenge us at this late

date?" The Black one—Crispus Attucks, Luis remembered his name from a lecture he'd attended while he'd been dating Dwayne—stepped forward. His companions clustered around him. "You're perhaps a minute late, or two."

Luis glanced around. He could see no one watching, except for Kevin. "International politics is so far from my pay grade it's not even funny. My job isn't so much about revenge anyway."

One of the white ones scoffed, sending dirt flying from his nose. "Isn't it?"

"No. It's about stopping a killer from harming more people. Which is why I'm here now. Do you remember the police shooting that happened in this spot ten years ago?"

The five victims of the Boston Massacre exchanged sightless glances. "We might. And why would we share it with you?"

Luis blinked. "Because whatever may have happened to you, in 1770, it's the twenty-first century now. And we can't keep letting it happen."

They looked at each other again. "I know not the name of the one who shot them." Attucks spoke now. "I cannot read. But I can tell you the man's uniform had the word Boston on it. *That* I have seen often enough."

One of the others waved a hand, making a sound like bones cracking against one another even though Luis could see flesh. "I saw a name on his pin." He patted his chest, right where a riot officer's name badge would be. "It was something Irish, and strange, although I took little note of it. We cannot affect these things from this side of the Veil, you know."

"You might be surprised." Luis raised an eyebrow. "You're having an effect now." Not that Irish names were in short supply on Boston's police force. "Can you remember anything about the officer? They're all dressed the same, I know. But did anything stand out to you?"

"Riot suppressors are all the same." Attucks spoke again. "They want blood, and they'll stop at nothing to get it. Any gathering of two or more men is a riot, and they wish bodies in a hole."

Luis wasn't about to argue with the man considered the first casualty of the American Revolution. "Was this one old or young?"

One of the victims, who hadn't previously spoken, cleared his throat. "It was difficult to see behind his shield, but his skin seemed to have some few wrinkles. It was round and florid, like unto a tomato."

"Thank you." Luis took a step back. "I know you don't believe it, but I'm doing everything in my power to make sure he doesn't get away with this."

To a man, they jeered. "He's gotten away

with it for ten years." Attucks waved his hand. "He will go to his own grave a free and proud man. But when he does, he'll be ours. You can count on that."

Luis ignored the way his skin crawled. He'd always tried hard to live up to his ideals as a cop, but if he'd ever needed incentive, Attucks had provided it. "I'll bring you proof, when he's caught."

"You do that, lawman." Attucks laughed at him, but there seemed to be little mirth in it. "But don't you think of walking past this boneyard without it."

"It's a promise."

Luis hurried back over to Kevin and told him what he'd seen. Then his knees buckled as the energy it had taken to speak with so many dead caught up to him.

Kevin caught him before he could fall. "I think that's enough happy fun ghosty time for you, bud. Let's get you home to Donovan." He kept hold of Luis' arm as they hurried toward the car, just in case.

Once they were in the vehicle, Kevin turned to him. "You seriously spoke with the first five people to get killed in the Revolution?"

Luis closed his eyes against his sudden, throbbing headache. "I don't think that's how they see themselves. They see themselves more as victims of police brutality. Both descriptions are true," he added quickly. "The Founding Fathers used what happened to those guys to help stir people up to the cause, and it worked because people were pissed. But for those guys, it was just another one of those times when Bostonians got unruly and the authorities reacted with excessive force to put them down." He shrugged. "We did get a description of the actual shooter. Name was Irish, although no one remembers what it was. It was a Boston cop, which explains why they're involved with a scheme to frame Donovan. And it was an older guy with a round and 'florid' face."

"Well, that narrows it down." Kevin slammed his hand against the steering wheel.

Luis yawned. "We couldn't use it in court anyway. And we can avoid looking at any younger cops as triggermen. I think what we have to do right now is focus on the state troopers, still. They're the ones we can mostly prove, and once we can convict we can lean on them to give up their cronies in the BPD."

Going after the BPD would probably cause problems with Patricia and the rest of Donovan's family, but right now, Luis didn't care. He'd take on anyone involved in trying to hurt Donovan.

Donovan didn't need to ask Luis why he was in the state he was when Kevin dragged him into the house that night. He recognized Luis' grayish skin tone and the way he shuffled his feet. Luis had been out talking to dead people again, and by the looks of it, he'd pushed himself hard. He hustled Luis into the bath, got him stripped, and dropped him into their big fancy bathtub.

It was kind of awesome being able to do that now. Donovan wasn't going to lie. He'd go back and give him the contact he needed in a minute or two, but first, he wanted to check in with Kevin.

Kevin had helped himself to a beer and was waiting for Donovan in the living room. Tria had taken a moment to greet the newcomer and was happily playing with Kevin's goatee. Kevin didn't seem to mind though. He just laughed and gave her as much attention as she seemed to want. "How's he doing?"

Donovan ran a hand through his hair and sat down nearby. "He's a mess. What happened?"

"Just a short little romp through one of the oldest parts of Boston." Kevin rolled his eyes. "I wish he wouldn't do this stuff to himself."

"Me too. I'm not sure he thinks he has a choice, you know? I mean it just started happening to him when we were doing that case in Sudbury.

It's not like he grew up with it or had any training or anything. It's something that happens, and he can either deal with it or complain." Donovan slumped in his seat. "I do hate how much it takes out of him though."

"Me too. It's also disconcerting as hell. He had a conversation with the victims of the Boston Massacre. No big deal." Kevin scratched Tria underneath her chin. "Who *does* that? More than that, who meets a major historical figure and then *takes a witness statement*?"

Donovan had to laugh at that. "Luis does. At the end of the day, he's a hunter. He hunts killers. Everything else is kind of secondary."

"Not everything." Kevin gave Donovan a significant look. "And right now, he's hunting for a killer who seems to be fixated on making life difficult for the one person in his life more important than hunting for killers."

Flames touched Donovan's cheeks. "I know. I hate that I can't help him."

"You are helping him. Trust me. You're giving him information, you're being honest, and you're believing in him. That's what he needs from you right now." He moistened his lips and looked away. "Listen, we got a clue I need to go track down. Tell Luis I'll pick him up tomorrow since we left his car at work, okay?"

"Cool beans." Donovan walked Kevin to the door, locked up behind him, and then went to check on Luis.

For a minute, Donovan thought Luis might have fallen asleep in the tub. Then Luis cracked his eyes open. "Hey."

Donovan sat by the edge of the tub and took Luis' hand. "I hear you had an exciting night."

Luis grimaced and closed his eyes again. "Yeah. Very exciting. I talked to some people who are dead. Which, you know, is kind of a thing for me."

Donovan splashed some hot water at Luis. "Yeah, okay. Except it doesn't usually put you on your ass like this."

Luis sighed. "Okay. Have you heard of the Boston Police Strike?"

"Wasn't that like a hundred years ago?"

"Give or take a year or two, yeah. Well, it kind of ran through me."

Donovan had to give it a minute for Luis' words to sink in. "The . . . whole strike?"

"The riot part. It happened in Government Center—well, Scollay Square, back in the day."

"Right. You know, my grandmother called it Scollay Square until the day she died. It was like she knew the place or something." Donovan tried not to think about that too much. "Anyway, the whole riot just—ran right on through?"

"Through me. Yeah. And then I interviewed a couple of dead witnesses. Maybe six? I don't know. I'm just a little beat." Luis took Donovan's hand. It was cold as ice. "But hey, I talked to a ghost who very deliberately kept a lost little kid entertained until his parents came and found him, so there's that."

"You know, sometimes I feel like the cognitive dissonance of our conversations is going to eat, like, half of my brain."

"I think it's going to eat all of mine. Don't ever let them send me for a CT scan. I don't want to know." Luis groaned, but then he laughed. "I shouldn't complain. It hurts, and it smells bad, and sometimes, I get to meet some of the most amazing people. I actually met Crispus Attucks tonight. Can you believe that?"

Donovan shook his head. "It's pretty amazing. What did he tell you?"

"Um, not to even walk past that graveyard until we've arrested the person who *did* kill those protesters. They saw one of the killings—two of the killings. And they have strong feelings about it. Apparently, they have a thing about state-sponsored violence. Who knew?" Luis managed a little grin. "If nothing else, they're waiting for the actual killer to cross over. If I don't find him, they will."

"Well, that's a cheery thought. I mean, it doesn't help me, but at least he'll get what's coming to him." Donovan grinned in spite of himself. "You think you could eat something?"

"I could try." He pushed himself out of the tub, and Donovan helped him into the kitchen.

He got Luis to eat some soup and then hustled him off to bed. Luis didn't need to be all that sexual for Donovan to feel good about having him beside him, but Luis could be very amorous after his ghostly encounters too. Tonight, he seemed to need to wrap himself around Donovan, even if he lacked the energy to do much. It was okay—Donovan could give him everything he needed and more.

He jerked them both together, long, slow strokes that left Luis gasping and shaking. It didn't take long to warm Luis' body and bring him to the edge of completion. Donovan took a little longer to get there himself, but he didn't want to dwell on the reasons why. He just wanted to focus on Luis, on them. Watching color and life come back to his beloved was enough to drive his worries away, at least in the short term.

After they'd both finished and cleaned themselves up, they went to sleep. Whatever happened, whatever absurdities Donovan's unknown enemies might manufacture, they couldn't take this away from him. He had the man he loved in his bed and in his arms. They had a home together. They had a life. They had a little cat, who was currently curled up on Luis' hip and purring.

The next day, Luis headed in to the office a little later than usual, with a bit of a spring to his step. Donovan knew he was the reason why.

He could only wish he had the same degree of optimism as he faced his own day in hell. Power supported him, and he knew it, but otherwise, it was hard to feel like anyone was even remotely helpful. Porras was around in the morning, before Power chased him off with a scowl and a threat to start docking his pay. He seemed friendly enough, but Donovan could do without the kind of friends who thought he'd murdered five people and didn't care.

He supposed it was a good thing that people who thought he'd killed unarmed protesters didn't want anything to do with him. He just wished they'd listen to the facts.

Still, Donovan had work to do. The day-to-day job of a state police Homicide detective didn't disappear just because his life was crumbling. He had a suspect in the Altobelli abduction, although he hadn't found the kid or the remains yet, and a fresh case had landed on his desk only this morning.

The issue, of course, was that only three cities in Massachusetts had the authority to investigate homicides. If someone died under suspicious circumstances outside of Boston, Worcester, or Springfield, investigation fell to the state police. Today, Donovan was looking at a messy rage kill in Medfield. It probably threw the good residents of Medfield for a loop, considering that the little town hadn't seen so much violence since King Philip's War, but Donovan headed out to investigate anyway.

If the local police chief, who waited with Dr. Wong for Donovan to show up, recognized him from the news, he didn't say anything. He just led Donovan over to the remains, which had been left unceremoniously in a heap near the prominent old church on the main drag.

"Do we have an ID?" Donovan asked, glancing up at the sky. It was going to rain soon, and he wanted to get the remains out of here before they lost evidence in the storm.

"We can't get an identification until the autopsy." Wong snapped his nitrile gloves on and flared his nostrils at Donovan, like a bull.

The police chief gave Wong a long,

measuring look. "His name is Trevor Matthews. He's nineteen, and he lives with his mother four blocks from here. I've already had someone go make the notification." He smirked over at Wong. "Your autopsy is all well and good, but his brother's the one who found him, and that brother's one of my officers. I sent him to tell their ma, which gave him the excuse to go home for the day so I can still pay him."

Donovan let himself smile, just a little. Most bosses wouldn't complain about letting a guy go home after his brother had just been found murdered. It was a rare breed of employer, especially in public service, who would work to find a way to avoid forcing that same employee to take more leave time than he had to.

"That's the great thing about being in a smaller jurisdiction, Dr. Wong," he said, before Wong could lash out and burn their bridges before they were built. "People know each other."

The chief took his hat off and shook his head. "Well, I'd have known Trevor here even if his brother didn't work for me. I've got a couple of guys down at the station, far away from the brother. You're going to want to talk to them."

Donovan could read between the lines. He set the crime scene techs to documenting the scene and followed the chief back to the station. There, he found two sullen teenagers with bloody knuckles, black eyes, and split lips. The kids couldn't have been more than sixteen.

He turned to his host. "Their parents been called yet?"

"Yup. They're on their way. Can't talk to them until they're here."

The parents arrived, and then lawyers had to be called. All the lawyers in the world couldn't do much. The kids were guilty, and by the time the district attorney got there to discuss matters with them, the whole story came out.

Trevor Matthews was a bully. He couldn't keep his hands to himself. He'd gotten probation after trying to force himself on one of the kid's younger sisters and killing her dog in the process. The justice system had failed her, and so the boys had taken it upon themselves to do something about it.

Donovan felt bad for them. It didn't make killing the kid right, but he still felt bad.

He formally arrested them and brought them to the Norfolk County Jail. They made it through their first court appearance before Wong had even finished processing their victim into the morgue, and didn't have to spend a night in jail. It didn't seem quite right to Donovan, but nothing about the case seemed quite right to him. Trevor could probably have been helped long before he started killing animals and hurting young girls. The girl in question wasn't going to be helped by seeing the system go after her brother, and no one benefitted when killers went free.

Even if Donovan could understand where they were coming from.

By the time he got back to the office, he couldn't think about the ugly stares from his colleagues or even about the plus-one to his clearance rate. He could only grieve. His phone pinged, giving him some welcome distraction.

The message came to his personal email, not from Luis or even Kevin but from one of Luis' less-discussed colleagues. Donovan hadn't spoken to Chris Wragge more than once or twice in the past year and change, but his curiosity was enough to break him out of his sadness.

Kevin Rourke got this image today from a contact of his. The original is in evidence. He says to keep it close to your chest and don't show anyone yet. You're going to want to smoke out the one trying to play you.

Donovan clicked on the attachment. Much to his shock, he found a photo of himself ten years ago, in riot gear, pulling a Black man out of the stampede running down Congress Street. The photo had a time and date stamp.

The photo was exoneration.

CHAPTER EIGHT

Luis got up early and went for a run. He needed to get some of this ridiculous tension out of his system. Sure, they had the photo. He knew people who wanted Donovan to be the bad guy would wave it away. Photos could be doctored, time stamps faked. It was evidence in Donovan's favor, but it wasn't airtight.

What he needed was the actual shooter, and finding that killer would be the hardest case Luis had ever worked. He had no real witnesses, no suspects, and nothing to go on. It was a cold case, which required a whole different set of training and skills, and it meant taking on a group of people who protected their own more fiercely than any other right or wrong.

Not that Donovan was benefitting from that protection. Not at the moment anyway.

A run would help him to clear his mind and regain his focus. Being in their house, which was full of Donovan's things and Donovan's scents, just clouded everything with emotion.

A run through the Chestnut Hill Cemetery gave him enough of a challenge to make things interesting while keeping him out of reach of homicidal drivers and curious onlookers. The cemetery had its share of observers, but the ghosts there tended to be fairly silent and not inclined to comment. One Victorian lady did take the time to give him the wolf whistle she could never have indulged in while alive. He wasn't sure how to feel about that.

Donovan had gone out by the time he got home. He'd left a note on the bathroom mirror. *Got a call about one of my cases. Couldn't wait. There's coffee in the pot for you. I love you.*

Luis' heart swelled as he stumbled toward the shower. Even with everything Donovan was dealing with, he still thought about Luis. He was an amazing guy.

He stepped out of the shower and padded into the bedroom to change for work. Just as he found his underwear, a stench from the grave threatened to bowl him over. An undertone of juniper gave away the identity of the visitor before Luis looked up—not that any other ghost had a tendency to pop in while Luis was naked.

"Captain Lightfoot." Luis slipped into his boxers and pretended he could look at the whole thing casually. Friends always dropped in without knocking. Of course they did. "Isn't it a little early for you?"

Lightfoot took a deep swig from his bottle. Luis had given him the bottle as a gift, after the dead serial killer had helped him solve a case. It never seemed to empty, and Luis couldn't quite figure out how that was supposed to work. He never figured out how the liquid didn't run through the skeletal parts of Lightfoot's mouth and throat either. He didn't understand the physics of undeath.

"No rest for the wicked. And I'm the wickedest of them all." He hacked out a wheeze of a laugh that rattled his vertebrae. "Of course look at ye. Ye're sat here still pulling on your clothes when there's mischief afoot—mischief ye could be stopping, and should be."

Luis pulled his pants on. "Well, you know, still living and all that. There's basic maintenance I have to do."

"Bah." There wasn't any heat behind Lightfoot's words, and he passed Luis his undershirt. "Yer man's in a bit of trouble, isn't he?"

Luis sucked in his cheeks. "He is. I'm not sure how far it goes, either."

"How now? Here I was thinking you're the big and mighty hunter, tracking down ne'er-dowells like me and bringing them to justice. How is it that one puny little punk escapes you simply because he carries a shiny badge?"

Luis found a dress shirt that looked good on him and pulled it on. "Because something like this can't be pulled off with just one cop. Hell, I can't even be sure it *is* a cop. It's got to be cops railroading him, but for all I know, the first shot was fired by someone completely outside the protest. Could have been self-defense for a mugging gone horribly awry, and we'll never know." He scratched Tria behind her ears and headed toward the kitchen.

Lightfoot followed him, just as Luis knew he would. "Of course, of course. But it wasn't. And the malcontents trying to railroad your boy know it."

"Too bad they murdered the guy who knew what was going on." Luis slammed his travel mug onto the counter with a little more force than necessary.

"Oh, it's true. It was too bad. Poor wee lad is all to pieces about it too. He's confused. Can't understand why half his stuff is missing and his foolish game system won't work."

Luis stared at the ghost. "Are you telling me that Harper is back?"

"Have ye potatoes in yer ears?" Lightfoot stuck an icy finger into Luis' ear, making him yelp.

"It's what I just said, isn't it? And if you're smart, you'll head down there and help the poor lad through this challenging transition." He held his gin bottle over his heart and adopted a pious pose.

Luis rolled his eyes, but he let himself grin just a bit. "I can't use it in court, but it's a step in the right direction. Thanks, Captain."

"It's what I'm for. Just think of me as your vaguely undead fairy godfather."

Luis mouthed the words, and then decided not to address the comment. Instead, he grabbed his mug and keys and headed out the door.

Once he got to the office, he lost no time in letting Kevin know they needed to head back to the Harper crime scene. Kevin was skeptical, but he agreed to the trip on the condition that he be allowed to drive. Luis had no problem agreeing to the stipulation. He had less than no interest in driving in the city of Boston.

They pulled up to the curb and headed upstairs. Luis had half thought someone would have broken the seal and looted the place, or possibly gone through to destroy evidence. Either the killer was too arrogant or too good to have left anything behind that hadn't already been picked up. Luis knew they hadn't gotten much.

Kevin glanced around. "You know this is making me nervous, right?"

Luis walked slowly, shoes echoing in the silence. The whole scenario felt like a setup, but he trusted Lightfoot not to do that to him. He didn't know why, except that Lightfoot hadn't steered him wrong before. He didn't know why Lightfoot would be sniffing around in Mattapan, a place he hadn't frequented in life, but he could get to that later.

He closed his eyes and tried to settle himself. "Jason Harper, my name is Luis Gomes. I know you're here. Come out and show yourself."

The smell came just as expected, faint at first and then stronger as Harper manifested before him. Harper hadn't been a good person in life, and the stink attached to him exceeded what his remains smelled like down in the morgue. The fatal wound that had killed him appeared as a gaping hole in his forehead. He'd been shot in the back of his head, execution-style, so the exit wound seemed to be in the right place.

"You can't come in here without a warrant. I know my rights, pig."

Luis rolled his eyes. "Those rights only apply to the living, Jason. Although I'm not here to mess with you. I'm here to help."

"I've heard that one before." Harper curled his lip, pulling it back farther than he could have in life to reveal badly receding gums. "And you can miss me with that 'only apply to the living' shit. We're here having a talk."

"We are here talking. Go take a look in the mirror."

Jason stomped over to the bathroom. It took a minute or two for him to get the lights on, which honestly should have tipped him off right there. Luis tried not to hold it against him. He knew he had a bias because of Harper's criminal background and because of what he had done to Donovan. He needed to overcome that bias if he wanted to get anywhere.

When Harper finally saw himself, his scream rattled the window, so badly even Kevin took notice.

"What the hell? You can't call an ambulance?" Harper rounded on Luis.

"An ambulance was called, Jason." Luis tried not to think about the oddness of his life. "Except it was too late. You are deceased. I'm very sorry."

"Fucking cops." He glared at Luis. "I knew I shouldn't have trusted none of you." He stormed back into the living room and flung himself onto the couch.

Kevin shuddered when he saw the dip in the upholstery.

"Hindsight is always twenty-twenty." Luis

scratched at his chin to buy himself some time. He couldn't exactly disagree with the young man. "In your case, it probably would have been a better idea." He cleared his throat. "I understand why you wouldn't—given your background, I'm a little concerned about why you'd cooperate with police to begin with. People tell me there were cops coming and going from your apartment all the time."

"Damn nosy neighbors. What was I supposed to do, tell them no? At first, I did. I told them to go fuck themselves, and I got creative about it too." He shook his head, sending noncorporeal droplets of blood and brain onto the upholstery. "But I have never met the cop who takes no for an answer, for anything."

Luis nodded slowly. "It's true. We're pretty persistent, whether we're the good ones or the bad ones. So you didn't voluntarily participate in the scheme to discredit Donovan Carey?"

"Not really. I mean, I could give a shit if some cop gets blamed for shooting people at the riot. I mean we all know *some* cop did it. It's not like any of them care if the wrong guy gets shot, right? Why should I care if the wrong one gets blamed? But I didn't want to get involved. You lie down with dogs you get up with fleas and all that.

"But then the old guy, he showed up with a

156

bag of smack and a hot gun. Said the gun had been used in a shooting up the road." Jason pressed his lips together and narrowed his eyes. He didn't care about the person who'd been shot, only that he'd been drawn into the cops' drama. "If I kept saying no, this shit was going to be found on my body after I tried to escape. So I didn't have a choice."

Luis sighed. "Yeah, I've seen it happen before."

"Shit, you probably helped cover it up. All you cops are the same, I don't care about which fancy suit you wear or which badge you carry. Some of the cops I saw were Boston cops, some of them were staties, you think any of them were any different? No. They were all exactly the same."

Luis nodded. "One of them killed you though."

Jason screamed again. The windows shook. "Yeah. Yeah, and when I get my hands on that bastard, I'm going to make what he did to me look like a picnic."

Luis interrupted him. "Do you remember who it was? I know it can be painful to remember back to the incident. I won't press you to remember, but if you can, it will help us to get him off the street."

"I could give a shit if he's on the street. If he's on the street, he can get his old ass here." Jason punched the couch. A green stain appeared where he'd punched, and Kevin paled.

The fight seemed to go out of Harper then, just a little. "The last thing I remember before I woke up and suddenly couldn't leave my house is two cops coming to visit. One of them was the first one that came to me. Dude is tall, about your age, white, and all the girls think he's hot. Name's Emerson. He's a statie. He was standing in front of me when everything went dark. The other one is an older guy, I don't know his name. He's the one who said he was going to plant that evidence on me though. I fucking want him dead."

Luis took a breath. "Okay. I know who the younger one is. I just need to figure out the older one. Is there anything you can think of that would help me to identify him, other than his charming personality and adherence to the letter of the law?"

Jason managed a little laugh. "Nah. He's an old white guy who doesn't like Black guys. They all start to run together after a while, you know."

"Oh, I know." Luis didn't have to fake his bitterness. "I've seen a few myself. Thanks, Jason. This has been very helpful. I tried to get to you before they could, when I figured out what was going on, but obviously, it wasn't fast enough."

"Yeah, well." Jason let his head loll back onto the couch cushions. "Since when do cops talk to dead people, anyway? Am I an X-file now? Couldn't they have sent Scully in a thong?"

Luis laughed. "No, Jason. That's still a TV show. As far as I know, I'm still kind of unique on the force. Someone told me you'd come back, and I came by to answer any questions you might have. I don't have all the answers, but you shouldn't have to deal with it alone."

Jason scowled. "But you're a cop. And I'm a crook."

"The lines aren't always the same when we're dealing with death." Luis shrugged. "I'm here to help when I can. Let me know if you need anything or have any questions."

They left the apartment. Once they were in the car, Kevin turned to Luis. "Okay, that guy *reeked*. How do you not just barf every time?"

Luis had to laugh at that, but he sobered up when he thought about what Jason had told him. "I think we've got a real problem on our hands. One of the cops who was there when Jason was killed was Emerson Porras, who's been pestering Donovan at work. I don't know who the other one is."

Kevin pursed his lips. "We'll have to figure out how to prove Porras is in on the conspiracy and make him spill."

Donovan moved the Altobelli case over to the "solved" board. The act was normally a celebratory one. They'd gotten their man. They'd found the bad guy, justice was served. This time around, there was no applause, no lifting of the spirits. Sure, Donovan had closed the case. They'd known it was murder, but not before Sharon Altobelli's remains decomposed to the point where a closed casket would be necessary. Donovan had suspected murder and not kidnapping, but he couldn't prove it.

And there were no kudos for being right without proof.

The hostile stares of his colleagues burned into his back. He tried to imagine a shield, like in a bad science fiction show, but it just wasn't cutting the mustard. *It's a good thing. They think I'm a murderer, and they hate murderers. That's why they're acting like this.* He hadn't circulated the photo, not yet. It would only be helpful if he could find the real killer.

Knowing he was in the right didn't make it any easier though.

He headed back to his desk and grabbed a random case file. He didn't care which one. Any case would do, as long as it got his mind off of his hostile teammates.

When he opened the folder, he saw a crime scene photo from ten years ago. A protester's body lay in the middle of a trash-strewn street. He stared sightlessly into the clear blue sky. His throat looked like something had torn it out, an animal or monster attack, but Donovan knew the truth. He'd been shot from behind. What Donovan was seeing was an exit wound.

So why was the protester on his back?

"Looking at your own handiwork?"

Donovan looked up to see a cold, pale face. Lt. Greg Orlov worked in Internal Affairs. Donovan hadn't had much to do with him. He hadn't needed to. Those who had described him as "essentially a vampire, or maybe a KGB agent. Either way, be glad you weren't there."

Donovan scoffed. "Not mine, thanks. Someone's though. I was just wondering, since we're on the subject. We know the victims were shot in the back—it was in the news coverage, it was in incident reports everyone saw at the time."

"Yes, this is true." Orlov leaned over Donovan's shoulder, peering at the crime scene photo. "This man—Leroy Thompson, age twenty-one—appears to be on his back. Why do you think that is?"

"I was just wondering that myself. Crime

scene processors know to leave the body as it is before processing a scene. EMTs would have checked for a pulse first—there were too many injured to help. And if they've got someone who's clearly deceased, they're going to move on to someone they can save."

"So you were there." Orlov's icy blue eyes sparkled with triumph.

"I was farther away, I have a witness to prove it. The FBI is investigating that, and you'd have to ask them for the names and whatnot. I'm staying the hell out of it because I know how important it is." Donovan stayed calm. "I do know how EMTs operate. Know how else you can tell it wasn't me, Lieutenant?"

Everyone around Donovan, everyone in Major Crimes, went perfectly still.

"How's that, Detective?"

"I'm not that good of a shot." Donovan pointed to the neck wound, even though he wanted to look away. "I'm certainly competent. I know my way around a gun. I'm not a sharpshooter. I aim for big parts, areas I know I can hit. I go for the torso or the lower body. This is a neck shot. The neck is a smaller area. It takes a ton of skill and training to be able to hit a person, especially a running person, in the neck with any kind of accuracy. If I remember correctly—and again, I'm staying out of the investigation—four of the five were hit in the neck."

"You could have gotten lucky." Orlov's face stayed still. If Donovan had impressed him, he wasn't letting him know.

Donovan turned his chair, so he was looking right up at Orlov. "Lieutenant, I've been accused of a crime I didn't commit by a suspect who was in another state when the crime he claimed to see took place. My colleagues treat me like a pariah on the word of a felon and a liar who *could not see* what he said he saw, I'm being hounded by the media, and I can't even trust my own union at this point. What about any of this says 'lucky' to you?"

"Hm." Orlov straightened up. "We'll see." He turned on his heel and walked away.

Donovan watched him go. His pulse thundered in his ear, but he made himself sit still until the creepy investigator was gone. Then he grabbed his phone and his wallet and headed for the exit.

"I'm grabbing lunch," he told the department admin, who didn't seem to care.

When he saw the track-suited figure leaning against his car, he almost went back inside. Fred Carey didn't look any different than he had the last time Donovan had seen him last fall. "You're not supposed to be here." Donovan strode over to his car and unlocked the driver's-side only. "Go away."

Fred grabbed the passenger-side handle. "That's no way to talk to your father, Donovan. I'm all the way out here to help you out with your little problem. Don't you think you should hear me out? It's not as though a man in your position can afford to turn up his nose at his friends."

Donovan hesitated. He shouldn't let Fred into the car. Fred wasn't his friend; he was a scumbag who'd once held a badge. Still, Fred had a point. It was entirely possible that Fred might know something. After all, if anyone was likely to know the kind of cop who would shoot innocent protesters it was Fred Carey.

"Fuck. Fine, get in." Donovan unlocked the car door.

Fred chuckled and slid into the passenger seat. "Take me somewhere nice for lunch, son. I'm an old man living on a pension, and with child support payments and everything—well, life ain't easy."

Donovan ground his teeth and drove. "You're getting Olive Garden." He clenched the steering wheel to keep from punching his father. "She named the baby Patrick."

"For Saint Patrick." Fred grinned.

"For Patricia. As in Mom." Donovan's

return smile was vicious. "So how's things?"

"Oh, you know. I see my friends now and again. I go to the club. I keep my ear to the ground. Your brother John made sergeant."

"Yeah, we had a little dinner for him." Donovan didn't bring up John's girlfriend because Chantal was Black and Fred would lose his mind. He didn't bring up how Luis had cooked the whole meal, because that would just bring up even more bad blood. "I'm proud of him. He likes what he's doing, and he's good at it."

They made small talk during the short drive to Olive Garden. Donovan, at least, was faking any joviality. He wanted to be here about as much as he wanted a hole in his head. Fred had been in the Boston Police Department for a long time though, and he still knew plenty of people. Donovan couldn't take the chance that he might have a clue.

Once their meals had been delivered, Fred finally got around to the reason they were there in the first place. "So it seems you've gotten yourself into a bit of a pickle, Donovan. This whole shooting protesters thing has come back to bite you in the ass."

Donovan gripped his fork so hard he bent it in half. "I didn't shoot anyone."

"Doesn't matter if you did or didn't, Donnie. People believe you did, and that's what matters.

Ten years ago, no one cared. A cop's word was valuable, and if he said a shooting was justified, that was all it took. Now—well, as long as your skin is black, you can do just about anything, and if a cop tries to stop you, everyone starts screaming about how you've hurt their little feelings." He rolled his eyes and stuffed a giant wad of pasta into his mouth. "Give me a break, am I right? You got drugs in your pocket, no one gives a shit about your feelings or your rights. You ain't got any."

Donovan sighed. They'd been through this a thousand times. He hadn't convinced his father then, and he wasn't going to now. Thankfully, Fred's gun and badge were long gone by now. Well, okay, he'd gotten to keep his gun, but the principle of the thing, the license to fire that thing in the name of the state—that had vanished under Fred's forced retirement. "I didn't shoot anyone. You don't have to believe I'm all that good a person. You know I'm not *that* good a shot."

"You could've been if you'd just practiced. I mean, hell, your cousin Alicia could do it. She's the best the SWAT team's got. She could hit a dime at three hundred meters. And the tits on her!" Fred chuckled. "But that's not why we're here."

"Good, because that's the last thing I want to think about."

"Don't bring up any of that fairy stuff

around me, Donnie."

"She's my cousin, Dad." Donovan shuddered. "Just . . . don't."

"Right. Anyway, here's the thing. Cops have always stood up for each other. Every once in a while the n—"

Donovan held up a hand. "We're in a public place."

Fred acknowledged this with a dip of his head. "Every once in a while, a bunch of dipshits would take it into their heads to wring their hands about civil liberties this, and police brutality that. But most decent people realized the only thing standing between them and complete anarchy is the thin blue line—that's us. Once upon a time, the Boston Police Department went on strike."

"Yeah, back in 1919. It turned out swell. Another riot, another five people killed."

"I think it was more than that. Whatever. It was lawlessness and misery, and it proved to people that they need us. And it proved to us, and to our brothers all over the country, that we can't trust anyone else to have our backs. People are always going to find something they don't like if they go poking around long enough."

Donovan poked at his bowl of pasta. "Okay . . ." He considered his words carefully. People's rights were important. So was civilian safety. No one could do things by the book 100 percent of the time. Even Luis, who cared more than most about civil liberties, wasn't perfect. Hell, he got tips from the dead.

"So cops won't rat out cops." Fred spread his hands wide, to encompass the whole table. "It's that simple, really. It doesn't matter what the issue is because we trust our brothers to have done what needed to be done. And when the chips come down, we all want the same courtesy. We definitely wouldn't want someone coming around and saying, 'Oh, I know Donovan shot those protesters,' when we might have helped an investigation along with a little bit of well-placed weed at the right time."

Donovan gave his father a flat stare. "Except I didn't shoot anyone."

"Whatever. You see my point. Except here, see—well, you've done some stuff that's made you kind of unpopular."

Donovan considered. "I solved some cases."

"Sure. And you solved some pretty prominent cases with who again?"

Donovan gave his father a flat stare. "Are you trying to tell me people are hanging me out to dry because I *was assigned* to cases with the feds?"

Fred curled his lip. "Not so much the assignment part. Maybe a little heavier on the *ass*."

168

"My God, you're crude." Donovan grabbed for his water glass. "You're saying people are willing to believe I shot five people in cold blood because I'm gay."

"If someone will do one deviant behavior, they'll do them all, sport. And you knew the risks of telling them about your weird little fetish." Fred sat back and gnawed on a breadstick, looking supremely unbothered. "You could have kept it all to yourself, but hey—you knew better."

Donovan's stomach gave a lurch, and he only kept his lunch from making a return appearance through force of will. "That's bizarre. I can't believe it."

"Believe it, Donovan. Even your own mother hasn't supported you."

"That's bullshit. I've talked with her plenty since this thing started. She's been supportive as hell." Donovan sat up straighter.

Fred was just trying to gaslight him again. This whole meeting had been a colossal waste of time.

CHAPTER NINE

Luis glanced at his screen when the message came through. "Patricia's here." He turned to Kevin. "Shall we go say hello to Donovan's mom?"

Kevin sighed and stood up. "I don't see why you couldn't have made this a more private visit." They walked down the glaringly white hallway side by side. Luis would swear the facilities department pumped in that new-office smell. "It feels like it would be safer and better for her—look less like she's snitching."

"The thought did occur to me. Still, it's official business. I talked to her about it, and she wanted to have it all during official hours, so it doesn't look like she's sneaking around passing around her ex-husband's records behind the scenes." Luis shrugged. "I guess it makes sense, even though I don't necessarily understand it."

Kevin didn't object, so Luis assumed he agreed and they continued to the front desk in companionable silence. He felt for Patricia here.

She wanted to do everything possible to protect her child. She always had, even when her version of protection had been toxic. She still had to walk a fine line because being too obvious about protecting him could cause him harm.

Luis was in a similar situation. He had to empathize with her, really.

She waited for them at the front desk in her uniform. She looked every inch the strong police captain Luis knew her to be.

"Captain Carey. Thank you for coming down."

She nodded once. "Let's have at it, shall we? I know we're all busy catching bad guys. We've had protesters out for a week with this and someone's got to keep them safe."

Kevin grinned, just a little bit. "No time like the present." They escorted her up toward one of the conference rooms. "We'll be recording this for everyone's safety, not because anyone suspects you of anything. I know the rooms can feel a little oppressive, but they're equipped to record and we're cheap."

Patricia let out a little laugh. "No worries. I know I've got nothing to be ashamed of. Not with this, anyway." She shook her head. "Such a mess. I swear I'll never understand why some people do the things they do, and I've been doing this work for fortysomething years."

"Now that, I'll never believe." Luis gave her a smile and showed her into the room. "It doesn't look physically possible."

Patricia just laughed at him. "Flattery will get you everywhere, Agent." She glanced at the one-way mirror. "Before we begin, here are the records you requested. They're copies, obviously, but they're yours to keep."

"Thank you, ma'am." Luis took the folder. "For the record, where were you on the day of the protest?"

"I had a night shift command at that time, so I was at home and in bed. Cell phone records should corroborate that. Crowd control did request every available officer to present for crowd control when they realized the protest was larger than originally expected, but I wasn't considered available as I'd worked too late and too long." She glanced at Luis' notes. "It was policy—intended to cut down on burnout and on police violence."

Luis nodded as Kevin responded. "Makes sense. Fatigued officers make bad decisions, just like anyone else."

"I know Donovan was there with the state police because he texted me to let me know he was there. Johnny was there too, he was a rookie. And Fred volunteered. He said he wanted the overtime."

Luis made a note of Fred's volunteerism in the back of his head. "Do you remember when you heard about the shooting?"

"After I woke up. I turned off my phone when I went to sleep. I know it sounds terrible, but it just would not stop pinging with alerts. I couldn't do anything about them, I couldn't respond to anything, so I turned it off so I could be rested and fresh for when I was ready to get back out there." She moistened her lip. "And it's a good thing I did. When I went back on shift, the riot may have been suppressed but we had serious trouble spots in Roxbury and Dorchester, disturbances all over Jamaica Plain, and someone setting fires all over Chelsea. It was like putting down the protest turned one riot into ten mini riots."

Luis sighed. "That's usually how it works. Did anyone say anything to you about the shootings at that time?"

Patricia looked down and away from Luis. "I had a lot of ideas back then . . . not great ones. So people who approved of the shootings felt I was a good person to come to with their praise." She swallowed hard and lifted her head. "No one came to me and admitted they'd done it. If they had, I would have insisted they turn themselves in and explain themselves. I wasn't there, so I probably would have given them the benefit of the doubt—especially before we knew the shootings were all in cold blood."

Patricia took a deep, shuddering breath and continued. "I'm not proud of the ideas I held, but I can't pretend I didn't hold them. And I still had a job to do. My job was, and is, to serve and protect the people of the city of Boston. If someone had come to me and said, 'Captain, I fired on a protester,' I'd have made them face discipline. Even at my worst, I still believed everyone had a right to be protected under the law."

Luis gave her a gentle smile. It shouldn't have been on him to forgive her, but he did. They'd found common ground, and she'd consciously chosen her son over racism and homophobia. "I know you did. And I believe you would have made them face whatever discipline existed at the time. Just to reiterate, at the time of the shooting, no rumors reached your ears that the shootings were anything but the result of panic."

Patricia sighed. "No, I never heard anything different. A few men who were farther away from the center of the shootings said it had to be justified because people were angry with police, and angry people get violent. At least two of them have been disciplined for domestic violence since the incident, so make of that what you will.

"A few people nearer to the center suggested they weren't sure what was going on at the time because things near the center were so chaotic. There was a lot of pushing, a lot of shoving. Some of the people involved with the protest didn't get along. Some wanted violence with police, some did not. It could have been panic. It could have been instigated. I don't know." She bit her lip. "I don't know if things would have been different if I'd been there that day. I truly don't."

"My guess is they wouldn't." Luis leaned forward and put his hand over hers. "A buddy of mine—I hope you get to meet him while he's in town—did an amazing paper on communal violence. It's rare for one person's presence to be able to affect the outcome." He smiled at the thought of Patricia and Dwayne meeting. "Yeah, someone has to throw the first brick, or whatever, but if it's not person x it will be person y." He straightened up a little. "Do you know where Detective Carey was stationed that day?"

"Donovan isn't part of Boston Police, he's not under my command. That said, records show his unit was stationed farther down the route and away from the shooting. I know for a fact I would have heard about it if he'd strayed from his post." She blushed a little. "That's the thing about police work being the family business. I hear everything, especially if it's not good."

How embarrassing, for everyone involved. "My foster dad was a detective in Miami PD. It was the same kind of thing when I joined the force. If I put one toe even the slightest bit out of place, you can believe Jose heard about it." Luis shook his head. "It's a lot of pressure, but you can believe I learned to do things right. No one wants someone going to their dad or their mom about them. What about John?"

"He was stationed up near the start of the march, near the State House. He's with Boston PD. You can check with Sergeant Wong, your friend. They were together that day, and he can vouch for him."

Luis made a note. He would check in with Sgt. Wong, Dr. Wong's brother. It had been too long since they'd chatted anyway. "And Fred?"

Patricia curled her lip a little bit. "He was assigned to one of the units lining the route. Like I said, he volunteered. He was initially supposed to be dealing with road closures, but the staties wound up taking that over so he got moved. He said he ended up down near the end of the intended route and didn't see much 'action.'"

Luis bit the inside of his cheek. He didn't want to attack Fred, not at this late date. Not when Luis had won. "And you have all of the records you could get your hands on."

"I do. You don't think Donovan's guilty, do you?" She straightened up. "You know just as well as I do that he's a gentleman."

Luis had to chuckle. Plenty of gentlemen turned out to be vicious killers, but he understood what she meant. "I know for a fact that Donovan couldn't have been the killer. It doesn't matter if he was capable or not, I have photographic evidence of him at his post saving people from the stampede."

"Then why are we having this conversation?" She stood up and put her hands on her hips. "This is killing him, Agents. People at work are refusing to be seen with him. That creep from Internal Affairs came over to his desk and tried to do a 'gotcha' on him, *in front of everyone.* You can clear him right now!"

Luis looked away as guilt stabbed through him. Kevin had to take up their defense. "The thing is, ma'am, the first thing people will say is that photographs can be altered. Someone murdered the person who accused Donovan, and while there's no way Harper could have seen what he said he saw, the words are out there.

"Someone is going to great lengths to make people believe the absolute worst about Donovan, Captain. And that's . . . well. I don't know why. I don't know who. But the only way we're going to be able to truly clear him, and keep him safe from this, is by finding the actual killer."

Patricia flopped down into her chair. "I don't like this. I hate it. It's going to come around to bite us, and we all know it."

Luis took a deep breath. "I am worried that it will get worse before it gets better. I don't know who's setting him up, so I don't know what their motivation is. I don't know how far they'll go to keep the blame on Donovan instead of where it belongs. Until I know that, I'm going to be jumping at every little shadow."

"Surely, you must have suspects." She knocked on the table. "You're not stupid. I know you've done this before."

Luis could only summon half a grin and hope it didn't come off like a smirk. "It's true. I've done this before. The problem is, no one knows their rights better than cops. And we do know the killer was a cop, or at least dressed like one. I have a lead on at least one suspect, but before I can move on him, I need to have more proof than *some guy said something about this guy.*"

"That's all they had about my son."

"It is. But see, we're the good guys. And if we want to not only destroy this person's reputation but actually put them in jail, we have to make sure this case is sealed tighter than a fifty-five-gallon drum with a body in it."

"Graphic." Kevin made a face.

"Sorry." Luis was not sorry. "This is the only way we can keep Donovan safe and clear him. I'm not asking you to trust me, really. It's just the only way we can proceed."

Patricia slumped. "I hate this."

"So do I."

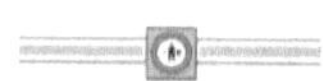

Donovan found a reporter hiding in the bushes when he got home that night. At least, he thought the guy was a reporter at first.

The intruder had a press pass from one of the less reputable online-only outlets, shoved a camera in his face and demanded to know when Donovan was going to be arrested for murder. Donovan had enough presence of mind to block without striking, so it would appear to people watching that the reporter was hitting him in the face with his camera.

Donovan knew how most of those livestreaming apps worked. He wasn't stupid enough to think the "journalist" was planning to wait until he got home and edit the footage.

"Look, buddy. I'm all about the free press,

but you can't go sticking things in people's faces. You're going to get yourself hurt like that." Donovan took a giant step backward, hands loose by his side. He was ready to fight if he had to, but he couldn't afford an aggressive posture right now.

The "journalist" tossed his camera aside and reached into his waistband. "It ain't me you've got to worry about, pig." He brought a gun up and aimed it directly at Donovan's face.

Anything resembling rational thought disappeared from Donovan's brain. He didn't have anyplace to go, no place to hide. He stepped in and grabbed the attacker's wrist, pulling him forward and slamming down on the journalist's elbow as he did.

A grotesque snapping sound cracked through the thick June air, but Donovan didn't rest on his laurels. He spun the attacker around and kicked his leg out from under him.

His intent was to take the attacker down and cuff him, but apparently, they weren't just teaching interview techniques and ambush photography in journalism school anymore. The stranger kept his footing and ran down the street. Donovan moved to give chase, but before he could, he saw Luis pulling into his parking spot.

Luis jumped out of the car and took off running, but he didn't get very far. The attacker had a head start, and Luis jogged back toward Donovan right away. He had his gun out, and his big brown eyes narrowed as he took in the scene. "What the fuck was all that?" He looked Donovan over, not being subtle at all about checking for injuries.

Now that the immediate danger was past, Donovan's knees buckled. "Guy was hiding in the bushes. Had a press pass." He gestured at the camera, which was still running.

Kevin came ambling up the walkway, already on the phone. "Hey, Agent Holcombe. I'm out here at Luis' place. Someone just tried to take out Detective Carey. I didn't get a good look at him, but I did see the gun. No, Donovan looks okay." He gestured at the camera, and Luis poked it with a pen to turn it off. "We got some of it on film, I guess. We're going to need the crime scene team."

The crime scene team. Christ on a crutch. Now Donovan's house was a crime scene. He stumbled and fell onto Luis, who held him.

"You're going to be okay." Luis murmured the words into Donovan's ear, not judging or pitying. "You're going to be just fine."

"This is so stupid. It's not like this is the first time I've been shot at." Donovan let Luis guide him over to the car.

It took a little while for the rest of the FBI

team to get there. Donovan just wanted to get back into the house and go about his business, but Luis wouldn't hear of it.

"When you think about it a little more calmly, you'll admit I'm right. Right now, you're not here as Donovan Carey, badass detective who's been through more than any five civilians." Luis managed a grin. "You're here as Donovan Carey, the guy who's just been attacked outside his own home. We aren't going to leave you outside alone while we clear the place, just like you wouldn't leave either of us alone under the same circumstances."

Donovan glared, but he couldn't argue with it. "I can't believe I'm letting these bastards take even one more minute away from me." He thumped his head against the headrest. "It's ridiculous. I need to get my life back!"

"Yeah. You do. But it's going to be a while before that happens." Holcombe wasn't unsympathetic, but she wasn't going to let anyone skate around the rules either. "Someone came here today to kill you, Donovan. Do you understand that?"

"Yes, ma'am." He bit down on his tongue to keep from mouthing off as Wragge and Borchard searched the house.

Fortunately, they were able to clear the rest

of the residence quickly. Donovan's assailant hadn't left much behind, just the gun, the camera, and whatever prints might have remained. Fontana took a formal statement from Donovan, and then the rest of the agents left to work on this aspect of the case. Luis chafed at not being able to go hunt the guy down too, but his place was at Donovan's side.

"The thought of him coming back for more is giving me hives." He scratched at his arm. "I'm sorry—I know you can take care of yourself. You're a grown man."

"But you also get kind of protective, and that's okay." Donovan watched as Kevin set up his laptop at the breakfast bar. "It feels good, you know? To know someone feels that strongly, I mean."

"Well, you know, you're kind of important. And a witness." Luis picked Tria up as she came to greet him. "This whole settled life thing is turning me into a caveman, I swear. I saw that guy, and I was not thinking about witnesses or questioning. It was more like, *smash now.*"

Donovan leaned his head against Luis' chest. "I'm glad you showed up when you did." He let Tria nuzzle his forehead. "It could have gone pretty badly otherwise. I was chasing, but who knows who he might have had out in the woods or something?"

"Yeah. It could have gone well, but if it hadn't, it would have gone *really* bad." Luis took Donovan by the hand and guided him to the couch. "I wonder if we shouldn't relocate you for a little while."

Donovan took a deep breath. He opened his mouth to object, but he found he couldn't. "The thought of not coming home to you makes me want to throw up, if we're being honest. But I have to think about this like it's a case. Because it is, I know." He closed his eyes. "It's what I'd tell a victim."

"Witness." Luis seemed to correct Donovan without thinking about it.

"That's why we came home so fast." Kevin ducked into the room, putting his gun away. "We're not slacking, Donovan. I promise you that. I just don't want to see you getting hurt while this whole thing drags on."

"And Anxiety Boy over here is proving a delight to live with, I'm sure." Luis grimaced and indicated himself. "For both of you. I hate to admit it, but it's only going to get worse after this."

"You're a delight." Donovan stuck his tongue out. "Look. I'm not going to fight you about this. I hate it, but I'm going to take your advice. I want to make it obvious that I'm not interfering with the investigation, but I also want to make sure I'm not someplace where it's so easy for them to find me. We don't even know who this guy was. So far everyone we've seen or heard from has been cop-adjacent, right? This guy had a beard down to his chest. He could have braided it. That would never be allowed in any police agency."

Donovan left the rest unsaid—the part where he didn't want Luis hurt either. He was pretty sure Luis and Kevin knew about it already. He didn't want to have his beloved's blood on his hands. All he wanted to do at this point was get the whole thing over with.

"Fred said something, when he weaseled me into giving him the time of day." He clenched his jaw. "He made a comment about how my... choice of companions... might have had something to do with why I was targeted." He looked back up at Luis and Kevin. "At first, I thought it was because I'd gotten paired up with the FBI on three cases, but then he let me know it was more the pairing *off* that did it."

Luis' face darkened, like he might explode. Kevin just curled his lip. "The man's an ass, Donovan."

"He's an ass, yeah, but there's a reason I didn't come out until last year. Most people haven't had a problem, or at least not that they've told me.

A couple of people have refused to work with me outright, because they didn't trust me to watch their backs and not their backsides. Not that they had anything I wanted to be looking at, but you know." He sighed. "At least one of them got kicked out of Major Crimes for it, so there might be some motive there."

Luis went still. "You know I'm going to need those names."

"I'd have given them to you if I had them. Lieutenant Power can probably tell you who they were. He's the one that told me, and even that was only recent. I just—okay, you don't like homosexuality, don't . . . pick up a person of the same sex and go have wild, fun sex with them? Don't come out to the Alley with me? I just don't see setting someone up as a murderer because you don't like what they do in their off-hours." Donovan's stomach turned. He'd known there would be consequences to coming out. He hadn't figured they'd be quite this terrible.

Luis rubbed at his face with his free hand. "I don't have to tell you, there's always some broken thought process when it comes to hate crimes. The idea that eliminating a person from another group—gender, orientation, race, or religion—somehow solves a problem is a fundamentally disordered thought. My suspicion is that because of the anniversary, someone in authority was already starting to ask questions, and at least one of the people behind this was looking for a scapegoat.

"They found a convenient scapegoat in you. If I were to put words in their mouths, so to speak, they probably said, 'Why not kill two birds with one stone? We need someone to take the fall for this, we'll give them Carey because he makes me feel uncomfortable about my own life choices.' And there we are." His tone had taken on that cold, clinical note he always had when he was in his profiler role. "Your choice of partner probably didn't help you much either—let's not pretend there isn't a wide streak of white supremacists running through law enforcement at every level." He looked up. "This is my fault."

Donovan grabbed his hand. "Like hell. Those guys made their own choices. They happened to be bad ones, and bad ones for me. But you didn't cause them to make bad choices."

"You're probably right." Luis didn't smile, but he gave Donovan's hand a little squeeze. Donovan hadn't convinced him, but Donovan knew he wasn't the kind of guy to get won over so easily. He still had plenty of self-image issues, even if he was better than he had been. "The important thing right now is that we get you to safety. How do you feel about staying with Dr. Wong tonight?"

Donovan dropped Luis' hand. "I thought you loved me!"

"I do. But it's the safest place I can think of. His brother's a cop who works off-shift, so there's an armed cop on-site pretty much all the time. And no one would ever think to look for you at his place." Luis grimaced. "You could stay with Holcombe, but her house is being redone and she's actually sleeping in her office right now."

"Christ. All right. We can do this. But you'd better believe I'm going to take it out of you when this case is all over."

Luis's smile was wicked, if a little strained. "Promise?"

Kevin cleared his throat noisily enough for Tria to get frightened off. "Right here, guys. Don't mind me."

Donovan laughed, in spite of the circumstances, and he headed off into the bedroom to pack. He had no idea how much stuff to bring. With any luck, he wouldn't have to stay away very long. His luck hadn't carried him very far lately, but maybe it would change soon.

CHAPTER TEN

Luis had loved the town house when he and Donovan had moved into it. He only had to spend one night in it alone to realize that he hated it without Donovan. Tria was a great cat, but she didn't quite cut the mustard as a boyfriend. For one thing, there was the interspecies difference. For another, there was the whole gender thing.

Finally, there was the whole thing where Luis didn't have Donovan right there in front of him and couldn't keep him safe.

He headed into the Chelsea office early, as much to get away from the emptiness of the town house as any desire to dive into the case sooner. He considered bringing Tria with him, so she wouldn't have to deal with the town house alone either, but decided against it. Law enforcement agencies weren't exactly cat-friendly environments.

Luis wondered if his own domestication had gone too far, if he was considering bringing his cat to work.

He went through a workout in the gym to take the edge off his anger and anxiety about Donovan's situation and then headed back upstairs to get down to business. He had one suspect, and he was pretty sure he had the guy dead to rights. While Jason Harper wasn't exactly the world's most truthful person, he had no reason to lie at this stage, and he was angry enough to want justice.

Harper's word counted for less in court now that he was dead than it had when he was alive, and that was assuming that Luis could convince a DA to go forward with the evidence Luis had found proving Donovan innocent.

He brought this up to Kevin once Kevin got in. Kevin had good ideas, as usual, but he wasn't overly hopeful. "It shouldn't be that hard to get warrants to look into some of Porras' activity. I mean we can investigate anyone, to a certain extent. The fact that he's been overly interested in Donovan lately gives us enough to poke around. If we want to get enough to tap his phones or something, we're going to need more than 'He was being creepy at my boyfriend.' "

Luis chuckled. "You'd think. I've heard stories, but those taps didn't hold up in court either." He rubbed his temples. "Christ. They really are going to find some way to frame Donovan for this, aren't they?"

Kevin tilted his head, just a little. "They can't. We've got evidence proving he was nowhere near the scene, an eyewitness who was with Donovan far away. It might not be enough to prove anything in the court of public opinion, but Donovan will get to keep his job and he'll stay a free man. That's the important thing here."

Luis ground his teeth. He was learning not to lash out when people tried to help, but it was hard. "He . . . well, yeah. That's the important thing here, but I don't think the people who set him up for this give a crap about the court of public opinion." He sat up straighter. "There's a reason they targeted *him*."

"Well, his dad seems to think it's because he's gay."

"Fred thinks I'm to blame for anything that goes wrong in Donovan's life." Luis chewed on the end of a pen he found on his desk. "It's not so much that he's gay, because remember he wanted Donovan to marry his mistress. It's the fact that he came out, that he was *publicly* gay, that's giving Fred a hard time. And maybe he'd be okay with some pasty little gym rat, who knows?"

"Do you think there's an element of homophobia to the frame-up?" Kevin straightened his neck.

"Porras didn't strike me as particularly

phobic. He was ambitious." Luis tried to remember back to the handsome detective. "Which could give him a reason to resent Donovan, actually. Here's a guy, approximately the same age and experience, who comes from a long line of cops. Now, I did poke at Porras' record briefly, and Donovan just has a better record than he does. But Porras may not see it that way, and I didn't do a deep dive. It's entirely possible that Donovan's better record could be the result of better opportunities.

"Maybe Porras figured getting rid of Donovan, or at least kicking his legs out from under him, would give him a chance to shine." Luis looked back up at Kevin. "I mean, it's a lot of speculation, but it gives us a direction to look."

"And once we have a glance at his phone records, we'll have a better idea of who his associates might be." Kevin snapped his fingers. "I'll get right on that."

"I'll get on a deeper dive into Porras' background and see if I can find any more evidence to bring him in. We know he didn't pull the trigger on Harper, but we know he was there. We know he knows who did." Luis reached for his phone. He had a trustworthy ally in Lt. Power, who would bring him all the information he had.

When Power answered, though, he wasn't interested in hearing what Luis had to say about

Porras. "I'm glad to hear from you, Agent. We've got a little bit of a situation here."

Luis' mouth went dry, but he kept his voice neutral and calm. "Oh?"

"I'm going to need you and your team to come out here to Framingham. We've had a witness come forward who is very eager to help in your investigation."

Luis could hear the strain in Power's voice. He knew the "witness" was in front of Power right now. "We'll be there as soon as we can, Lieutenant. See you soon." Luis blinked, hung up, and turned to Kevin.

He explained what had just happened to his partner, and Kevin frowned. "That doesn't sound good. It sounds like a hostage situation to me. But we'll go down there. We should bring Holcombe too."

"Hell yeah, we should." Luis wanted to call in SWAT because Power sounded like he was in serious danger, but he knew he was overreacting. He couldn't stop himself from overreacting, but at least he could recognize the signs and do something about them. "Let's see where this goes."

They collected SSA Holcombe and filled her in on the way. Holcombe couldn't know about the ghosts, of course, but she had gotten more or less used to hints and confidential informants by now.

In this case, Porras' sudden interest in Donovan was enough of a reason for suspicion. "I don't like this. It's absolutely a setup. I'm concerned about who's behind it though." She tapped her fingers against the armrest in the back seat. "Do you think Porras is ambitious enough to be this underhanded?"

"I don't want to think he's this bad." Luis sighed and looked up. "But he's our best lead by now. We've got neighborhood people placing him at the scene even on the day of Harper's murder. We've got his sudden interest in Donovan. If he's the guy who brought down a dirty cop mass killer, he suddenly becomes a very attractive candidate for promotion or candidacy into the FBI—in his mind, anyway. I'm confident that he knows who did the deed, even if he didn't kill Harper."

Holcombe whistled. "What we've got here is a massive conspiracy against one state trooper. It makes me uncomfortable—but it is what it is."

"It's not just a conspiracy against one state trooper." Luis shook his head. "There was already going to be renewed attention on the case because of the anniversary. We've had a lot of change in the past ten years, and society as a whole has become less tolerant of police brutality and officer-involved shootings. This is reading to me like someone saw an opportunity, looked around for a convenient

196

scapegoat, and found Donovan. If we find the actual killer, we find the conspiracy and everyone wins."

Kevin turned in his seat to look at Luis. He seemed to avoid a collision with a nearby Prius through instinct alone. "Do you think you've got the stomach to see this through? Because this is still Donovan. This is still your boyfriend, the guy you're all shacked up with and stuff."

Luis rubbed at his solar plexus. Against all he understood, it hurt. "Yeah. I mean, I don't feel like I've got much choice. For one thing, the people doing this are out there giving all cops a bad name, which affects us too. It's up to us to take them down because it's not like anyone else is going to do it.

"For another, Their true motivation is probably self-serving but at the end of the day, they've decided on Donovan as their scapegoat, and they're not going to stop until he's gone. I can't live with that. I'm not saying I'm the only one who can stop it." He held his hands up. "I'm not that guy. And I trust the rest of the team, the rest of the Bureau, to do right by both Donovan and the original victims here. I'm just saying I won't be able to live with myself if I don't do everything in my power to stop it. I'm already getting antsy about not doing enough—if I tried to sit out I might actually explode, and that's messy.

"And finally, I'm here now. I'm in the work. Leaving in the middle of a job makes me itch all over. I just can't do it." Luis shook his head. "Both you and Donovan have had to force me to eat and sleep when I'm on a case. Can you imagine if I tried to leave this case in the middle, knowing what's at stake? Come on—I'd literally come right out of my skin."

Holcombe snorted. "Because that's healthy. I guess you don't get into investigations because you've got a healthy mindset though." She gave a little laugh. "For what it's worth, we're here with you right up through the end."

Holcombe filled him in on what they'd learned from the video and gun they'd found at the town house yesterday. They were still analyzing the gun, but the video had given them a name. Martin Gagnon really was a reporter for JusticeBuzz, one of the more fringe online-only outlets. His assault of Donovan had been livestreamed to approximately a thousand viewers, with five hundred thousand watching after the fact. While Gagnon was still in the wind, Fontana had little doubt he'd catch up to him in a day or so.

Gagnon wasn't connected to the police. He wasn't connected to Harper. He was just a guy who saw a dirty cop and felt the need to take the law into his own hands. Luis couldn't do anything but shake his head. If he did anything at all to affect the search for Gagnon, the guy stood a real chance of walking free, simply because of Luis' relationship with Donovan.

They pulled into the parking lot and strode past the reception desk toward Major Crimes. The guy stuck working reception must have seen their faces and decided staying clear would work out better for him. Either that or he'd had advanced warning. Either way, he didn't give them a hard time.

Holcombe led the way to Power's office. Luis couldn't be unaware of Donovan's face, pale and sweating, but he couldn't stop and comfort him. Whatever was going on, it was bad. Luis had to keep his armor up and comfort his beloved later.

Quite the scene waited for him in Power's office. Power was seated at his desk, sweat glistening on his dark skin. He wasn't alone. Porras sat in one of the chairs across from the head of the department. Sitting in one of the other chairs, flanked by a man in a suit who could only be an attorney, was Fred Carey.

Luis fought the urge to punch the old man. This, then, was why Donovan was sweating in the bull pen. Anything that involved Fred had to be bad. It was also likely to be dirty and underhanded because that was how Fred operated.

When Fred gave Luis a giant jovial smile, Luis knew Fred was in this up to his eyeballs. "Why if it isn't Agent Gomes. Shouldn't you be working on a drug case somewhere?"

Luis didn't bother pretending to smile. "Watched any good films lately, Fred? I know you've got some interesting tastes. I'm sure your recommendations would be helpful."

Fred turned bright red, even on his bald spot. He'd probably forgotten when Luis had ferreted out his secret gay porn addiction. Luis had not. "You just leave my porn tastes alone, wetback."

The attorney cleared his throat. "Mr. Carey, as your attorney, I must inform you it's in your best interests to stick to the facts and avoid racial epithets."

"Yeah, well, good thing I'm paying you to be a lawyer and not the PC police, isn't it?" Carey smirked but folded his hands on his belly. "Anyway, I thought it was time I came forward with what I saw. I mean, it's been ten years and all that. Times have changed, blah blah. And I know it's my own son, but I have to do the right thing. Don't I?"

Power glared, but gestured. "You signed the document, and I've prepared copies for the FBI. It's a notarized affidavit." He gave Luis a significant glance.

"I wanted you to know that I was out there the day of the protest. I was on the sides, on crowd control. And I saw, with my own two eyes, my son, Donovan Carey, pull his gun and shoot five protesters dead in the street."

Donovan knew nothing was going to go his way today when he saw his father enter the bull pen, escorted by Porras and some guy who looked like a lawyer. No one looked at Fred or at Porras. Everyone looked at Donovan, staring at him like he'd grown an evil second head.

When Luis showed up, with Holcombe and Kevin, Donovan put his personal effects into his briefcase. He didn't have a lot of stuff lying around here. He had a couple of framed photos, one of himself and Luis with Nicky and one of his mom with his new baby brother. That was it. He stacked his cases neatly on his desk and sat, staring at his screen, until Power called for him.

Fred, Porras, and the attorney left the office before Donovan got called in. His feet felt like they were encased in lead, but he shuffled the long walk toward his boss' office all the same. Everything was inevitable now, and being slow wasn't going to stop it.

He closed the door behind himself. "Yes, sir?"

A shadow passed over Power's face, and once again, he looked profoundly old. "Have a seat, Carey. You already saw who was here in this office."

Donovan closed his eyes. "I did." He wouldn't reach for Luis. This was still work.

Luis' hands found his shoulders anyway. They were the lone warm spots in the room.

"Do you know why they were here?"

"No, sir."

"Detective Porras told me Mr. Carey had come to him, through his attorney, with a confession. Mr. Carey states that he saw you shoot those five protesters ten years ago, in cold blood." Power held up a piece of paper. "He swore to it in a notarized affidavit."

Donovan's stomach gave a lurch. "That's impossible. I have an eyewitness to prove I was nowhere near the shooting. I have several, with documents to back it up and photographic evidence. I was helping people avoid being trampled, not sitting there taking potshots."

"Do you think I don't know that?" Power slammed the document back down onto the desk. "I've seen all of that. I've seen every piece of evidence the FBI has provided so far. I know damn well you're innocent of what you've been accused of. And I know damn well that it doesn't matter a good goddamn."

"It matters." Holcombe shrugged and accepted her copy of the affidavit. "It just doesn't matter in a way that's useful to you right now."

Power turned to Luis. "Make that make sense, Agent."

Luis sighed. Donovan looked up into Luis' eyes, which blazed with rage, but his voice was gentle as he spoke. "Donovan is obviously the target of a conspiracy. What we don't know yet is how far the conspiracy goes or why he's being targeted. We have our suspicions, but it isn't helpful to voice them until we have more proof than 'This guy is a jerk so I think he's doing x.' " He bent down and kissed Donovan once, chastely, on the forehead. "They've given us some helpful information with this move, actually, but that doesn't make any of this any better."

Donovan swallowed and looked back at Power. "What does 'any of this' mean?"

Power looked away. "Their next move is to go to the media. 'In the interests of transparency.' "

Donovan shook his head. "That doesn't make a lick of sense. Fred hates the media. 'Openly helping crooks and killers get away with murder' is what he says. He also thinks they should be hanged. He'd never go to the media."

"Well, he is." Kevin curled his lip in disgust. "Because he cares so fucking much about making sure the people of Massachusetts know the police are working for them and not each other. You know, in light of recent scandals."

Donovan's hands and feet felt numb. Yeah, sure, recent scandals. Fred had been involved with a few of those scandals. And why would he approach Porras, anyway?

Power cleared his throat. "So since he's going to the media, we have to suspend you. With pay, obviously, but that's probably very little comfort."

His words sounded like they came from a million miles away. The whole office seemed distant and unreal. In fact, the only thing Donovan knew for sure was real and certain was Luis' hands on his shoulders. Otherwise, he might float entirely away. "I'm innocent though. You know this."

"I do. But we have to suspend you because the investigation isn't complete." Power bowed his head. "I didn't want to do it because I know these are false accusations just as much as you do. There's no reason to do this to my best and most productive investigator. But with them going to the media, they're forcing my hand. I have no choice here—if I don't suspend, Internal Affairs opens up an investigation of me and this whole department. That ties our hands on every case we're investigating—everything gets put on hold. Do you understand that, Donovan?"

Donovan nodded. He couldn't get actual words out. His tongue was a weight in his mouth. He understood. He'd probably make the same decision under similar circumstances, but it didn't make it any easier now.

"I need your gun and your badge." Power couldn't look at him.

Donovan fumbled for both. His hands weren't working right. He handed the gun to Luis, who made sure the safety was on before passing it over to Power.

"All right. Now that that's done and over with." Power took a deep breath. "Why would your father involve himself with this?" He laced his fingers together. "I know things haven't been great between you for the past nine months or so, but this goes beyond a little family drama."

Donovan still couldn't speak, but he looked up at Luis and nodded. Luis knew. He could tell everything. Donovan could have no shame or secrets anymore.

"Donovan and Fred haven't been close for a long time, since things went south between Fred and Patricia. It's not my place to get into any of that here, certainly not without Patricia's involvement, but I can say they were distant at best before Donovan came out. When Donovan came out, and revealed he was dating *me*, Fred became enraged. He entered into a manipulative scheme to try to force Donovan to break up with me and go back into the closet. It didn't succeed, and both Donovan and Fred's mistress sought restraining orders against Fred."

"But not you." Power raised an eyebrow.

Donovan remembered the discussion. He'd wanted Luis to get the protective order too. Luis just shook his head. *They don't usually give them to guys like me against guys like him. And I almost hope he tries something. It'll give me a good target.*

"He's not interested in interacting with me. He wants Donovan back in the fold." Luis' voice was clinical. "If he's involved with this conspiracy, it will have its roots somehow in his relationship with his family. Fred is an old-fashioned guy with deeply archaic ideas about control and society. He'll do anything, no matter how immoral, to get the world back to where he thinks it 'should' be. And that apparently includes participating in a conspiracy to frame his son for murder. I wouldn't be surprised to see him offer to recant his testimony in exchange for Donovan's submission to certain terms—for example, returning to the closet and denying his sexuality."

A wave of dizziness struck Donovan, and he found his voice again. "You think he'd actually lie about that just to try to scare me straight?"

Luis hesitated for a moment. "We need more evidence, but consider what he's done in the past. He happily played on your deepest insecurities to try to manipulate you into marrying his pregnant mistress. He manipulated your mother to try to force her to stay in the marriage and not leave him, in spite of his—well, we'll call them failures as a spouse." His tone shifted, and it sounded like he was looking at someone else. "I'm going to take his photo around the crime scene and see if anyone can identify him. I'd also like to get a sense of his whereabouts during the protest."

"We have his records during the riot." Power scowled. "No one can say for sure where he was because his unit was assigned to rove."

"There are other ways, sir." Kevin spoke up this time. "And honestly, this little stunt gives us more leverage. Porras' sudden interest in Donovan made us suspicious of him, and he was identified as having been near Harper's home the day of the murder."

Power sucked in his cheeks. "There's no reason for that. He wasn't working any cases in the city."

"We know, Lieutenant." Holcombe smiled thinly. "What Mr. Carey did here today was give us the probable cause we needed to get a warrant to tap phones. It won't give us immediate results, but it will get us somewhere." She glanced at Donovan. "Unfortunately for Detective Carey, it's going to be a difficult road for a while. Where are you staying, Detective?"

"I'm staying with the Wongs."

"Good. It should keep you off the radar, and we've got a reason to stop by the Wongs' place to check in on you." Her smile turned warmer. "We're not going to hang you out to dry, Donovan. It's going to be hard, but you're innocent and we know it."

Power cleared his throat. "It's going to be harder for me to show visible support. You're already aware of the interest Internal Affairs has taken in this investigation. We're going to need to be very circumspect, but I do support you. We're going to get to the bottom of this, I promise you."

Donovan nodded. He couldn't find the words for any better response. He couldn't say he understood or that he believed Power. He didn't. His whole world had just come crashing down. He knew his father was bad. He hadn't known, hadn't understood it would go this far. "I'm going to just . . . go."

"That's fine." Power tugged at his tie. "Maybe someone should drive you?"

"That won't be necessary." Donovan straightened up. There was no way in hell he was going to let his colleagues see him getting driven away. It was bad enough they knew he was being suspended. They believed he was guilty, simply because he'd been accused. He wasn't going to give them the satisfaction of seeing him broken. "I'm able to drive myself, thanks."

He regretted his decision as soon as he got on the road, tears blurring his vision. He couldn't un-make it though. He drove all the way back to the Wongs' place in Hyde Park in the right-hand lane, gripping the wheel in both hands, terrified to get pulled over.

Who knew who else might be in on the conspiracy?

Donovan wasn't exactly surprised to find Steve Wong at home since Steve had been working second shift lately. He was surprised to find Steve waiting at the kitchen table with a cup of coffee for him though.

"Hey." Steve gestured to the cup of coffee. "I wanted you to know I heard from two people."

Donovan bit back on a rude retort. Steve was his host. He wasn't going to snap at him. "Yeah?"

"Yeah. I heard from Luis, and I heard from your mom. Luis gave me a quick update on what happened. I want you to know there's no love lost between your old man and some of us on the force. I haven't made an issue of it because, you know, why? But seriously, screw the union. You need it, you want it, it's done. Both because it's the right thing to do and because if he'll do it to you, he'll do it to us in a heartbeat.

"Your mom wants you to know she's loaded for bear. She's got your back, no matter what. She's at City Hall right now, having a 'discussion' with certain people about this situation. Her next stop is the State House. I wouldn't want to be in your old man's shoes when she's done with him."

Donovan sat and wrapped his hands around the coffee mug. "It's good of her to try, but I don't see it doing a whole lot of good. I mean, the department and the media have both decided I'm their guy, you know? I don't think the facts have anything to do with this case."

Steve winced. "Don't give up hope yet. I know it seems pretty bleak and I can't imagine quite what it feels like, but you've got a lot of people standing with you. It's only a matter of time before your dad and whoever the hell he's backing step over the line."

Donovan managed to force himself to smile,

but he knew the truth. A conspiracy like this was too slick to ever get caught. Fred knew too many people, too much about the system to slip up badly enough to have anything splatter onto himself. Donovan's career was finished.

CHAPTER ELEVEN

Luis needed another workout after work just to vent his fury. Brick Fontana, in a surprisingly considerate gesture, volunteered to come downstairs and hold the heavy bag for him. A couple of agents wandered in, saw what was going on, and ran away as quickly as they could. Luis didn't care. Until they could be part of the solution, they should stay away and avoid being part of the problem.

Okay, that was probably an unhealthy way to think about his colleagues. As long as he kept his mouth shut about that mindset, he could worry about fixing it later.

He headed back to the town house with work to do after because there was no way he was going to rest with Donovan out of the house like this. Luis trusted the Wongs. Okay, he trusted Steve Wong, and Dr. Wong's apparently friendly feelings toward Donovan would have to be enough. More than that, though, Wong's strict attention to protocol and rules would ensure Donovan's safety in this case. Luis didn't need to worry about that.

Except Fred had just raised the stakes. Fred had just told an outright lie that would make Donovan an even bigger target for hundreds of people all over the country. Luis didn't think Fred was stupid enough to try to physically harm Donovan right now—it was too soon, and Donovan was in too much of a spotlight. That didn't mean that plenty of angry antipolice folks with something to prove wouldn't want to take the opportunity to hurt him. He'd be an attractive target for vigilantes within law enforcement too, whether they were the actual killers looking to make sure Donovan continued to fill his role as a scapegoat or a cop who wanted Donovan to pay for being "dirty."

Luis' stomach roiled, and he threw up in the bushes near the door before entering the house. *Fuck.* He needed to get a handle on this, and quickly. He'd always taken his job seriously, but this was Donovan. If he failed, he'd be letting down the one person who'd given him everything.

The scent of food hit him as soon as he opened the door, and he reached for his gun before stepping inside. He took his hand off the handle when he recognized Patricia's blonde head. "If I'd known you were coming I'd have stopped and grabbed dessert." He locked the door behind himself.

"I didn't trust that one of those bastards didn't have eyes on your phone." She wrinkled her nose and gestured to the counter. "Sit. Eat. We've got a lot to discuss."

Luis picked up Tria and gave her a scratch before obeying. "I told you what happened today."

Patricia dished him out some stew. Stew, whether beef or lamb, was Patricia's one real dish. Fortunately, she always had some on hand to thaw and heat up in an emergency. "You mentioned. I might have asked a few questions. For the record, the Wong place in Hyde Park is now the safest place in Massachusetts. The governor's house isn't this well protected."

Luis relaxed a little bit. "Thank you."

"He's my son. I love you, Luis, but I didn't do it for you." She ruffled his hair. "Never hesitate to ask for help when it comes to him, Luis. I know your family's a little different, but believe me when I say, there's nothing I'll put in front of my children."

Luis smiled as warmth suffused his being. "I know. Still, this whole situation is awkward. For everyone." He took a mouthful of stew. "Where do your men stand?"

"There's a few who don't seem to have much to say. My guess is that they're very much old guard types, the kind that Fred would have adored. I caught one of my men with a stars-and-bars tattoo and had him transferred to another unit. I can't trust them.

"Some of the crew have been pretty forthcoming. One girl is seeing a guy who works in Internal Affairs. Investigations are supposed to be kept confidential, but everyone knows there's no such thing. She'll let me know if there's anything to find."

Luis raised an eyebrow. "Wouldn't you know?"

Patricia scoffed. "Please. I didn't even know he was cheating until I couldn't deny it anymore. When it came to him, I was—well, let's be kind and say I was willfully ignorant. And because I outranked him, a lot of folks were careful to keep anything work-related separate so it wouldn't 'cause friction.' " She rolled her eyes. "We see how well that worked out, but whatever. It's all in the past."

Luis acknowledged this with a nod, but a knock on the door kept him from following up. Luis sprang to his feet and headed for the door, gun drawn. At first, he thought he was just being paranoid, but Patricia followed with her weapon at the ready too.

At least he wasn't crazy in *that* way.

He peered through one of the windows on either side of the door and caught a glimpse of Dwayne Mason, glancing nervously to either side. He put his gun away and opened the door, even as Patricia watched. "Dwayne?"

Dwayne slid inside and gave Luis a quick hug. "Sorry I didn't call. I didn't want to tip anyone off that I was coming."

Patricia looked from Luis to Dwayne and back again. "Strange company you're keeping these days, Luis. Isn't this the guy who's stirring up all the fuss about the protest in the first place?"

Dwayne stood up to his full height. "Captain Carey, I presume. I have to say I'm surprised to find you here, considering your husband just falsely accused someone of murder."

"That would be my ex-husband, thank you very much." Patricia put her gun away, but she still stepped into Dwayne's personal space. "And that doesn't explain why you're showing up here."

Luis stepped between them. "Patricia, this is Dwayne Mason. He's a good friend of mine and a former partner from my grad school days. Dwayne, this is Patricia Carey. She's Donovan's mother, and yes—she's a Boston Police captain. Fred never reported to her. Why don't we go inside and speak like normal adults?"

Both Patricia and Dwayne bristled, but Tria hopped in and demanded to be picked up. This diffused some tension, and when Patricia served up a plate of stew for Dwayne things lightened still further.

"I don't want to impose." Dwayne held up his hands.

"Relax. I raised four children, along with a whole host of nieces and nephews and Lord knows how many young cops besides. I only know how to cook in portions large enough for a precinct. There's plenty." Patricia handed him a fork and knife. "I know we've had our differences, and public differences at that. But Luis probably wouldn't have invited you in if you were hostile to my Donovan, so I honestly can't care about any of that anymore."

Dwayne smiled, just a little. "I haven't spoken much with Donovan, actually. Just once or twice. He seems like a good guy. I did talk to one of the people he saved, back during the protest. I'm still not a big fan of policing, at least not the way things stand today. I do think Donovan has a real intention to protect and serve everyone. That's how Marshall Wilson made it sound, anyway." He turned to Luis. "He'll testify, by the way. It took a little work to track him down, but he's willing to tell the truth."

Luis almost fell over with relief. "Thank you, Dwayne."

"Don't thank me. I'm here for the truth, just like you are." Dwayne grinned. "I believe you about Donovan, okay? And after that press conference today, I'm on board. Ordinarily, what happens between cops, it's not our problem. We don't think too much about it. It's something for the lawyers to work out. This, though—this is something else. This is some sick stuff. And until you told me he was your ex, ma'am, I had no reason to think you weren't part of it."

Patricia turned away. "If I had a time machine—well, but then I wouldn't have my four kids." She shook her head. "I'm trying to stick with 'everything happens for a reason.' It's not working so well some days. I didn't watch Fred's press conference. Was it that bad?"

"The man should get an award for his acting." Dwayne curled his lip. "So much wailing and gnashing of teeth—oh, how could my son be such a disappointment. On and on. Some people are going to fall for it. It's despicable. What I can't figure out is why."

Patricia scoffed. "Things were tense ever since I threw Fred out of the house. Then when Donovan came out and admitted he was dating

Luis—well, Fred was just about beside himself. To say he wasn't Luis' biggest fan would be putting it mildly."

"It's the tan, isn't it?" Dwayne gave Luis an appraising glance. "I keep telling you."

"I thought I was the one who told you." Luis kept his tone light, although the comment hit him like a stab wound. People could tell him this wasn't on him as much as they wanted, but Fred likely wouldn't have taken part in the conspiracy if Donovan hadn't renewed his relationship with Luis.

"Hey." Patricia snapped her fingers at him. "I know that look on your face, Luis. This is not your fault. Fred makes his own choices, and I've known him since high school. Believe me when I tell you, he doesn't take input from anyone but Fred, okay?" She put an arm around Luis and turned to face Dwayne. "It's not about why Fred's involved. It's about proving it and clearing my son."

"It's deeper than that though." Luis sighed. "First of all, if we want to have any credibility when we clear Donovan, we have to understand Fred's motives."

"Of course you think that." Patricia ruffled his hair again, a fond smile creasing her face. "That's your whole career right there."

Dwayne chuckled a little. "She's not wrong. Of course, you're a damn fine detective so I'm going to say go with what you know. We might be able to clear Donovan in court without clear motives for Fred, but not in public opinion. People need a reason to believe why a man would lie on his own son."

Luis closed his eyes. "I need to know his record. I need to know what people in the community know about him. I know he 'retired' from the bomb squad. What else can we find out about him?" He glanced between his two companions. "I need to know about any and all complaints against him, anything *at all* that someone could hold over him to force him to participate in something like this."

Patricia paled, just a little bit. "You think someone could be pulling his strings?"

Luis hesitated. "I don't think it's outside the realm of possibility. Dwayne's right. Family bonds are important. I'm not Fred's biggest fan, but it's going to take a lot for a guy to get up there and outright lie about his own son being a killer. And we do know it's a lie, so there has to be some reason for him to do it. And it's not just because he doesn't like Donovan's boyfriend."

Patricia nodded slowly. "Yeah. I think I can get those internal records, or at least find out if there's enough there for you to subpoena them."

"I'll talk to some of the community organizers. They've got lists of cops people know to avoid." He held up a hand when Patricia gave him a sharp look. "I'm not here to get into an argument with you, Captain. Just please, take it as a given that people in a community know who to avoid and talk amongst themselves. I'll get back to you on that one, Luis."

"Thanks." He took a deep breath. He was on a tightrope and there was no net, but he could handle it. He'd done this before. "And if someone could maybe pass a message to Donovan for me, tell him we're working this avenue and we're going to hopefully bring him home soon."

Donovan got a text the next day. The text came from his cousin Alicia. He looked at it a little funny because Alicia had been closer to Luis ever since they met, but he couldn't think of a reason why she would be involved with the conspiracy against him. Then again, he hadn't been able to think why his father would get involved either.

Can U come over to my house? I want to talk with u.

Donovan winced at the liberal use of the

letter *u. Sure. Can I bring a friend?*

Alicia responded right away. *Only if u trust him and he's not that creepy doc.*

Donovan had to laugh at that, even though his situation was dire. Then he went and found Steve, who had today off. He explained the message and asked if Steve wanted to come out to scenic Waltham with him. Steve considered and finally agreed, on the grounds that Donovan probably should have witnesses anywhere he went for the next little while.

Donovan didn't want to think about the implications of that.

His stomach sank when he saw the number of cars at Alicia's place, but he recognized Patricia's among them. "My mom's here." He relaxed a tiny bit.

"That's not surprising. It looks like a family reunion." Steve wiped his hands on his jeans. "I'm going to stick out like a turd in the punch bowl."

"Not entirely." Luis appeared at Donovan's side and pulled him in for a kiss. Donovan's knees buckled as he finally got what he'd needed for so long. Okay, maybe it wasn't what he truly needed. Maybe it was just the next best thing—Luis' scent, his warmth, his touch—but it would have to do. "Thanks for helping out, Steve. I appreciate all this."

"No worries. It's the least I could do. Is there a grill I can work or something?"

Luis grinned and showed Steve to the backyard. They'd gotten to know each other when Fred had manufactured a breach between Luis and Donovan last fall, and it was good to know Luis had other friends in the area. Sure, Donovan was a little jealous, but he had to be proud of Luis and how far he'd come.

Luis returned a few moments later, joined by three of Donovan's cousins and Donovan's brother John. Liam Kennedy was an officer with the City of Cambridge. Tony Kennedy was an officer in Fall River. Joe Kennedy was an officer in Salem. All of them wore plainclothes today, and all of them gave Donovan firm hugs and pats on the back. They shook Luis' hand too, which made Donovan more comfortable.

Patricia and Alicia were in the living room, and just as Steve had suggested, it did look like a family reunion. No one in that room wasn't related to Donovan on his mother's side—the only Careys were Donovan and his siblings. He wondered idly if Steve would be stuck out in the yard all day, but someone went to bring him in.

"All right." Patricia didn't have to raise her voice. Everyone knew how important this was. Patricia was the family matriarch, and once she spoke, everyone else silenced themselves. "Is there anyone here who doesn't know why we're here?"

Alicia spoke up from the couch. "Uncle Fred is a creepy douche?"

A few people laughed, and even Patricia smiled. "All right, all right. How about the specific reason why we're here?"

An uncle—technically, Patricia's first cousin, but he'd grown up in her home like any of her brothers—stood up. "Yeah. To be specific, your jackass ex-husband decided to start spreading shit about Donnie here. And we're here to figure out what to do about it."

Rumblings of assent ran through the crowd, and Donovan's hair stood on end. Luis tensed beside him, but he didn't raise any objections.

Donovan leaned in. "Shouldn't you maybe say something?"

Luis shook his head. "I want to know what they plan to do. And if they're planning to protect you, well then, I'm not stopping them."

Donovan did a little double take, but Liam stepped in. "Something ain't right here. Fred's an ass, we've known he's an ass for a while now, but seriously? This riot's old news. Why's he stirring the pot on something that happened ten years ago? Even if Donnie had done it all those years ago— which he didn't—the time to do something about it would have been then, not now."

"There's no statute of limitations on murder, Liam." Aunt Barbara, who'd retired from the state police, threw a piece of popcorn at Liam. "You know that—I taught you better." She turned her gaze toward Donovan. "Not that you did it, of course. I just don't want my boys thinking sloppy."

"Of course." Donovan blushed.

"What's the feds' angle here?" Another cousin, Jimmy from Boston's Transit Police, spoke up from the back of the room. "I get why we're all here, and Luis is Donovan's boyfriend, which is cool and stuff, but he ain't family yet. He's here as law enforcement, so what do the feds have to do with any of this?"

Luis met Jimmy's eyes, which was hard to do without looking down on him. Jimmy was five foot three. "I'm here because it's Donovan. The feds were brought in because there was enough interest in the original killings to open up a federal case— with all the cuts to the Civil Rights department at the DoJ, they farmed it out to us."

Donovan squeezed Luis' hand. "That's an awful big clue right there, isn't it?"

"Yup." Luis nodded once. "We've established that Donovan didn't do it, but since charges haven't been brought, we can't introduce the evidence at trial. We have to find the person at the center of this mess to arrest and bring to trial, so we can cut the head off the snake and hopefully bring some justice to everyone."

Alicia scoffed. "You don't cut the head off of a snake with a trial, Luis."

A few people murmured their assent.

Steve grimaced and stood closer to Donovan. "Did that mean what I think it meant?" he whispered to the two people he knew best.

"Best not to ask," Luis replied. "We're talking family here."

Cousin Vinnie, who worked all the way down in Providence, stood up. "Alicia's right. Look, things happen in a riot. I wasn't there, I don't know what went down. We might never find out because ten years is a long time. I know what's happening now, and what's happening now is my cousin's jackass father is trying to feed him to the wolves because Donovan took care of his mother when Fred was an ass to her. It doesn't take a PhD to see that. No offense, Luis."

Luis held his hands up. "None taken."

Donovan could see the ice in his eyes, although he kept his tone light.

"Now what I say we do is we go find the perverted little pissant and have our own little tea party. Give him some concrete overshoes, chuck him into the harbor, and I guarantee you this whole thing will never happen again."

A few cousins clapped. Most, especially the women, stared. "I can see why you work in Providence," Jimmy said after a second.

"Hey, what are you trying to say?" Vinnie puffed his chest out.

Patricia put her fingers into her mouth and whistled. The murmuring, which had been about to grow into a shout, died instantly.

"Look. While I won't pretend the temptation hasn't occurred to me—maybe fifty-seven times in the past twenty-four hours, maybe fifty-eight— offing Fred doesn't help Donovan right now." Patricia swept her gaze over everyone. "It makes Donovan look even guiltier than Fred's trying to do. What we need is to find anything we can about Fred. He's trying to discredit my son. We need a wall, people—a wall around Donovan, a wall they can't get around."

"The wall should be, you know, truthful." Luis rolled his shoulders. "That's definitely a thing we want to keep an eye on."

"This is our top priority." Patricia kept speaking. "We keep him safe. We keep the people who are testifying in Donovan's favor safe. That means if I give you a call and say 'Vinnie, I need you to get someone from Boston to Providence right the hell now,' you do it no questions asked. I

228

don't want dirty cops working for me. I never have. But I will burn every edifice to the ground before I will let them sacrifice my son to political expediency."

Donovan knew his skin had to be glowing bright, although whether it was with pride or shame, he couldn't say.

"Did someone say something to you?" Luis' eyes bored into Patricia's. Donovan had seen that same look from Luis before, although not usually in a family setting.

Patricia sniffed. "As a matter of fact, they did. It was Power's boss. I want to be perfectly clear. The powers that be are more than willing to hang Donnie here out to dry if it means they get the civil rights people off their back." She smacked her fist into the palm of her hand, the crack crashing through the air like lightning. "Are we going to allow that?"

Everyone started cheering. Donovan couldn't take anymore. As his cousins, aunts, and uncles started drawing up plans, Donovan slipped outside into the backyard. Luis followed, which Donovan had more or less expected.

"Shouldn't you be in there with them?" He pursed his lips and jerked his head toward Alicia's house. "I thought it was all about planning and getting the case won."

Luis put his hands on Donovan's hips and touched his lips to his. "You're lashing out because this whole thing sucks and it feels like everything's spinning. Which—I get." He held Donovan close. "I'm not here today as law enforcement—although I'm glad I heard some of what's in their minds. I'm here because I miss you, I love you, and I don't get a lot of chances to be with you and support you in person. I wanted to take the chance when I could."

Donovan sighed and buried his face in Luis' shoulder. He didn't like being out here in the open, where anyone could see him being all vulnerable like this, but he didn't have a choice. He needed this time, and he couldn't get it any other way.

"I know." He didn't dare lift his face up. "They're going to shoot me in the foot, aren't they?"

"It's a possibility. I'm hoping it will work out." Luis sighed. "Donovan, I am scared. Your dad escalated things in a way that's got me more afraid than I already was. I don't like the way some of your cousins want to chuck him into the harbor, and I definitely don't like their apparently poor grasp of how bodies decompose underwater, but I am terrified that I won't be able to find the concrete evidence I need before this gets to a point where you get hurt. I'd rather risk them doing something to your dad than something happening to you. And

I'm sorry, because it's your dad, but you're so much more important to me than he is."

Donovan laughed. He took Luis' face in his hands and kissed him, deep and long and loving. "Luis, I stopped caring what happened to Fred after that whole thing last fall. He's my father, and we probably had some good times together, but I can't even remember them after everything he did to my mom, to you, to me, to Kate—it's all just such a mess. Never mind all this. I just don't want my Kennedy family fighting with my Carey family like some kind of Massachusetts version of the Hatfields and McCoys."

Luis laughed. "We'll see if we can keep that from happening. If nothing else, it'll keep them occupied while we sneak off somewhere."

"Now you're speaking my language." Donovan tried to pretend he was feeling more enthusiasm than he was. The last thing he wanted was for his families to go to war with each other.

If they did though, it would be because of Fred, not him. He had to cling to that thought. It would keep him going through the rest of the investigation.

CHAPTER TWELVE

Luis was no stranger to feeling helpless. He'd grown up with that feeling, ever since he came to the US and his father started to change. Luis had learned early on that the way to deal with feeling like he had no way out of his problems was to grab hold and take control of whatever *was* in his grasp, and this situation with Donovan was no different.

He didn't need to be psychic to know Fred was in this up to his eyeballs. He wouldn't have sat here and bided his time, waiting for an opportunity to strike out at Donovan. Fred was the kind of guy who nursed a grudge, sure, but he was also impatient. Luis had seen as much when he'd been an undergrad.

It gave him two possibilities. Either Fred had found out about the conspiracy against Donovan through some other means, like overhearing something at his favorite watering hole for racist cops, or someone had specifically approached him. If someone had specifically approached him, it was because Fred had something to be worried about from the riot.

Luis reached out by phone, email, text, and even in-game chat to everyone with any kind of access or authority he knew. Sure, Fred had done something unthinkable, but he'd also given Luis a target. He called in favors. He leaned on friends, colleagues, and former lovers. He even reached out to people he'd interviewed in prison. Someone had to have dirt, and Luis wanted it.

A little part of him, the part of him that still spoke in his father's voice, reminded him that he could have avoided all of this if he'd done even half of this legwork six months ago, before any of this started. If he'd done something about Fred when he first realized Fred was going to be a major problem, they might not be having this conversation.

He ignored his insecurities. He was a professional—he knew his brain was lying to him. For one thing, the thought of a cop lying to frame another cop (never mind a family member) never would have occurred to him. The whole thin blue line thing was real, and Luis had run up against it too often to fling it out the window. For another, he'd thought Fred was out of their lives. Fred had taken his lumps and gone away. He'd lost, and permanently.

And finally, Luis himself was the logical target of Fred's rage. It made no sense for Fred to target his own son if he wanted to bring Donovan back into the fold. The fact that he'd targeted Donovan meant either he'd given up on Donovan or he feared something more than he feared the loss of control in his own family.

Guys like Fred didn't just give up on loss of control. So—he had to have something to hide.

He got results within a day, and from one of his jailhouse interviewees before anyone else. Ronnie Culpepper, who'd been a problem solver for drug runners in Providence before getting his life sentence twenty years ago, had been an interesting case study for Luis. They'd stayed in touch, and when Luis called looking for information, Ronnie was only too glad to comply.

"Yeah, I remember Fred Carey. He wasn't what you'd call a dirty cop—I mean he wasn't someone I could bribe or cut in on a deal or nothing like that. He was fine as far as that went, but he had his issues."

Luis felt like a cat, staring at a mousehole. He couldn't be too obvious. "With women."

"Oh, yeah. You couldn't make a deal, but all you had to do was send a pretty girl past him, and it was off to the races for old Freddie." Ronnie scoffed. "He was always predictable, you know? It was easy. But she had to be white. If he even suspected she might not be, he'd bring her in for hooking and rough her up for her trouble. My boss had a couple of girls wind up with teeth knocked out, one with a broken arm."

Luis winced. "I don't suppose any of them would be willing to go on the record."

"It goes back thirty years or more, buddy. I'm pretty sure the statute of limitations has long since expired. Look up Stacy Newman or Bridget Lo. They both wound up getting out of the business and going legit. You can tell 'em I sent you. They won't mind."

As it turned out, both Stacy Newman and Bridget Lo were very willing to talk to Luis, and to go on the record too. "I'd have been scared about it twenty-five years ago." Newman coughed a little. "Maybe ashamed, I don't know. I'm still not exactly thrilled about dealing with law enforcement, but you know what? Fred Carey is a big fat pig, and if I can help take him down I'm going to do that."

Allegations of brutality were well and good, especially with the added dimension of dereliction of duty. It told Luis he was on the right track. It wasn't enough to bring charges.

Alex Morales was able to get a bit more detail about those brutality complaints when Luis called him. "It turns out Organized Crime took a look at him not long before he retired. He was going for a consult position, but it turns out there were a few too many complaints about him." As he spoke, a message landed in Luis' in box with a massive file attached. "You know how he retired from the bomb squad?"

"Yeah. I remember him being on the bomb squad when we were in college. I don't remember hearing that he'd served in the military or anything, but I didn't think they'd have told me or anything like that." Luis opened the file and had to lift his jaw shut with his hand. "Holy crap, that's a lot of complaints."

"Yeah. And that's back in the quaint old days when people rarely filed complaints about police. They didn't fire him, but they did kick him into a less public-facing role. Obviously, we decided we didn't need that kind of consulting." Alex snorted. "I did a little looking into the other name you mentioned, since I was in the system anyway."

Luis smirked, even though Alex couldn't see it. He didn't ask about Alex's presence in the system because he didn't want to know if it was authorized or not. "Let me guess. Same thing, different day?"

"Oh, Detective Porras has been suspended four times for inappropriate use of force. One of those incidents resulted in paralysis, another required facial reconstruction surgery."

"Christ on a—" Luis quieted himself as he heard Kevin move. "How in the hell did he keep his job?"

"You know the drill. 'I was afraid for my life.' 'The suspect was resisting.' It's always the same. Sometimes it's even true." Disgust dripped from Alex's words. "I had a complaint filed against me once, by a suspect who'd stabbed me. The Bureau still had to investigate it. That's how this works. But you get the wrong investigator, or the wrong person in charge, and it just goes nowhere."

"I don't see Power being the one to let him stick around, but I get the impression Power isn't necessarily driving the bus in this situation." Luis pinched the bridge of his nose. "This whole thing is a mess."

"How's he taking it?"

"As well as he can. I want to be with him, but because I got stuck with the job, we've got to keep apart. Not just because of that either. Some blogger tracked him down at the house and tried to shoot him, so we moved him to a safer location until we can get to the bottom of all this. It sucks. But hey—we got into police work for the glamor, right?"

"Damn straight. I'll remember that the next

time one of you senior agents makes me go dumpster diving." Alex laughed.

"It builds character." Luis had to grin at that, but he sobered up before hanging up the phone.

More reports came in, with details of Fred's brutality becoming clearer as information rolled in. Luis had always known Fred wasn't a great guy. Sure, Luis' own dad had been worse, but it wasn't exactly a competition and he knew Donovan hadn't had it easy. Fred was prone to bursts of rage, and apparently, he felt strangers on the street were appropriate targets for emotions he couldn't release at home.

He didn't *only* lash out at ethnic minorities. Some white people had earned his fury as well, largely in crowd-control situations. As Luis explored the records further, he found he could predict who Fred would assault. It wasn't rocket science, after all. Abusers were abusers. They didn't go after people who had power they could use against him.

To think Donovan had come from this kind of man . . .

He turned his mind away and toward something more productive. He needed to keep his focus if he wanted to help Donovan.

Kevin, for his part, was working to track down witnesses to Harper's shooting. He came back to the office shaking his head. "What gets me about this case is the utter arrogance of the people involved." He threw himself into the seat with more force than usual. "They were just brazen. They didn't try to hide their faces or who they were. Sometimes, they just walked right up in full uniform. I cannot understand how these people thought that was okay."

Luis turned his laptop around so Kevin could see the screen, where the files Alex had sent were readily available. "This is how. Up until recently, there hasn't been even the slightest bit of accountability."

Kevin stared at the screen, face etched in sadness. "This guy got shot in his own home. I mean, yes, he was a crook. Not a good guy at all, but he'd paid his debt to society and all that. He had just as much a right to sit in his own living room and play dumb video games as anyone else does. And these guys—who he trusted, he'd made a deal with them—just walked in and shot him when he became inconvenient."

Luis turned his laptop back around. "They're killers. The fact that they have badges doesn't make them any different from any other murderer. Murderers don't care about their victims. Their victims are less important than the reason they're killing. Sometimes the reason is

240

actually valid—it's them or me, they're going to kill my kid. Most of the time, it's because the killer just values something else more than they value a human life."

"We're supposed to be better." Kevin punched his desk, hard enough to dent a drawer.

"See, I think that myth is part of why there's not enough accountability when cops go bad. We should be held to a higher standard, but at the end of the day, we're human just like everyone else. Some of us are just plain bad, some of us are good, and most of us could go either way under the right circumstances." Luis stared at the screen. "These two here? They're just plain bad."

Anyone could see that Fred and Porras were bad, and Luis' ability gave him the awareness that Porras at least was a murderer. The only thing he needed was proof. Nothing in Porras' file was enough to get him forced onto desk duty, never mind kicked off the force or arrested. Even his suspensions hadn't held up. And Fred wasn't a cop anymore, so proving he'd been guilty of police brutality wouldn't do more than open the City of Boston up to lawsuits.

They needed more.

Donovan glowered at his tablet. Sure, it was great to be living in the future, where he could have a thousand books in the palm of his hand. It was less wonderful to be stuck hiding indoors in the middle of June because people were lying about him in ways that caused other people to want him dead. Having a thousand books was wonderful. Being forced to read because he had to stay indoors and out of sight sucked.

He would never, ever recommend a safe house to a witness or survivor again. Assuming he ever got his job back, he would tell them to take their chances with whatever had gotten them into their situation in the first place. It couldn't be as bad as hiding out in the medical examiner's place, twiddling thumbs.

Okay, he'd probably still put people into safe houses. He'd just be a lot more understanding about the whole thing.

He checked his email—personal email, since he was locked out of his work account while he was suspended. He could just imagine the messages piling up. Hopefully, no victims or family members were trying to reach him. Well, they almost certainly had to know what was going on. It wasn't like Donovan's suspension wasn't at the top of the news for pretty much every outlet.

Cop's Dad Accuses Him of Murder!

Someday, Donovan was going to get his hands on Fred. When he did, no amount of family feeling would save him.

What was Luis doing right now? Donovan knew Luis was working his ass off for him. If anyone could get to the bottom of this mess, it was Luis. At the same time, Donovan couldn't sit here and pretend the silence didn't make his skin itch. He understood why Luis had to keep his distance. They already knew Fred would attack their relationship as part of his defense. They needed to be able to prove they weren't conspiring.

Was Luis hating the separation as much as Donovan was? Was he already packing up and heading for warmer climes? Donovan knew damn well he was the only thing tethering Luis to New England.

His phone rang. He jumped to answer it, not caring who might be calling. He'd blocked Fred's number, so the caller could only have good news. "Hello?"

"Donovan, how's it going?" If Patricia had gotten any sleep at all in the past few days, it didn't show in her voice.

"Mom, are you okay?" Donovan sat up straighter and reached for the gun he didn't have anymore. He bit back a curse and reached for his personal weapon. If his mom was hurt, he wasn't going in unarmed.

"I'm fine, honey. I don't know the mother who sleeps much when her child is in danger. I spoke with Luis a little while ago. Did you know your—did you know that Fred has a record of police brutality?"

Donovan squirmed. If anyone should have known about Fred's record, it was Patricia. Patricia hadn't wanted to know though. Everyone had wanted Fred and Patricia's employment to be kept strictly separate, especially Fred and Patricia themselves.

"I don't know. I guess I'd heard his ordinance disposal skills weren't what put him on the bomb squad, but I didn't think about it much either."

His mother sighed. "Son of a bitch. I swear, the man brings more shame onto the people around him with each day that passes. Do you think he's got something to hide?"

Donovan gave a laugh and closed his eyes. "Mom, I think he's got plenty he *should* hide. I also think he's never heard the word *shame* as it applies to him. Can you imagine him hiding something because he thought he'd done something wrong?"

Patricia cackled. It sounded like glass breaking. "No. But he might hide it because he knew other people would think he'd done something wrong. I don't want to think like that about the father of my children. I know we're through. I hate the man. I despise him, and the only good thing he ever did was give me the four of you. But I don't—I can't let myself think he'd go out and bash heads in just for the color of their skin."

Donovan kept his eyes closed. "You know what? I'm sorry, Mom, but I can see it a little too easily. It might not even be because of color. It could be because of orientation or just looking 'suspicious.' He had a lot of ideas about how to assert authority, ideas that I just thought of as old-fashioned until I went to Florida." He wiped his palm on his jeans. "One of the reasons I went into the state troopers instead of Boston PD was because I didn't want to be too closely associated with him, to be honest."

He heard Patricia gulp. "How did I let that go on? Right under my nose?"

"Mom, it's not your fault. You guys didn't talk shop. You couldn't—not without things getting weird about rank. If you had, you'd have known what he was up to long before now. We're all learning new things these days. We can't beat ourselves up because they're new. We just have to move forward as best we can and do better, okay?" What had Donovan learned, now, that could have kept him out of this situation?

Well, he'd learned his dad was the kind of guy who'd lie about his own son to save his own skin. Donovan hadn't discovered what was useful about that information yet, but he'd get there.

"Hey, Mom. Dad wouldn't do this just out of spite. I mean if he wanted to hurt me because of what's going on with me and Luis, he'd have done it back in the fall. Who do you think would have leverage on him that could make him do something like this?"

Patricia let out a strangled-sounding laugh. "You know, Luis said the same thing. The two of you have been together too long. In all honesty, I can't think of anyone. It's not like the man ever listens to anyone else or has even the most passing acquaintance with the idea of shame. I can't imagine him having anything he'd ever want to hide. Hell, when I confronted him about bringing home a social disease, he had the temerity to tell me I was wrong for being upset about it."

Donovan shuddered. The thought of the mess his father had created filled him with horror, and not just because he didn't want to think about his parents ever having had sex. "There has to be something, though. He hates me, sure, but not enough to want to parade his queer son around on all the news channels."

"It's not like that." Patricia caught herself.

"I'm sorry. I shouldn't be making excuses for him anymore. It's exactly like that. He's an ass, he's always been an ass, and he'll always be an ass. I agree it seems strange for him to want to spring you into the public eye now, but there must be a reason. I just can't think of it."

Donovan looked at the ground. He couldn't understand what must be going through her head. She'd been married to Fred for decades, raised four children with him, only to find he was a liar she never truly knew at all. "Well, if you think of anything, let me or Luis know."

"I will, dear. Oh—and I'm looking to get you a lawyer."

Donovan's heart froze in his chest. "Ma, I'm not guilty."

"I know that, honey. Still, it's my job to keep my son safe. And I don't trust any of those bozos in the top brass as far as I can throw them. We don't know how far this goes. Luis is good at his job, but he might not be good enough to pull the rug out from under a conspiracy even the most senior state troopers seem to want to make real." She sniffed. "I'll let you know what I find. Love you, son."

"Love you too, Mom." But Patricia had already hung up.

Donovan stared at the phone for a few seconds. He guessed he could understand where his father got his need for control from, at this point. He was a piece of driftwood on a current, hurtling toward a waterfall, and he just had to trust that someone was going to catch him before he went over the side.

Someone knocked on the door. "Detective? There's a very bad man at the door for you." It was Dr. Wong, who still seemed oddly out of place and formal even though they were in his home.

Donovan grabbed for his gun again. "Bad how?" He sprang to his feet and opened the door.

He didn't have to look far to see who the *bad man* might be. His room was at the top of the stairs, and the front door at the bottom. There, in the doorway, waited Dwayne Mason, standing patiently with his eyes blazing.

Donovan pinched the bridge of his nose. "Dr. Wong, this is Dr. Dwayne Mason—"

"I know who he is. He leads protests against the police for a living!" Wong was almost vibrating with displeasure.

"He's a friend. And a good friend of Luis'." Donovan raced down the stairs, holstering his gun. "Hey, Dwayne. Sorry about that. What do you say we go grab a drink somewhere? It's dark enough that we should be able to get away with it."

Dwayne's responding smile was tight, but he agreed to the exit. Donovan wasn't sure leaving the house was in his best interests, but he was willing to give it a try.

"That must be the medical examiner." Dwayne relaxed a little bit as he and Donovan headed toward the main drag and one of the dimly lit bars that populated it. "Luis mentioned he was kind of lacking in social graces. I'm surprised Luis hasn't decked him yet."

"He's come close, actually. But he found a work-around. You should have been there this one time, back in the fall. Wong made his team flip over a whole rowboat trying to get to a body. Luis had to jump in and save them all, because at least one of them couldn't swim. It was a whole mess."

It was hard for Donovan to reconcile Dwayne's easy, gentle laugh with the rhetoric the professor spouted on TV on such a regular basis. "I can see it happening. Anyway, Luis told me where to find you. I wanted to catch up with you and hopefully pass along a message." He slipped a piece of lined yellow paper into Donovan's hand. "Burn after reading or whatever. He must really love you to be doing all this cloak-and-dagger shit."

Donovan blushed. He knew he must have a dopey grin on his face. He just couldn't bring himself to care. "I'm a lucky man."

"You most definitely are. Listen, I'm trying

to pull together some people who were there the day of the protest. Some of them say they were rescued from the stampede by a guy who sounds like he looked like you. Luis was able to get his hands on records from the EMTs and the hospitals proving that those people were injured, and you were listed as a witness on documentation from at least two of those ambulances. I don't see why this is still happening. Why is anyone listening to the angry old white guy?"

Donovan sighed. "Because he's my father. And people don't think he'd lie about his own son. They have to investigate the charges because the word of a retired cop carries weight."

"This is ridiculous." Dwayne rubbed his face. "Some of the other people I've been talking to were there that day, but they were closer to the shooting. They don't know you."

"Well, they shouldn't. Since I wasn't up there and didn't shoot anyone, and I don't usually work in the city of Boston. They've got their own Homicide team." Donovan scratched his head. Whatever Dwayne was getting at, he couldn't figure it out.

Dwayne shook his head. "Well, yeah, but that's kind of the problem. They aren't going to go to bat for you, and get involved with police business, unless you come and talk to them. Can you come downtown and meet with them three days from now? I know it's a little unorthodox. Luis just about had a heart attack when I suggested it. He's firmly convinced there's a monster hiding under your actual bed looking to shoot you, by the way."

Donovan almost laughed, and then he remembered. "Well, his mom got killed when he was young. It's probably making him a little paranoid right now." He made a snap decision. "I understand he'd like to wrap me up in Bubble Wrap and Kevlar, but if I have a chance to help myself here, I have to do it. I'll go. Let me know where and when."

"I'll send you a text when I've got the space confirmed." Dwayne shook his hand. "You doing okay here with that creepy coroner? I know Luis said he's mostly harmless, but the guy seemed like a real jerk."

Donovan grinned. "Yeah. I'm getting by. His brother's cool, and hopefully, we'll get through this okay. I just miss home, you know?"

"Hopefully, we can make that happen for you." Dwayne shook his hand. "Now smile so I can send Anxiety Man some proof of life." He pulled out his phone and got a picture.

Donovan read Luis' note as soon as he got back to his room. It wasn't much. The detective in

Donovan didn't take long to figure out Luis must have scrawled it out quickly, probably as soon as he learned Dwayne was coming over.

Just wanted to tell you I love you and can't wait to see you.

There was a little stick-figure drawing of a three-legged cat instead of a signature.

Donovan didn't burn the note. He put it into his wallet, so he could take it out and look at it anytime he wanted.

CHAPTER THIRTEEN

Luis went back to the Harper crime scene with Kevin at night. For whatever reason, ghosts seemed to have an easier time at night. Luis could probably find out why if he put a little bit of effort into it, but it hadn't ever seemed all that important before. Maybe he'd have to fix that sometime soon, but right now, he had bigger fish to fry.

He wasn't surprised to find Harper's presence stronger in every way, although he didn't seem to be able to leave the apartment. Kevin gagged from the stench, which made Luis wonder exactly what it was Harper had done that no one had caught him for. Maybe that was why Harper had stuck around.

"Mr. Harper." Luis looked straight at his target, which he seemed to find jarring. "We need to talk."

Harper scoffed. "You can't just come into a man's space and make demands. I may be dead, but I've got rights. This is my space. I decide what goes and what doesn't."

Luis remembered back to the pool in the Freedom Hotel. Those ghosts had years to hone their talents and build power. Jason Harper hadn't been dead for two weeks yet. Luis had managed to take out stronger dead than him—but if he did, he wouldn't be able to get the information he wanted. "There've been ten calls to Eversource since your death from the other units in this building. Have you been messing with the electricity?"

"Not on purpose. It's none of your business anyway. There's no federal crime against being a dead guy in an apartment. I'm just trying to get my game to work." Harper picked up his controller, making Kevin's eyes pop out. He couldn't make the unit function though.

Luis reached into his bag and withdrew a bottle of high-quality bourbon. "It doesn't quite make up for having been killed, apparently by police, but apparently, it doesn't run out either. I didn't come here today about the wiring, Jason. I'm not that invested in what you do with your afterlife."

Harper glared at him. "If you're 'not that invested,' then why are you here? I thought you were supposed to help me move on or something dumb like that."

"People stick around for different reasons.

Sometimes, it's to get justice. Sometimes, it's just to make sure they're not forgotten. Sometimes, it's so the crimes they committed are finally known, in full, and then they can move forward with the rest of whatever the hell it is they're supposed to do. I've got a friend—a dead one—who hasn't figured out what it is that's supposed to help him move on in two centuries. I'm not sure he wants to move on. I'm not sure he cares."

"I don't care either." Harper puffed himself up. Considering his condition, it just made him look bloated. "I never believed in any of that shit anyway. So you can just go right the hell on back to wherever you came from, and take D'Artagnan there with you."

Harper was better read than most guys with his record. "I hadn't thought of Agent Rourke that way, but now that you mention it, I guess I see the resemblance." Luis nodded. "Look. If you want to sit here and haunt this floor for the rest of time, that's your business. I need to ask you more questions though. So I'll just ask them, and you answer them, and then you can get back to getting mad at the TV and burning out the neighbor's light bulbs."

Harper flared his nostrils. "You really can't leave me in peace? It's not like you can use my testimony in court."

"No. But it will tell me where to look to get the evidence I can use. The cop who watched you get killed—Emerson Porras. How did you know him?"

"Was that his name? Porras? I just remember his first name. It doesn't matter what his name was because the next time I see him, I'm going to fry his brain like an egg."

"Good to know." Luis should probably have cared more about the threat, but he wanted to do the same thing more or less so he let it slide. "Where did you meet him?"

"I don't know. I met a lot of cops. I wasn't exactly Mr. Law and Order when I died, you know?" Harper chuckled. "I did a lot of stuff that got me put around the guys in blue. It's not a secret. I don't really care who knows it."

Luis made a note. "But he didn't stand out to you in any way at the time that would make the arrest memorable."

Harper seemed poised to retort, but then paused. "You ever been on the other side of an arrest? Because they all start to run together after a while. The first time, I was scared shitless. I was maybe ten, and I pissed myself. By the time I was twelve, it was all old news to me. The cop comes along, he roughs you up a little, you bounce around in the back of the car or the van, and then that's it.

It doesn't matter why you did it. It doesn't matter *if* you did it. Because I didn't steal a car when I was ten, but if I was going to get accused of that crap and get punished for it when I was ten, I was going to get paid for it when I was twelve, you know?"

Luis nodded, biting his tongue against impatience. "Yeah, I do. Much as I wish it were different, I'm not going to pretend it is." He didn't have time to sit here and talk about all the ways the system failed. "There has to be some way you and Porras connected. I'll look into the arrest angle. If I show you a picture, can you tell me if the person looks familiar to you?"

Kevin stepped forward, burying his mouth and nose in his shirt against the stink. "Here you go." He handed Luis a folder and waved at a window vaguely to the left of Harper.

Harper watched him go. "He really can't see me, can he?"

"Nope. He can smell you though. Every ghost has a unique aroma. It's related to who they were in life. Anyway, here's the picture." Luis opened the folder to show the most recent picture of Fred Carey they had on file.

Harper's empty eyes seemed, against all possibility, to widen. "That's the guy! That's the guy who was here with Emerson! That's the guy who shot me!" He reached out for the picture, but

Luis kept it away from him.

"No destroying, please. I need to get confirmation from people I can put on the stand. I know you get that." Luis managed a ghost of a smile. It was all he could manage.

How was he going to tell Donovan his own father had murdered someone in cold blood, and there wasn't much they could do about it?

"Who is this guy? Is he mobbed up?"

Luis shook his head. "His name's Fred Carey. He's a retired cop. Boston Police. His son is the guy you accused of murdering five protesters in the riot."

"Oh, and he's pissed about it." Harper blinked. "But wait—he's also the guy who threatened to kill me and make it look like I was trying to attack a cop if I wouldn't accuse the dude."

"Exactly. That's why this is such a big deal." Luis sucked his cheeks in for a second. "I'm absolutely positive that you understand the implications here. You're not a dumb guy, Jason."

"No. I'm not." Harper's eyes blazed for a moment. "But I can't do anything about it when I'm trapped in this apartment. It's like being on house arrest."

"You'd know." Luis had to give a little smile at that. "Look. Did he say anything, or do anything, before he killed you?"

"No." Harper shook his head hard. "He knew what he was going to do. Emerson seemed to want to talk, but I could see something was up with him. This guy—I never did find out his name or anything—this guy just came in and shot me once my back was turned."

Luis closed his eyes. He'd always known Fred was an ass. He hadn't known Fred was capable of something like this—but he found he wasn't surprised either. "Thank you, Jason. This was a big help."

"How? You can't do anything with it. Even if you could somehow put me in front of a jury, it's my word against his. We both know exactly how that would go."

"You just let me worry about that part, okay?" Luis closed the folder. He didn't want to have to look at Fred's face more than he had to right now. "It's my job. You've got other things to think about for the moment."

"Like what? All I've got right now is time?" Harper grabbed the bottle of bourbon Luis had brought for him.

"I'm not a metaphysician. I'm just a guy who woke up one day and could see and talk to dead people. If I were you, I'd try to figure out why I'm stuck here and what I could do about it. Not everyone gets stuck as a ghost. Not every ghost sticks around for long. Once you figure out why you're here, you can figure out if you want to stay or if you want to find out what's waiting for you. I'll help you if I can, but I'm not an expert in life after death. I'm just a detective."

"I still don't get why you're willing to help me." Harper took a swig from his bottle. "Cops are cops, no matter what color. And I'm not a great guy."

Luis shrugged. "I know you did some stuff you weren't ever caught for. It probably wasn't something I'd have been enthusiastic about while you were alive. You still had a right to not get murdered. As for the ghost stuff—I haven't found myself in that position yet. I just try to treat people the way I'd like to be treated."

Harper managed a small smile. "I'll see you around." He raised the bottle in a kind of salute.

Luis gestured to Kevin, and they made their escape from the haunted apartment. "So it was Fred after all," Kevin said once he was done gasping for fresh air. "My God, the guy keeps getting worse. There's no bottom when it comes to him, is there?"

"It doesn't look like there is." Luis hadn't ever been fond of the smell of a city in June, but he'd take it over the stink of Harper's apartment.

"So now we know the who—at least with Harper. That should help get us to the who of the protesters too. All we need to do now is prove it."

Kevin scoffed and got into their vehicle. "Solving the Israel-Palestine Conflict might be easier. Come on, man. Fred's a piece of crap but he's not stupid. And Porras is an ass, but he's also a detective. He knows how to clean himself out of a crime scene."

"We just have to hope Maxwell is better." Luis kept his tone light as he walked. "We've got witnesses who have put Porras on-site. Once we finish going through Porras' phone records, we'll be able to put him in contact with Fred. Then we just have to build from there."

"A jury will absolutely buy that explanation." Kevin rolled his eyes. "I know I'd totes vote to convict based on the fact that two guys spoke on the phone once."

Luis couldn't exactly discount his skepticism. "Totes?"

Kevin's pale cheeks reddened. "Leave me alone, I have a teenaged daughter."

It gave Luis something to laugh about as they drove back toward Chelsea. It wasn't much, but it was a start. Luis would take it.

Donovan wasn't shocked when he was "invited" to come up to Chelsea to meet with investigators. He'd figured it was coming eventually, and had even been anxious to get on with it. At the same time, he couldn't help but feel a little bit like a dog on a chain. If he got through this, and somehow managed to get an opportunity to investigate again, he would absolutely be more considerate of witnesses' and victims' time.

He didn't have much better to do, and the trip to Chelsea would get him out of the Wongs' house, so he headed north with as much speed as he dared. His guest badge still gave him access to the office, so he didn't have to go through some ridiculous sign-in process just because he'd been suspended. *Thank God or Holcombe for small favors.*

Luis was waiting for him at his desk. Goddamn but he looked good. He even wore that lavender shirt Donovan loved on him. Of course, this was an office. Donovan couldn't throw his arms around Luis and claim every inch of him with his tongue. That would be unprofessional.

Luis' smile told Donovan enough about the things he wanted to do to Donovan. "Hey. Let's, uh, get this out of the way." He jerked his head toward the conference room.

Donovan's pants felt three sizes too small,

but he nodded. "Yeah. Yeah, we can do this." He walked beside Luis. "I miss you."

Luis swallowed hard. "I miss you too. Tria tries to chase me to bed at night, but it's not the same." He opened the door. "Let's get this party started."

Holcombe was there, as was Kevin. Donovan's boss, Lt. Power, waited there too. The poor guy looked like he hadn't slept since Donovan's suspension. He stood up and hugged Donovan before sitting down again. "It's good to see you, Carey," he said, recovering some of his stoicism. "It's not the same without you in the office."

"It's not the same without being there. I know we've been saying I should consider some vacation time, but this isn't what I had in mind." Donovan tried to keep his tone light. "I mean Dr. Wong's place is nice and all, but it ain't a beach."

"I'm sure someone can be persuaded to whisk you away someplace a little less . . . er, crowded, once this case is over." Holcombe cleared her throat. "I believe the quote was 'I'm dragging him off to Key West and no one can stop me?' "

Donovan blushed even more deeply, and even Luis blushed. "You weren't supposed to hear that," Luis muttered.

"It's the FBI, Luis. We hear everything. All

right, gentlemen. Let's get down to business. We have some important information to discuss, and some plans to make." She glanced at Luis, hesitated, and then turned to Kevin. "Agent Rourke, if you'd like to begin."

Donovan got warm under his collar, but he kept his mouth shut. Holcombe might have been dismissive of Luis when he first arrived, but their relationship had improved dramatically since then. If she was turning to Kevin, she might have a good reason for it.

"Right." Kevin sat up straighter. "Anyway. So we wanted to update you on some sensitive information, and we need to make a plan of action. The thing is, what we're about to tell you isn't something we can file charges on yet. And if any of the people involved suspect we're aware of their involvement, we run the risk of them destroying evidence."

Power rolled his eyes. "We know how investigations work, Agent. We've conducted one or two of them ourselves."

Luis grimaced. "Apologies, Lieutenant. We don't mean to be dismissive or belittling. It's . . . well, it's hard to say what we need to say, and Kevin is actually stalling less than I would be. You already know we'd become suspicious of Detective Porras."

"It had come up." Power sat back and raised an eyebrow.

"Right. Well, people in the neighborhood did identify him as having been at the house on the day of the Harper shooting. We're looking into his phone records and arrest records now." Luis took a deep breath and then met Donovan's eyes. "He wasn't the only one there that day. Witnesses also identified your—identified Fred Carey from photographs presented." He looked away. "I'm sorry, Donovan."

Donovan's mouth went dry. He gripped the edge of the table, but then he let go. "I guess . . . I guess I can't be surprised he would be involved in something like this. He's never been all that enthusiastic about people of color, or people who are involved with crime. Jason Harper was a career criminal who spent more than half of his life either in jail or on parole." Something deep in Donovan's brain screamed at him. This was his own father he was talking about.

He pushed on. Sure, it was Fred. Family bonds didn't matter much to Fred, and Donovan needed to forget them too.

"I'd think witness statements would be enough to get a warrant though." He cleared his throat, but it didn't help with the dryness.

"Some of the witnesses are less than reliable.

We're talking about going into a decorated cop's home and searching it. Not that he doesn't deserve it, but before we can get that, we need to get something else to make sure the judge can't get away with denying us the warrant." Holcombe moistened her lips, just a little bit. "We did get one to agree to let someone have a talk with him. While wearing a wire."

Her words sank in for Donovan. "You want me to wire up while talking to Fred." His stomach turned.

"You don't have to." Luis put his hand over Donovan's. "I don't want you to put yourself at risk, not in ways you don't feel comfortable with. I'm willing to be the one going in there. I can probably goad him into saying something he shouldn't."

Donovan scoffed. "Dude, he'll shoot you before he even opens his mouth."

"He's not that stupid." Luis gave his hand a squeeze. "He's probably not that stupid, anyway, and if he does, we have an excuse to take him down. It's a risk I'm willing to take."

"But I do think it's less of a risk to send Donovan in." Holcombe glared at Luis, and Donovan realized they'd already had this discussion. "Not because you're his son, we already know that's not a factor or it's less of a factor than whatever else is going on with him. But because you're suspended, he's likely to believe you're a safer contact than Luis. He won't be able to resist using the opportunity to taunt you, which is likely to give us a chance to find information he wouldn't give us otherwise."

Donovan blinked at her. "I'm sorry, I didn't realize you'd met Fred."

"Someone was able to convince a few people to talk who hadn't been willing to file complaints in the past." She glanced at Luis. Donovan couldn't help but feel proud, even under the circumstances. "You should be proud to take after the Kennedy side, Detective. The point is, your father has certain predictable behavior patterns, and most of us feel you're the safest and most likely person to get the information from him. Are you willing to do that?"

Donovan didn't hesitate. "Yes."

Luis looked like he was sitting on a chair full of thumbtacks. "He's already put you in enough danger."

"Yes, he has. But it's not going to get better if I'm hiding, you know? I'm going to do whatever it takes to bring that son of a bitch down. He's no better and no different than any other suspect. I don't get my badge back, or my life back, until he's taken down."

Power cleared his throat. "Not that I have

much authority here while Detective Carey is under suspension, but I give my approval. My concern, however, is that the focus seems to be on the murder of Jason Harper and not on clearing Detective Carey's name. How does solving Harper's murder get him out from under this cloud of suspicion? I appreciate that it's a murder, and we can't have murderers running around with badges, but I have Internal Affairs breathing down my neck and they've been eating too much garlic."

Luis chuckled at that. "Graphic. The only people with a motive to murder Jason Harper would be the ones who put him up to slandering Donovan."

"Or, you know, any one of the people he might have had bad dealings with in his life on the street." Power folded his hands in front of him. "He was a gang member, Agents, not a choir boy."

"But it wasn't gang members seen going in and out of his apartment for weeks before he accused Donovan, or before his murder." Kevin shrugged. "That's the problem with being a cop. If you're not undercover, we tend to have a certain look. Makes us easy to distinguish. Also, the cops spotted were white, which stands out in Mattapan."

"Fair enough." Power nodded. "When do you want this meeting of the minds to take place?"

"Tonight or tomorrow. Whichever you can get him to agree to." Holcombe looked at Donovan. "I want to wrap up this mess as fast as we can while still getting it right. It's a sin and a shame what's being done, and I'm almost afraid to find out what's happening out there while those men are getting away with murder."

Brick Fontana brought in recording equipment, and Donovan called Fred before he could lose his nerve. He'd blocked Fred's number, but the feds didn't have any trouble finding it for him.

Fred, because he was the most predictable man to have ever lived, picked up on the first ring. "Well, if it isn't Donovan, Prince of the Fairies. I wish I could say this was a surprise, but who are we kidding? I knew you'd be calling. Enjoying your shiny suspension? Did FBI man drop you like a hot rock when you weren't a cop anymore?"

Donovan gritted his teeth. Not only was his father taunting him openly with what he'd done, everyone could hear it. His family's dirty laundry was out there on display for everyone to hear. "I'm not sure why you decided to do what you did. But we need to talk about it."

"Oh, he wants to talk." Fred laughed with evident delight. "First, he gets a restraining order because he doesn't want to talk to his old man, now he wants to talk. You can't have it both ways, Donnie Boy. You have to pick a side."

Donovan took a deep breath. He could keep his temper. "Let's meet up. Say, the Fox Hole. Seven o'clock."

The Fox Hole was a favorite watering hole of his dad's. It would also have plenty of space for agents and others to be available if Donovan needed to be rescued.

"I don't know, Donnie. I'm not hearing a whole lot of contrition here. But you know what? I'll do it. Just because you recommended a public place and not that town house of yours. I wouldn't want to meet up with you in private. After you killed five oh-so-innocent rioters in cold blood, who knows what you'd do to me?"

Donovan sighed. "We both know I didn't kill anyone."

"Prove it, Donnie Boy. That's how this works, isn't it?" Fred laughed again and hung up.

Brick cut off the recording, and everyone in the room let out the breaths they'd apparently been holding.

"You did a great job." Luis patted him on the back. "Awesome work."

"I want a shower." Holcombe wrinkled her nose. "No offense, Donovan."

"None taken, ma'am. I feel the same way."

"Luis, why don't you show Detective Carey to the showers? I'm sure he'll feel much more comfortable going into the meeting after cleaning up a bit."

"I know where—" Donovan cut himself off as Luis hauled him to his feet.

"Right away, ma'am."

Donovan only figured out what he had in mind by the slight pinkish tinge to Luis' cheeks. Funny—Holcombe looked perfectly innocent the whole time.

CHAPTER FOURTEEN

Luis didn't get to be in the bar when Donovan met with Fred. If this were any other situation, any other case, he wouldn't have had to be told. Hell, he'd have been the one suggesting it. Instead, Holcombe had to explain it to him like he was five, because evidently Luis' brains had all leaked out his ears when Donovan was endangered.

Now he sat in an unmarked white van out behind the paint shop next door, listening to background noise in a dive bar in Southie while Evan Borchard sat beside him and cleaned under his fingernails with a paper clip.

Luis watched in disgust. "You know," he said after staring in horror for several seconds, "nailbrushes were invented for a reason."

"Gotta do something to kill time." Borchard shrugged and gave Luis a little grin. "Have you ever considered meditation? It's a great way to chill the fuck out. I'm just saying."

Luis scoffed. Borchard must have cheated

on every exam he'd ever taken if he was stupid enough to think Luis could *chill out* while Donovan was in there, unprotected.

"You're from Boston. I'm from the South. I've forgotten more about chilling out than you'll ever even pretend to know."

"Actually, I'm from Wisconsin, now that you mention it. And you're the least chill guy I've ever met. I've met cats less high-strung than you. I mean, I can see why you'd be a little on edge under the circumstances, but giving yourself a stroke won't help you or him." Borchard gave Luis a pleasant, if fake, smile.

Luis opted not to argue with him. "You're from Wisconsin?"

"The fact that I actually pronounce my *R*s didn't tip you off?"

"Kevin pronounces his when he so chooses. I figured you were just being professional in the office." He shrugged.

Finally, the microphone picked up something other than men calling out for Sully. The sound of Fred's voice set Luis' teeth on edge, but he'd signed up to hear it. He couldn't exactly complain.

"Well look, if it isn't the prodigal son." Fred's laugh sounded dirty, even over the mic. "Come home with his tail between his legs, like I always knew you would. Smart boy. You picked one of the few places in Boston where a killer cop like you can still show his face."

"Cut the shit." Donovan didn't so much sound tired as resigned. "We both know I didn't kill anyone. Why are you doing this?"

"Aw, Donnie, I'm hurt. I'm doing this because I want truth, justice, and harmony to prevail. Isn't that what we're supposed to be about here? I mean, you kicked your old man to the curb because I was somehow supposed to be manipulative and underhanded, but now, you want me back because I'm speaking the truth and you want to shut me up?"

Luis put his hand on his burning stomach. Fred's mocking, singsong tone was going to give him an ulcer.

"Mind your blood pressure." Borchard hissed out the words, a snake in the darkness of the surveillance van. "Treat it like any other case. Donovan's a pro."

In the bar, Donovan was proving he had more professionalism than Luis. Either that, or Fred's taunts truly didn't hurt.

"I'm not sure you have any idea what the word *truth* actually means. I don't think you ever did. And hey, it's your life. If that's how you get by, whatever. I just want to know what you actually get out of any of this shit." Donovan sipped from something. He'd probably complain about cheap beer later.

"It's like I said. I get the truth."

"Can it. There's no one else here. No one can even hear you over all the noise in this place. You got what you wanted. I'm suspended, the agency is probably going to sacrifice me to appease the media, whatever. You've successfully lied to destroy my career. All I want to know is why."

"Donnie, Donnie. Did you really think you were going to sit there all high-and-mighty with your nose in the air and act like you were somehow above me?" Fred's voice changed, growing harder and sharper. "I'm your father. I told you what to do, and you defied me. You brought me shame. You embarrassed me in front of the whole force. And then—then! You blabbed to your mother, which only made things worse. Did you think I'd forgive that? Did you think I'd forget that?"

Luis froze in place, straining to hear. If he could see Fred's body language, he'd get a much better idea of what the old man was hiding. Fred wasn't stupid. He wasn't going to outright confess, not here and now. He still could let something slip that Luis could use though.

"Seriously? You got knocked off your pretend throne, you're not king of the castle anymore, so you decided to shoot yourself in the foot and create a fraudulent investigation? You know as well as I do that this whole thing is going to crash down around you soon enough."

"Ain't like you're getting your job back though. In fact, I'm pretty sure they've already promoted someone to take your place." Luis could hear the shit-eating grin through the speaker. "Nice kid. He was working on the night shift until you got canned. Good luck for him, huh?"

Luis sent a quick text to Power's cell. *Did Porras get promoted to days?*

Power's reply was immediate. *Over my dead body. He's trying though.*

Luis bit down on the inside of his cheek and kept listening.

"And hey, if it turns out someone else got mistaken for you, then great. At least Detective Porras did his duty by bringing his concerns to his superiors. He gets what he wants, I get what I want. You—well, you get your face smashed into the mud. Which brings me back to *what I want*. You're such an idiot, Donnie. Such an idiot, I can't believe you're my kid. You think anyone was going to have your back once you started waving that rainbow flag? The state troopers don't play that way. They want good men—actual men—who follow orders.

"And if you think the feds are going to

277

swoop in and save your ass, you can forget about it. They don't have jurisdiction in Boston, and there's no way the brass in Washington's going to give even half a shit about some sissy state trooper in Boston whose own father turned him in for murder." Fred laughed and clapped his hands. "It's too perfect. I mean, sure, maybe under the last president—maybe. Now though? Now they'll probably fire your little boy toy just on general principles."

Luis balled his hands into fists. He didn't realize he was standing until Borchard grabbed his arm. "Deep breath, Gomes."

Luis inhaled, held it for four seconds, and exhaled. He didn't feel any better, but he was able to sit back down.

"Sure. That's all well and good. I mean, I'm not sure where the ego's coming from, but you being afraid of gay men isn't exactly news." Donovan yawned. "The thing is, I just don't buy it. Sure, you're petty and absurd, but since when do you sit on your thumbs waiting to do something when you're pissed off? Why are you actually doing this? Who put you up to it?"

Fred's voice got closer to Donovan, like he'd leaned in close. "Here's the thing, Donnie. You think you know me, but the fact that you're even asking me that question means you don't know me at all. No one, and I mean no one, owns me. I'm my own man. I do what I want, when I want to do it. You remember that the next time I give you a direct fucking order and you disobey it, you got that?"

Donovan let out an unimpressed little laugh. "Fred, you don't get to give orders. If you go to the FBI, right now, and confess to having set the whole thing up, they'll probably stop looking into it. If you let it go on long enough, they're going to find what they're looking for."

Fred guffawed. "That's cute. What, exactly, do you think they're looking for, sport?"

"I don't know. I'm out of the investigation. But you know those wacky feds. They get a bee in their bonnet about something, and they don't stop. Now I'd never dream of telling you what to do. I am telling you that the longer you keep lying, the bigger it gets. The bigger it gets, the harder the punishment hits when it finally does. And I know I don't want to be splattered when it hits the fan."

Fred scoffed again, but his voice held little of its original self-assurance. "They've got nothing on me, kid. I'm a professional. I've been doing this shit for years. I am the law. If I say something happened, it's because it fucking happened and I can prove it. Don't you think, even for a second, you can prove otherwise."

Luis heard a chair slide back against a

wooden floor, and then after a minute, Donovan muttered, "He's out the door."

A moment after that, Wragge spoke from outside the bar. "I saw him getting into a vehicle. Running the plates now."

Information popped up on Luis' screen. "Looks like an old Boston cop, maybe a year to retirement. Bob O'Malley, works in traffic and special operations."

"Fabulous. We'll have to take a look at his activities during the riot." Holcombe cleared her throat. "Well, now that we've got that, let's regroup and discuss back at the office."

Luis waited for Wragge to get into the van and drive them back to the Chelsea office. Donovan rode with Kevin, just in case they were being tailed, and Holcombe went with Brick. Luis hadn't spent much time with Wragge and Borchard, and he couldn't say they seemed particularly comfortable having him around either.

Maybe it was the way he kept bouncing his knee, as if he could somehow make the van go faster.

"He'll be fine." Wragge glanced back at him.

Luis held his breath, as if that would somehow keep them safe if Wragge plowed into the back of a tractor trailer or something.

Wragge didn't seem to notice. "He's got

Rourke with him. It's going to be okay."

"Maybe try yoga." Borchard looked Luis up and down.

Luis held back a long diatribe about yoga, but only barely.

He removed the wire from Donovan himself as soon as they got to the office. He wasn't willing to let anyone else do it. Donovan put up with it, a good-natured grin on his face. "You going to make it, Luis? I know it was hard, but we got through the thing."

"Barely." Borchard snickered and patted Donovan on the back. "I thought he was going to explode all over the van. Then I would have had to clean it up, which would have sucked."

Luis flipped him off. "Seriously, are you okay?" He knew Donovan wasn't going to tell him anything for real, not while they were in front of all these people, but he had to ask.

"I'll live. I could happily go the rest of my life without ever seeing the old man again, but I'll live. I'm glad we got what we went for though."

Brick scowled. "How? He didn't confess to anything."

Donovan shook his head. "You say that because you don't know Fred. He admitted to his motivation, he admitted to being in on it with Porras, and he admitted to being involved with planting evidence."

"It's true." Luis perked up a little bit. "We know we're on the right path, at least. And here's the other important part—he admitted he lied. If nothing else, we have him on tape admitting he lied, admitting to why he lied, and confessing that he masterminded the whole thing."

Holcombe hummed. "We do. I'm not sure it will hold up in court, but we have corroborating evidence. That said, I have some other concerns." She sat and cradled her head in her hands. "Sorry— that place gave me a headache.

"Listen. I think we have enough to force the state troopers to reinstate Detective Carey. That's kind of the bare bones, minimum qualification for success. What we don't have is enough to press charges against anyone for fraud, determine the extent of the fraud, or find out how deep this goes." She looked up at Donovan.

Part of Luis wanted to step in and object. Donovan had suffered enough. He'd been forced to leave his home, have his name dragged through the mud, been accused of an odious crime, and had to suffer through knowing his own father had been the architect of it all.

But Luis was also an investigator, and the murder of six people in cold blood wasn't something he could just let slide. He couldn't even ignore the murder of one person in good conscience, and the five protesters were above and beyond even that.

Donovan rolled his shoulders. "You're right, Agent. I think we need to see this through as far as we possibly can."

Donovan did move back into his own home. Staying apart was stupid now that he was officially cleared. Maybe the brass in Framingham didn't know, or didn't see it that way, but they would once Luis' team wound up their complete investigation. Donovan was grateful to the Wongs for putting him up as long as they had, but he also needed to be in his own space with his own partner, doing his own cooking.

Then there was the fact that Luis was getting so wound up without him his colleagues were getting worried about his health.

Luis didn't seem quite as excited to have him back as Donovan expected. At first, this bothered Donovan, but then Luis stopped him and asked him a question.

"Are you back here just because Borchard told you I was going to have a stroke? Because I swear to God, if he convinced you to endanger yourself because of how laid-back he thinks I should be, I'm going to put my foot so far up his—"

Donovan laughed and took Luis into his arms. "No. I'm here because I want to be. I'm not endangering the investigation, and I want to be with you."

Luis met his eyes. Donovan could see so much there, guilt and love and fear and relief. "Are you sure?"

"As sure as I've ever been of anything."

And that was that.

He was still suspended, of course. The feds wanted to examine just how deep the conspiracy went, and so they were holding off on presenting anything to Internal Affairs. They informed their own bosses, who approved of the plan to continue investigating. Against all odds, they allowed Donovan to participate to a limited extent.

"You're a victim in this." Holcombe shook her head as she set him up with a desk in the same bull pen as Luis and the others. "You're not as much of a victim as the people who were killed, but you're still a victim. I can't let you go out into the field or anything like that, but you're also a damn fine investigator. I certainly can't expect you to sit quietly at home and watch daytime television all day. We have records from your father's phone and from Porras'. What I want you to do is go through and figure out when they started hanging out together. If you can get at some of the other conspirators that would be fantastic, but the priority is Carey and Porras."

There were a *lot* of records to comb through. When Donovan had first made detective, this had been part of his job. Now, he got rookies and interns to do it. Apparently, the FBI had neither of those, so they delegated to Donovan.

He got it. He wasn't going to fight it. It was better than hanging around at the Wongs and hoping he could avoid having to talk to Dr. Wong again. As Donovan started his search, he made notes about his observations, just so he wouldn't forget in the sheer volume of tedium.

The first thing he noticed was that his father talked on the phone a *lot*. Fred had always been a chatty guy, more social than the average cop. Donovan recognized a lot of the names associated with the numbers. Some of them dropped off after the big breach in the fall, when everything went to shit and Patricia finally dumped Fred. None of those names, guys Donovan had known since he was a baby, had reached out after the fight, but apparently, they'd dropped Fred like a hot rock too. Good to know.

Porras, on the other hand, hadn't showed up

in Fred's records until early January. Records indicated Fred made the first move, too, in the form of an outgoing call. Donovan had to think about that one. Porras hadn't really been on his radar back then. He'd kind of known who he was, one of the night shift guys who he'd see once in a while.

He sent a text to Power. *Call me back when you have some privacy, please.*

Power called ten minutes later. "Detective Carey. It's good to hear your voice. I got a call from Agent Holcombe this morning. She said you're helping out now. That's excellent news."

"It is, sir. I'm looking forward to hopefully getting back to work at my own desk soon, but for now, at least I'm doing something useful. Listen, I have a question for you. You're probably more in the know about this stuff than I would be. Did Porras have any outstanding incidents in December or early January that would bring him to anyone's attention?"

Power hummed for a second. "Well, there was something. He got a two-week suspension around December fifteenth. According to a suspect, he'd bashed his face into a car so often he needed reconstructive surgery to breathe through his nose again and still doesn't look like his ID picture. Internal Affairs looked into it and found that the suspect was resisting, but that Porras still

286

responded with more force than strictly necessary. There's still a lawsuit pending."

Donovan drummed his fingertips on the desk for a moment. "That's along the lines of what I was looking for. Do you know who it was from IA that handled it?"

Power paused for a moment. "Not off the top of my head. But I'll find out for you, okay?"

"Thank you, sir."

Donovan sent a quick note to Holcombe and Luis, explaining what he'd found and the steps he'd taken. Then he exported the phone records into a spreadsheet, saved it, and started to play.

It only took a minute to create a macro to indicate whether a name in his father's phone records was a state trooper, a Boston cop, someone with a prison record, or "other." Donovan ran the macro on Porras' phone records too. Then he did a count.

His father had been a Boston cop, so it made sense for him to talk to a lot of Boston cops. It didn't make a whole lot of sense for him to be talking to too many younger cops though. For that matter, it didn't make a lot of sense for Fred to have connections to Porras.

Porras' records made a little more sense, in that a younger guy looking to move up would naturally seek out mentorship. Then again, a younger detective looking to move up the ranks as a detective wouldn't necessarily be looking for career advice from guys on Boston's bomb squad. One state trooper's name popped up more than a few times.

Donovan knew him. Greg Orlov, from Internal Affairs.

Orlov wasn't someone likely to know Fred from back in the day. Orlov was Donovan's age, give or take a year. Why the hell would he be having any contact with Fred? For that matter, why was Orlov getting friendly with a guy who'd only just been the subject of an Internal Affairs investigation? Donovan had been a detective for a good long time. He knew when something didn't pass the smell test.

He called Luis over. Luis, who'd been digging through some other dusty file, jumped up like a coiled spring. "What's going on?"

"I've got Porras and Fred both getting awfully chatty with this jackass from Internal Affairs." Donovan leaned back and let his eyes unfocus a little. He'd been playing with the spreadsheet just long enough for his eyes to start to hurt. "I know him. He was poking around my stuff and pestering me right before I got suspended."

Luis lifted his eyebrows and pulled a chair over. "Isn't that exciting?" He was almost purring as he spoke. "I bet, if we ask nicely, we can get a copy of his record and case file." He pushed his chair back over to his own desk, where he sent a quick email and then returned.

"Don't you have to get a warrant?" Donovan glanced at Luis.

"I'll let Holcombe deal with that. We're starting to get into an area where we need to play very nicely with state and local jurisdictions, make sure all our *Ts* are crossed." He managed a thin smile. "I know I sound annoyed. I am annoyed. We're here having this conversation because they didn't give a shit about their victims' due process, to include yours. But we still have to mince around the special rights of a bunch of dirty cops because they're somehow more important than the people they hurt." He shuddered. "Don't mind me, I'm just rambling."

Donovan glanced around them. They were alone, but he lowered his voice anyway. "Did you get—you know—other information?" He waggled his fingers in what he hoped was an approximation of spookiness.

Luis sighed. "Yeah. I know they did Harper. I don't know who did the protesters yet. They haven't stuck around, which is good for them. If we can get a conviction for Harper, I'll be happy, although I'll be more comfortable getting someone for the protesters too." He tightened his mouth. "I'm sorry. I know it's your dad."

"It's not like you're not used to the idea of criminal dads." Donovan sat back a little. "How do you deal?"

Luis looked up at the ceiling. "It's different. I barely remember a time when he wasn't in jail, and during that time, he was still someone who should have been in jail. I mean, yeah, he was better when we were in Brazil, but that was a really long time ago and I have no idea what he was like when I wasn't home. I guess what I'm saying is I've had a minute or two to get used to it. It's different for you because your dad comes from a group you've been reared to respect and it's all new. I need to be more considerate of that fact."

Donovan chuckled. There wasn't much humor in it, but he still had to laugh. "You know, it's weird. I didn't think he was bad growing up. I mean, he was strict, and he could be a dick, but he wasn't that much worse than a lot of other guys' parents, you know? And then, I got older, and I realized just how bad he was failing. It's been a long time since I could see him as someone I could respect—before we got back together, really.

"But I still never thought of him as a dirty cop. I always thought he was at least good at what he did. I'm finding out stuff through this investigation that's making me sick to my stomach, and I don't know what to do. He killed that guy, Harper, in cold blood. Just to hurt me."

Luis reached for his water bottle. "Er. Donovan, I don't think it was just to hurt you. I think it goes beyond that." He took a deep breath. "It doesn't fit. I know you don't exactly view profiling as a science, but your dad's behavior hasn't changed in seventy years. It's not going to change now. He's not going to wait nine months to get revenge because you came out. He might take an opportunity that presented itself, but he's more the kind of guy who's going to just lash out right away."

Donovan nodded. "You're right. Who do you think he's hiding though?"

Luis opened his mouth. He closed it again. "I don't want it to seem like I'm railroading your dad, or trying to put something on him. I'm not. I don't want to be right here. But I'm looking at the records of the day of the protest, and I'm looking at his service record and the litany of complaints against him.

"Donovan, I can't be sure Fred isn't protecting himself here."

CHAPTER FIFTEEN

Luis stared at the screen and tapped his pen on his desk. He would not go down to Mattapan, summon Harper's ghost, and shake him until he cried uncle. For one thing, the guy had already dealt with enough police violence. For another, it would be a waste of time, and time was something Luis just didn't have anymore.

"Would it have killed Harper to have used a regular phone on a consistent basis?" He threw his pen at the cubicle wall, picked up a new one, and started chewing on the cap.

Donovan gave him a side-eye. "You do know the answer is probably yes, right?"

Kevin hid a snicker as Luis deflated.

"I know," Luis said while Brick, Wragge, and Borchard looked away. "I know. It's just— damn it. We know who killed him. We know why. We just can't prove it. We've got witnesses who put them at the scene of the crime around the time of the murder, but if we want to nail them we have to prove the conspiracy."

Holcombe emerged from her office, eyes bright. "You're sure these witnesses will testify they saw Porras at the crime scene?"

Luis decided he didn't want to know how his boss had heard his comments. "Absolutely, ma'am."

"They'll testify about Fred too, ma'am." Donovan glanced up from his workstation. "I'm just saying."

Holcombe grimaced. "It's true, and I'm sure they'll be delighted to see him arrested. But Fred's currently a private citizen. Porras is a state trooper. Fred can go where he wants when he wants, provided he's wearing his pants and it's public property. Porras is another matter."

Kevin shuddered. "I'll thank you never to mention the idea of Fred Carey without his pants again." He clutched at his gut. "I've got a delicate constitution, you know."

"Agent Rourke, hush. I've seen you put your hand into a drum filled with liquefied human remains to pull out an identifying piece of evidence. Your constitution is as delicate as *Old Ironsides*. If we're going to get the evidence we want, we have to focus on the weaker suspect."

"Porras." Luis straightened up and put his feet flat on the floor. He still had that fluttering, panicked feeling deep in his gut. If he pretended he was grounded and calm, maybe his psyche would catch up.

Donovan curled his lip. "I'm pissed I didn't realize he was more than just some little weasel, you know? Why did I not pick up on it?"

"Because you didn't realize you needed to be looking for that stuff." Luis glanced over at him. "You're at work. You don't think you need to be looking for some guy who's going to join with your father to fuck you over by framing you for something that happened ten years ago. It just doesn't happen. It's so far out of left field, you'd have to be a textbook example of paranoid personality disorder to think of it, okay?" He turned back to the others. "So. What do we know about Emerson Porras?"

Wragge flipped off his screen. "We know he's a dick." He turned his chair to more fully face the rest of the team. "To be more specific, he's had multiple complaints of police brutality, he's got a reputation for unchecked ambition, and his solve rate is on the low end of 'middle of the pack.' His police brutality complaints don't appear to have a strong basis in race, but that just means he's not picky about who he beats up."

"Okay." Holcombe chewed on the inside of her cheek. "Anything else we know? Family, hobbies, relationships?"

"It seems like Fred reached out to him after he got a two-week suspension. The common factor in their phone records was a guy from Internal Affairs named Greg Orlov. Most of us think of him as Mayo, because he's oily and smells a little bit like sulfur." Donovan squirmed. "I know it's a little unprofessional of me, but you're not *supposed* to be friendly with Internal Affairs. It's not healthy."

"No, you're supposed to keep a certain level of distance with them." Kevin nodded. "So if this Orlov guy is making connections between a state trooper and a retired cop . . ."

"He has to be in on it. And we'll investigate thoroughly. Don't you worry about it." Holcombe smiled tightly. "The priority is getting a killer cop off the streets. Porras is the key to this whole thing. Focus, folks. We unlock him, we find what we need to take them all down."

Luis stared straight ahead. "I met him. He was . . ." He stopped himself. "He seemed eager to make himself known. I don't know if that makes sense. He wanted to make a good impression on a fed. He wanted to make damn sure I knew who he was. Which—it happens sometimes, you know? People have watched too much TV, they think we do a lot of intrigue and international spy stuff. They think it's more exciting than what they do."

Donovan snorted. "Depends on what they do. I think what you do is creepy as hell, sweetie."

Luis had to laugh. "Thanks, darling. Maybe they're hoping they get assigned to art crimes? I don't know. Anyway, he definitely stood out. But it could give us a way to bring him in without having to wait around for a warrant."

Borchard winced. "Gomes, you know we have to do things by the book here."

Holcombe nodded. "If he comes in voluntarily—say, for an informal discussion—we don't need a warrant. Or we can buy time for someone to go get one. We've definitely got enough to get an arrest warrant for him for Harper's murder. We've got witnesses placing him on the scene and cell phone records implicating him in the effort to frame Detective Carey. I want to go deeper."

Brick jumped to his feet. "I'll work on that warrant."

"I'll call him about coming in for an informational interview." Holcombe's smile turned predatory. "With any luck, we'll get to the bottom of this in the next few days."

Something deep in Luis' chest surged. After a minute, he recognized it as hope. It had been a long time since he'd felt like part of an actual team. Seeing the others scramble to accomplish tasks related to this case made him remember what it had felt like when he'd first become a profiler. "I'm going to keep trying to find a way to link Harper and Porras. It has to be in here somewhere."

"I'm right here with you, buddy." Borchard waved. "Fun times."

Harper's arrest record was extensive and crossed many jurisdictions. Looking for records of times he might have come in contact with either Porras or Fred was like looking for a straw-colored needle in a haystack, complicated by Luis' knowledge that the encounter might not have left an official record at all. He knew all too well that some cops might develop an informant through "warnings" or letting a suspect think paperwork had been filed when it hadn't.

It was Borchard who found it. "The first record of Harper coming into contact with any of our suspects is actually with Orlov, before Orlov went into Internal Affairs. Harper was 'present' at the arrest of a Chris Mattheson for possession of a class A substance with intent to distribute, but was not arrested himself. Orlov was the arresting state trooper. Mattheson was ultimately convicted. We next see Harper as a witness against Lena Fallon, a state police detective accused of planting evidence on a suspect in a domestic assault case in order to bring the suspect in without the victim's testimony.

This is not long after Orlov was assigned to Internal Affairs." He looked up. "Fallon lost her job, even though the suspect tested positive for the substance she supposedly planted on him."

Donovan recoiled. "That's... I won't pretend there aren't dirty cops out there, but come on. That's despicable. Who does that? It only hurts the other cops doing their jobs, makes us look worse than we are."

"Something else to investigate." Holcombe shrugged. "Porras will be here at two. Let's look alive and build as much as we can against him. Donovan, I want you in a conference room. I know you're cleared, but we don't need him to know you've been cleared just yet."

"Got it." Donovan cleared his things out and moved into one of the conference rooms. Luis watched him go, but didn't interfere. This was too important.

He still brought him lunch though. He wasn't going to have Donovan in his space for long.

Porras showed up at two. Luis would rather have had more to go on. In an ideal world, he'd have preferred to have surveillance photos, DNA, *anything* harder than eyewitness testimony to shove into Porras' face. They'd have to go in with what they had.

He'd gone after cops before, but it wasn't his

favorite target. He still preferred to think of his colleagues as the good guys, even though he acknowledged there were some shortcomings in the criminal justice system. The problem with dirty cops was that they knew all the procedural moves Luis had to make in order to catch them. Since they were the bad guys, they weren't restricted by any such problems.

Holcombe wanted Luis in the room with her when she spoke with Porras. She explained to Porras it was because he'd spoken to Luis first. "I hope you don't have any hard feelings." Porras grimaced as he shook hands. "I mean, I got that tip, and I had to follow it where it took me, you know?"

Luis smiled and gestured toward the other guest chair in Holcombe's office. "Hey, I get it. I'd do the same thing in your position. I'm disappointed, but the job is the job."

It wasn't a lie. It just didn't mean what Porras thought it meant.

Holcombe smiled at Porras, looking every inch like a bureaucrat with a fresh recruit. "So, Detective Porras, Agent Gomes tells me you've expressed an interest in the Bureau. I have to say, solving a ten-year-old mass murder would absolutely be an argument in your favor. It's impressive, how you managed to solve it right around the anniversary. Tell me, were you already working the case, or did the tip just spontaneously come to you?"

Porras beamed. He fucking preened under Holcombe's praise. Luis had to resist the urge to punch him.

"Well, ma'am, I've always been a little curious about it. I mean, it never did sit right with me for the protesters to just go with their murders unsolved. That's not justice, is it? But, no, I guess Sergeant Carey's been carrying a lot of guilt around for ten years. That tends to happen with cold cases. In the heat of things, people feel fear or family loyalty. After some time has passed, though, things change and witnesses are more willing to come forward." He leaned forward. "Would there be opportunities to work on cold cases, with the Bureau?"

"Oh, there are plenty of cold case opportunities with the Bureau. Agent Gomes here has worked more than a few. He's assigned to an active murder right now though. How are you coming with that, by the way?"

Luis kept his tone neutral. "I'm pretty sure we're close to an arrest, ma'am."

"Awesome work, bro!" Porras offered him a high five. He wasn't as oblivious as he acted though. His palm was sweaty when Luis smacked it. "I can't wait to do some work with you, man."

Luis scratched his chin. "Well, maybe you can give me a hand with this one. I'm trying to figure out how the killer and the victim know each other." He glanced at Holcombe for permission. When she gave him a little nod, Luis continued.

"See, the victim is this career criminal. Not the kind of guy most folks in law enforcement are going to mourn, but the guy put himself front and center into a civil rights investigation so we kind of have to pay attention, right? Anyway, we know the killer is a cop. What we can't do is figure out where this particular cop and this particular career criminal first came into contact."

Porras' pupils shrank, and his skin lost some color. His voice stayed strong and steady though. "I'm pretty sure I can help you with that. If you've got the arrest records, I can go through them. Think of it as being like an audition, right?"

Holcombe cleared her throat. "We've already got those. I think we'd like to hear a few more details, Detective. Such as how Lieutenant Orlov put the two of you into contact with each other in the first place, and why. But first, I'd like you to place your hands on the desk where we can see them."

Luis held back a grin as Porras complied, jaw slack. "You have the right to remain silent," he said, grabbing his cuffs.

Donovan had to be proud when he saw Porras being led out of Holcombe's office in cuffs. He didn't have time to revel in the feeling though. Acid bubbled up in his stomach as every possible permutation of every difficulty raced through his head. What was going to happen when Porras didn't show up for work? Wouldn't that be a huge red flag for Orlov? Wouldn't he alert Fred?

It was all out of his hands. He could only do what he could do, and he knew the FBI knew what they were doing. He had work of his own, and now that he wasn't hiding what he was doing, he could bring Luis with him to do it. He didn't know why he felt more comfortable bringing Luis on this trip, but he did.

Dwayne had set up a meeting in a little Pentecostal church not far from where Jason Harper had apparently died. Donovan hadn't known where his accuser had lived, but Luis could and did tell him now. "He's still up there," Luis told him. After a pause, he added, "If it helps, he didn't get much choice in the matter."

Donovan pulled into a parking spot near the church. The place could have used a paint job, but it fit into the neighborhood well as it was. He could remember everything his father had said about this part of town, and how he'd believed it at one point. He knew better now. Who was going to put their hard-earned money into painting a place they didn't even own?

"There's always a choice." He put the car in park. "It's not always a good choice, but there's always a choice."

Luis bobbed his head from side to side. "Meh. Don't get me wrong. Harper was no saint. But the people behind this whole thing—"

"You can say Fred. It's okay."

"Fred told him if he didn't go along with it, he'd kill him and plant evidence on him to make it look justifiable. So his choice was to lie about someone he didn't know, and wasn't going to like anyway because of your profession, or to die." He shrugged and got out of the car. "I don't necessarily like the guy, but I can see why he'd make the choice."

Donovan got out and locked up behind them. "Worked out well for him in the end."

"Lie down with dogs, wake up with fleas, I guess. Landlord's going to have a hell of a time trying to rent the place out though. He's mad as hell." Luis led the way into the church basement.

Dwayne greeted them both with hugs, which surprised Donovan. When a tiny elderly woman with white hair came forward to hug Luis, Donovan did a double take. "Something you're not telling me, Luis?"

"Donovan, Dwayne, this is Camila. She lives downstairs from Jason Harper. We met the day he was killed." He looked down at the older woman and spoke in Portuguese. Donovan couldn't understand what they were saying to each other, but whatever it was made Luis' eyes bulge and the old lady laugh.

Luis covered his surprise with a cough. "Dwayne, do we have a lot of folks here tonight who have difficulties with English? I can translate for Portuguese and Spanish. I'd have trouble with Haitian Creole though. I've heard it, and I can get by if I have to, but I can't translate."

"I can handle that one if I have to. My mom was Haitian." Dwayne grinned. "I'm glad Donovan was able to bring you. I didn't think you'd be okay with this, honestly. He seemed to think you were a little anxious for his safety."

"Oh, I have been." Luis blushed scarlet. "I won't deny it, but he's also a grown man. I can't exactly lock him up. We can catch up later—I don't want to waste people's time. They volunteered to come here."

Camila looked Donovan over and gave him an approving nod and then took a seat in the front row.

Dwayne took center stage, with Luis and Donovan. To say the crowd was diverse was an understatement. Most of the faces belonged to people who looked Black or Latinx, but Donovan saw a few white and East Asian faces in the crowd too. Some were young children. Some were elderly, and some were from ages in-between. The only thing they all had in common was an apparent desire to stare at Luis and Donovan, and not necessarily in that order.

Some people did need translation; some didn't.

Dwayne started out by explaining why they were having the meeting. "Thank you all for coming out here tonight. I know I'm not exactly known for being friendly to the police." A few people laughed, Luis included. Donovan liked Dwayne, but he wasn't there yet. "The fact is, everyone's got a job to do, and so do they. Police brutality isn't just cops doing their jobs, it's what happens when police don't know how to do their jobs. It's what happens when bad people get jobs as cops.

"Not too long ago, someone tried to set this guy up as the guy who murdered five nonviolent protesters ten years ago."

As the translations finished, people nodded

and murmured assents. "How does he have the balls to come in here then?" yelled a woman who didn't look much older than her late teens.

Luis cleared his throat. "Hi. Luis Gomes, FBI. We know it was a setup because the people who set him up were sloppy and got caught. They left witnesses, they left other evidence, there will be a very public trial. I'm looking forward to it for a whole lot of reasons. Some of them are even professional. The people who set him up also murdered Jason Harper, just a couple of blocks from here. Donovan Carey is innocent."

A low rumble rose up near the back, and Donovan's stomach dropped. If he couldn't get these folks to believe him, how was he supposed to get a jury?

Dwayne cleared his throat, and people calmed. "The murder of Jason Harper, and the people who set Donovan up, are both solved cases. The problem is, it's not enough."

People agreed enthusiastically with this, cheering and applauding even before the translations were done.

"It's not enough for you. It's not enough for me. It's not enough for the FBI, surprisingly enough. And it's not enough for State Police Detective Donovan Carey."

A middle-aged Black man stood up. "Why

not?" He glared at Donovan with undisguised hostility. "If you're innocent, and the people who did you wrong are getting caught, why isn't it enough for you? Why are you bringing us into it?"

Donovan wiped his hands on his pants. "Because the person, or people, who killed those protesters is still out there." He swallowed. "It's been ten years. And honestly, when the shootings happened, I thought it was some stupid kid who panicked. A lot of us on the force did, you know? I figured they'd come forward, or they'd get found out, and someone would take their goddamn gun and badge because they shouldn't have it, and that would be it.

"I also grew up in a family of cops. Literally everyone in my family has a badge, except for like one aunt who's a prosecutor. She married in though, so she doesn't count. I knew there were some bad cops out there, but I honestly believed it was something that happened in other places. I know better now, and not just because it's happening to me."

Donovan looked around the room. He couldn't quite read the faces. He didn't think he wanted to. He didn't want to know if he was getting the words out wrong, so long as he got them out. "Listen, please. I know now that those shootings were cold-blooded murder and that we're capable of figuring out who did it and bringing them to justice. That's my whole job. I can't do it alone.

"I know some of you were there that day. Hell, I was there that day. I wasn't anywhere near the shooting, and I can prove it. Some of you were though. What I need from you—what we need from you—is a description of the people who attacked the protesters."

Another middle-aged Black man, this one seated near Luis' friend Camila, stood up. "I know where you were that day." Unlike his companion, he didn't seem to have trouble with English. He spoke fluently, although with an accent. "You were near where the stampede happened, when people ran from the shooting. You pulled me out of the crowd when I fell, and got me to an ambulance. You couldn't have shot anyone. You had your hands full with me, and some others."

Donovan's knees almost collapsed under him. If he hadn't had the podium for support, he'd have collapsed to the floor. He couldn't remember the man's name, but he remembered the face. "Thank you. How are your knees, sir?"

The man grinned. "I've had an operation or two, but they're much better."

Dwayne grinned and turned on an overhead projector, like the ones they'd had in high school.

"Does anyone remember having been up here near the State House?"

For a moment, there was silence. Then a short, pretty Latina stood up. "Yeah, I was there. Got my arm broken for it too. Some young guy. He tried to cover up the name on his uniform, but it's hard to do that when you're swinging a baton hard enough to crack skulls."

"I still get migraines." A Black man with dreadlocks stood and parted his long hair, revealing a ghastly scar. "I remember his name though. Porras."

Luis frowned. "Porras was the shooter?"

Donovan could understand his confusion. Porras was human scum, but he wasn't an assassin. He liked to hit people. He wasn't the type to pull a gun and start shooting. He could see Porras using his nightstick to break heads, but not murdering people in cold blood.

"Nah." A white woman with a pixie cut stood, hugging a hoodie closer to herself despite the heat. "I was next to Dorcas when she was shot. I saw the fucker who did it, and it was an older guy. The name on his uniform was Carey, but he didn't look like you." She looked down. "He was built different. Shorter. He had a mustache. He was stocky too. Kind of a barrel chest."

Her words hit Donovan in the chest.

310

Luis jumped into the crowd, pulling out his phone. "Ma'am, is this the man you saw?"

The witness paled and swayed on her feet. "Yes. That's him. I'd never forget him. I still have nightmares about him."

"And would you be willing to testify to that in court?"

She flinched, but then she set her jaw and nodded. "Yes. I—I have to."

A younger woman turned to her, eyes blazing. "You couldn't have said anything at the time?"

"Ma'am, she probably tried to. I don't know that anyone was listening." Luis turned to the resentful witness. His voice was gentle. "Times have changed. People are listening now."

He jogged back up to the front of the room and wrote his work number and email address on the transparency, so it appeared on the screen. "People are listening. *I'm* listening. Detective Carey's listening. Dwayne's listening. If you have information about what happened at that protest ten years ago, share it. Please. If you have something else you'd like us to take a look at, please call. I can't promise action, but I can promise I'll hear you out and do what I can to make sure you know what the next steps are."

Donovan could only watch as people

reacted. Some turned away in disgust. Others took pictures of Luis' information, to save for later. Still more wanted to approach him directly, waiting in a line.

Had this many people seen Fred murder five people in cold blood? Had this many people known Donovan's father was a murderer before Donovan did?

He escaped to the men's room and threw up.

By the time he made it back, Dwayne was helping Luis get people's contact information. Camila and her family were waiting patiently nearby. Initially, they'd been waiting for Luis, but when they saw Donovan, they approached him instead.

The man Donovan had saved shook his hand first. "You probably don't remember my name. I'm Marcel. Thank you for saving me that day. I'd have died without you."

Donovan blushed. "It's literally my job. You had every right to be safe at that protest. I'm glad to see you're doing better. I see your mom has already met Luis."

Marcel laughed. "Mama meets everyone. She's never been one to hold back. Eighty-six years old and still going strong. She's forgetting her English, but she's on top of literally everything else. God forbid a neighborhood kid forgets his homework! I can see Agent Gomes is busy, but she has a message for him. Do you think you can pass it along for her?"

Donovan nodded. "Sure, whatever you need."

"She says the neighbor upstairs, the dead one, is being noisy. She'd like for him to come by and move him on, or at least make him more polite if possible. There's no excuse for being rude in the afterlife."

Camila patted Donovan's arm and murmured something in Portuguese, then tottered out of the church. Donovan stood, frozen, while Dwayne gaped.

Marcel seemed oblivious to their obvious distress. "She says she'll make him a nice dinner when he comes by. You all have a good night now."

CHAPTER SIXTEEN

They'd let Porras spend the night in the Nashua Street Jail, pondering his fate. He wasn't forced to bunk down with other inmates. As a cop who hadn't been convicted yet, he would be in too much danger in the general population. Instead, he got a small cell all to himself. Other inmates knew he was there. They could tell who he was. They just couldn't touch him.

It must not have made for a very restful night.

Luis' night hadn't exactly been calm and quiet either. Donovan had carried Marcel's message. Luis had come close to having a heart attack, which more or less matched Donovan's reaction or so he said. Dwayne had been shocked, gaping like a fish out of water, and Luis had to do a lot of fast talking to explain himself after that little bombshell. He thought he'd been so careful about keeping that part of his life a secret, but apparently, he was just as clumsy with it as he was with everything else.

Either that, or he'd simply underestimated the observational powers of little old ladies.

Either way, he had to do something about Harper if he was still causing problems. It made sense for someone who had been a neighborhood problem in life to continue causing trouble after death. Luis could be as sympathetic as he wanted with regards to Harper's demise, but Harper hadn't ever displayed any kind of concern for the people around him before. There was no reason for him to start now.

Plus, Harper clearly wasn't thrilled about being stuck. Captain Lightfoot hadn't exactly been the most civic-minded of men, but in death, he found fulfillment and pleasure. Harper wasn't inclined in that direction. Luis should help him on if he didn't want to be here, regardless of his effect on the neighbors.

The only problem with that line of reasoning was that Luis had no idea how to move someone on.

He'd been present when ghosts moved on, but that was different. He hadn't done it on purpose. He hadn't been the cause. He'd simply helped make things happen that released the spirit, usually by solving a murder. Justice was a foreign concept to Harper and had been since he was a child.

Since his anxiety over being found out wouldn't let him sleep, he spent more time researching Harper. He hadn't been trained as a psychic or medium or whatever. He was, however, a forensic psychologist. If he couldn't solve the problem one way, he'd solve it another.

By the time it was late enough to go to work, he'd consumed most of a pot of coffee, made another one for Donovan, gone for an early morning run, made breakfast, and made decent inroads into understanding his subject. Harper wasn't the first inner-city kid to fall through the cracks and come to a bad end, of course. With the benefit of hindsight, Luis could see a hundred places where intervention might have set him on the right path.

Then again, plenty of inner-city kids had rough starts and didn't go on to deal drugs, hurt people, and get roped into a scheme to implicate cops in crimes they hadn't committed. Hell, Luis had started out in a slum, exchanged it for another one, and witnessed shocking violence at an early age. He'd turned out pretty well, all things considered.

Luis' job, with regards to Harper, wasn't to focus on the harm he'd done. Not anymore. Luis' job was to help him move on to whatever afterlife awaited him. Most of the time when he'd seen people move on, it happened when they achieved the goal that kept them stuck. Luis didn't know Harper well, but he thought he had enough information to try.

First, though, he had to deal with one of Harper's killers.

Porras was ready and waiting for Luis and Kevin by the time they arrived at work. They must have roused him early to bring him up to Chelsea. He wasn't nearly as handsome in his orange jumpsuit; it made him look jaundiced. Huge dark circles stood out under his eyes, telling Luis just how welcome his neighbors in pretrial detention had made him feel.

However tired or nervous he might have been, he managed to summon up a smirk for Luis and Kevin and tossed a wink at the one-way mirror where he knew Holcombe was watching. He didn't know Donovan was also observing, but the principle was the same.

"I bet you're real proud of yourselves." Porras shook his head, a little sneer marring his handsome face. "Think you did something special, huh?"

"Not particularly." Luis kept his face deadpan, even though he seethed inside. The rational side of him found it funny that he could be friends with the ghost of a dead serial killer without judgment but was filled with seething rage toward a fellow cop.

"Mr. Porras, you've been advised of your rights, but we do feel it's incumbent upon us to advise you of them again. You have the right to remain silent, you have the right to an attorney. You are aware of your rights, correct?"

"Yeah. Of course. I've done this before." Porras chuckled and leaned back as far as circumstances allowed. "I don't need a damn lawyer. I fucking hate those guys."

Most cops did. Luis had an ambiguous relationship with them himself. He wasn't about to allow Porras to think they were building a rapport though. "And you're aware this conversation is being recorded."

"Yep. Like I said, I've done this before. Let's get real here. You want to talk about that dirtbag Jason Harper, right?"

Luis made himself shrug casually, even though he wanted to punch Porras in the face. "Harper's death is a matter of some interest, yes."

"Why? The guy's a scumbag. He was a scumbag from the time he was nine. He wasn't ever going to change. He wasn't ever going to turn his life around or somehow do something good for society or anything like that. This ain't a movie."

Porras waved a hand, which looked absurd in his shackles. "We did the world a favor."

Luis ignored, or pretended to ignore, the use of the first-person plural. "Mmm. Well, we're not here to make value judgments, just to get the facts of the case. I know you understand. It's the job. Let's talk about those facts. You admit you were present the day of the murder."

"You don't know it was daytime." Porras scoffed, turning his nose up at Luis. He hadn't realized people actually did that, but he could see it in real time.

"Actually, we do. He spoke with his parole officer at eight thirty in the morning, and we found the body at one." Kevin gave him a thin smile. "That gives us a fairly narrow window for time of death. Neighbors put you on the scene sometime around nine, and Dr. Wong puts time of death around then."

"And that's what they pay you FBI guys the big bucks for? My nephew could've figured that one out, and he's six." Porras tossed his head. "So what? Who actually cares? Like I said, he's a dirtbag, and it just makes the case against your little boyfriend there even stronger."

Kevin looked over at Luis, like he couldn't believe what he'd just heard. "No, Porras. It doesn't. Here's the thing. We've got witnesses to prove that Donovan didn't shoot anyone, that he was far away from where the shootings took place. We've got time- and date-stamped photos, we've got time- and date-stamped documents from the EMTs, we've got injured protesters who identify Donovan Carey as the one who helped them, we've got EMTs who identify Donovan Carey as the state trooper helping injured protesters—not harming them—and we've got people who survived the shooting openly stating Donovan wasn't the one who shot them. All of whom are willing to testify in court."

Porras paled.

Luis leaned forward. "You can't shoot them all, Porras. Especially not from Nashua Street."

Porras took a deep breath and straightened up. His skin had turned almost waxy. "Okay. So maybe Golden Boy there isn't the one who shot them. It's not illegal to speculate, right?"

"Speculation is one thing. Forcing a guy to testify to something he didn't see, and couldn't have seen, is something else. We've got Harper on video up in Maine when the shooting occurred." Luis sat back, doing his best to portray himself as perfectly relaxed.

Maybe Borchard was right. Maybe Luis did need to learn how to chill.

"Here's the thing, Porras. Right now, we've

got you for murder, obstruction of justice, and conspiracy. For some reason, you decided to conspire to frame an innocent man for the murders of five innocent people ten years ago. I don't know if anyone explained what I do, but a big part of my job is getting at the why behind criminal behavior."

"And here I thought they just kept you around for your looks." Porras winked.

Luis stared at Porras for a moment. "Keep that sense of humor. It's going to do you good where you're going. I can only think of one reason for you to lie about Donovan Carey being the shooter." He paused to let his words sink in.

Emerson Porras wasn't a stupid guy. "Hey—I wasn't even there that day. I was stationed out in Western Mass, on traffic duty. You can check the records. I wrote tons of tickets that day."

"You're full of shit, Porras. You were there that day. Twenty different people filed complaints against you for brutality. The thing is, none of them involved firearms. All of them involved your nightstick." Kevin leafed through a thick stack of papers. "You broke arms. You broke legs. You broke ribs and punctured one person's lung. You broke skulls and gave one protester seizures that have lasted to this day."

Porras beamed. "What can I say? I'm good at what I do. They'll think twice before disrespecting law enforcement again."

Luis pinched the bridge of his nose. "Think before you speak, Porras."

"I'm not ashamed. And I'm not sorry. We're literally holding this country back from anarchy. Without us, this whole country would be tearing each other's throats out. Sometimes we have to get a little rough to get our point across."

Luis forced his anger back. It wouldn't get him what he wanted. "If you're not ashamed or sorry, why frame Donovan for murder?"

Porras shrugged. "It honestly wasn't my idea." He bit his lip, and then he shrugged. "If I'm fessing up to one thing, I might as well admit to everything. I wouldn't be here if you didn't have plenty of evidence, am I right? I'm not Carey's biggest fan. I think he got promoted faster to fill a quota. I'm out there risking my ass on the side of the Pike every day, and he gets bumped up to detective just because he's got family in the agency and likes to take it up the ass? Then he gets promoted to day shift in, like, three years, and I'm still stuck down there, never seeing my friends, living like a goddamn vampire? It's not right."

Luis kept his mouth shut. He let Kevin scratch his head and give Porras the quizzical look. "Hm. It's my understanding that Donovan Carey was in the closet until last year."

"Whatever. It's not right, okay? They don't belong in law enforcement. Meanwhile, I get suspended for even looking at a suspect wrong. So I get suspended, and then I get a call from this guy. He knows I'm frustrated, and he's got a plan to help me move up. I get to look like a goddamn genius because I've solved this big *thing* that happened ten years ago. Golden Boy gets taken down a few pegs, which my buddy *really* wanted, and all those people bitching about how cops do their jobs get to feel like we're listening to them. Right?" He looked between Luis and Kevin as if he truly expected to find a sympathetic ear.

Luis refused to let any emotion show on his face. It would jeopardize the confession he needed, and it would affect how the confession was received at sentencing and on appeal. Plus, if he let himself emote, he ran the risk of beating the ever loving shit out of Porras, and how ironic would that be? "Okay, Mr. Porras. Like we said, we're not looking for value judgments. We're just looking for facts here. This *guy* who reached out to you. What was his motive for wanting to frame Donovan?"

"Like I said, it was just taking Donovan down a peg or two and shutting people up about telling cops how to do our jobs." He shrugged. "Not my problem. The enemy of my enemy and all that."

"We're going to need you to identify the 'guy' in question." Kevin met Porras' eyes head-on.

"You already know who he is, G-man. I know you're just fucking with me now. It's what I'd do. But hey, I'll say it for the record. It's Fred Carey. I guess he and Golden Boy had some kind of falling-out, and he wanted to put him in his place or something. Family drama isn't exactly my idea of a good time, but we both wanted the same thing, so whatever." Porras smirked right at the mirror.

Luis glanced that way too. He had to imagine Donovan could somehow draw support from his impassive glance. Then he turned all of his attention back to Porras. "Mr. Porras, do you have knowledge of the identity of the killer from the protests ten years ago?"

Porras scoffed. "Nope. And I don't care either. As far as I'm concerned, that person should get a medal."

Kevin put a hand on Luis' arm. "All right. We'll get this written up for you to sign and take you to the judge."

Porras gave him a big thumbs-up. "Sweet."

Elation warred with nausea as Donovan stood behind the one-way mirror and watched Luis and

Kevin interrogate Porras. How many other guys in Major Crimes felt the same way as Porras? How many of them would also stab him in the back to advance, just because of his sexuality or just because of his family?

And where the hell was Porras getting all that bravado?

He couldn't focus on that now. He turned to Holcombe, more to fight the bile than anything else. "It's great that we've got him on murder, and we'll probably get Fred on it too. People who were there were pretty firm about the shooter having the name Carey on his uniform, but not being built like me."

"The problem is that there are a hundred men with the last name Carey on the Boston Police payroll back then, and maybe fifty on the state police roster." Holcombe sighed. "And your father's defense attorney will—rightly—make the point that a guy who admits he set up Donovan can't be trusted when he says Fred committed a crime too. We need more."

"His service weapon was gifted to him when he retired, but he'd be a fool if he kept it." Donovan paced in the small observation room. "He's a lot of things, most of them bad, but he's not a fool."

"Donovan." Holcombe stepped in front of him, meeting his eyes. "It's okay to still have good memories of him. And it's okay to mourn those memories too. You understand that, right?"

Donovan stopped short. "Yeah," he said after a second. "I mean, he taught me to fire a gun. He taught me to play baseball. He taught me to enjoy things like watching football and that kind of stuff. But some things—I mean, he was never good to my mother, for one thing. He didn't hit her, but he was still bad. And he hasn't gotten better with age. I just—I'm not conflicted or anything. It's more like I feel sick that someone who could do something like this gave me half of my genetic material."

Holcombe grimaced. "Yeah, I'd imagine that would be a pretty tough blow. Are you going to be okay?"

"Probably." He rolled his shoulders. "When I think about all the people he's harmed, all the people he's probably done similar things to and gotten away with it—yeah, I'll be okay. I'm lucky. I've had good people on my side who were willing to hear me out, help me, do whatever it took to help me clear my name. There are plenty of others who didn't. I've got to do whatever I can to try to even the scales a little, don't you think?"

Holcombe gave him a gentle smile. "You're a good man, Donovan. Come on. Let's see what we can do to bring your father in."

Donovan was able to get Luis alone a little later and thank him for dealing with Porras' confession. "I know it can't have been easy, sitting there and listening to him."

"Oh my God, I was worried you'd think I was being too calm." Luis melted, just a little bit. "I just hoped you knew how much I wanted to throttle him. I still want to throttle him. Jesus Christ. How're you doing? Are you okay? Hearing all that bullshit must have been a challenge."

Donovan chuckled. "I wasn't sure if I should be happy we got him or puke about how bad everyone seems to be. But hey—you stood right by me and proved them all wrong. Thank you."

Luis stayed late in Chelsea that night because he needed to put some more work into getting the warrant to arrest Fred and Orlov. Donovan had to go home alone, which didn't fill him with joy, but he'd deal with it. He knew how Luis got when he had a challenging case, and the nature of this one made Luis more obsessive than usual. Donovan would make dinner and have it ready and waiting for whenever Luis stumbled in the door.

He'd just finished cooking—just pasta, nothing fancy—when someone rang the doorbell. A quick glance at the app on his phone showed him the visitor was Fred Carey.

Donovan froze. It was one thing to get a visit from a homophobic, manipulative father with a history of interfering in his life. It was another to get one from a mass murderer who happened to share his blood.

At the same time, Fred was here. The security system Luis had set up was recording everything, or at least it would once Donovan pressed the right buttons. Donovan could either let him kick the door down or go out there, meet with him, and control the situation.

He sent Luis a quick text. *Fred's here. I'm going to see what he wants. I love you.*

Then he told the app to record, went to the door, and confronted his father.

Fred, being Fred, sneered and tried to shoulder his way inside. It might have worked when Donovan was a kid, but now he just closed the door firmly behind him.

"Why are you here? I have a restraining order. And, yes, the authorities have already been contacted."

"Who're they going to believe? The decorated retired officer who told the truth or the killer cop who's somehow managed to evade justice for a decade?" Fred laughed and stuck his thumbs into his waistband. "What's the matter, Donnie? Don't you want your old man to see the new place? I'm sure it's just fabulous." He added an exaggerated lisp on the word *fabulous*, just in case Donovan didn't get his point.

"It's a decent place, for two cops. Why are you here?" Donovan refused to rise to the bait. If he kept telling himself he refused to rise to the bait, he figured he might actually succeed.

"Ah, come on, Donnie. An old man just wants to talk to his son. I mean, you're the prodigal son, sure, but even the father in that Bible story welcomed his son back with open arms. Of course, the son had to abandon his life of sin first."

Donovan rolled his eyes. "You're the one with the most to repent for, don't you think? Having affairs while you're married, spreading diseases, getting women pregnant at your age—"

Fred slammed his hand against the door, making a loud slapping sound that set the neighbor's dogs to barking. "I'm the father. What I say goes. If I say you need to repent, you need to fucking repent. You're the one who wouldn't listen, who stuck with that man-whore instead of marrying that girl I told you to marry. You'd be a father by now if you'd done what I told you."

"Maybe on paper. Hey, if I'd slept with her, would I have picked up a case of whatever the hell you passed on to Mom? Because I've got to say, that's not the kind of family sharing plan most folks have in mind."

Donovan knew the slap was coming, so he was braced for it. He didn't block it or fight back against it. He didn't want to jeopardize the FBI case against Fred. It wasn't an easy choice though.

"Sometime in between when I moved out of the house and now, you learned how to talk back to your father. I can't say I like the change. I know where to look for the source though. It's that queer you're hanging around with. I'll tell you this much. You drop him—you drop Luis, never see him or speak to him again—and I'll walk back what I said about you."

Donovan's heart leaped into his throat. Fred couldn't possibly be saying what Donovan thought he heard. He had to know he was being recorded, right? There was a sign for the security system right there by the front stoop.

"You're joking."

"Oh, come on, Donnie. You and he haven't even been together very long, and you broke up once! You aren't seriously picking some Brazilian queen with a murderer for a father over your actual family?" He grabbed Donovan by the shirt. "You've already seen what a bad idea that is. I already took your whole career away with a few short words. Do you want to see what I'll do if you really push me?"

Donovan detached his father's hand from his shirt and laughed. He couldn't help it. "I'm sorry—what? *You*, casting stones at someone else for murder? That's rich."

Fred's face went florid. "You'd better not be making accusations you can't back up, boy."

"Yeah, that would be illegal. And if I involved someone else, that would be conspiracy. And if it involved accusations of a crime someone else was being investigated for, it would be obstruction of justice. And if I killed the person who knew I'd accused you falsely, that would be murder." Donovan kept laughing. "Just imagine what a mess that would be for me, if I got caught. Good thing I'm not doing that."

"You're fucking delusional. All that gay sex stuff has scrambled your brains."

"Keep thinking that. In the meantime, why don't you tell me why you did it all?" Donovan brought himself under control and tried to keep his body loose. He wasn't afraid Fred would shoot him, not anymore. Instead, he needed to keep Fred here long enough for Luis and whoever he could drag along to find him and arrest him.

"Because it was funny, Donnie. Because it was funny and you needed to be taught a lesson." Fred poked Donovan in the chest. "You've gotten way too big for your britches. You need to remember your place, and it's my job to remind you."

Donovan scoffed. "You killed a man—a man who was cooperating with you—because you were mad at *me*? That's some bullshit right there."

"Who's talking about murder here? Yeah, I told your boss that you killed those protesters. They were dragging their feet about suspending you. What the hell do I pay my taxes for, right? You made your choice, Donnie. You could have your family or your little boy toy. Don't come crying to me because you made the wrong one."

"No one's crying. I've got plenty of family, all I need actually. What I don't need is deadweight pulling me down. And believe me when I tell you, Fred, down is the only direction you're going." He stopped himself from revealing more, but only barely.

He couldn't let Fred know he'd been involved with the investigation. The FBI didn't even want to make an announcement about Porras' arrest. Donovan refused to be the one fucking that up for them.

Fred spat at Donovan. It hit him in the shirt. "We'll see about that, you little traitor. You're going to be sorry you were ever born."

"Was that a threat?"

"It was a promise." Fred turned on his heel

and stormed off.

Luis returned to the town house ten minutes later. The giant black SUV had the siren light on, but not the sound. "Goddamned Boston traffic," he groused. "I missed him, didn't I?"

Donovan sighed and kissed Luis. "It's okay. I kind of suspect he was fishing for information, you know? He hit me, but he didn't seem inclined to shoot me."

"This time." Luis glowered toward the parking lot. "I think I hit the ceiling when I got your text. Did you record the convo?"

"I did." Donovan chuckled. "Of course I did. No way I wasn't going to. Did he miss the security system sign or what?"

"We never meet the smart criminals." Luis laughed and let Donovan guide him indoors.

CHAPTER SEVENTEEN

Luis reviewed the video with the rest of the team, seething the whole time. He didn't care that the rest of the guys were watching Fred bad-mouth him. They already knew what Fred was. Hell, they knew what Luis was too. He'd been pretty up-front about it from the time he showed up. Luis' rage was reserved for Fred, for the situation in which Donovan found himself.

Fred had dared to blame Donovan, and his relationship with Luis, for Fred's actions. Luis knew abusers usually blamed their victims for their actions, but this took the cake. *I had to lie about you and try to destroy your career, Donovan, because you just wouldn't listen to me.*

Holcombe stopped the video when Fred drove away. "Well, we have him on video confessing to making the false accusation. He's not admitting to murder."

"Witnesses put him at the scene." Kevin ticked off evidence on his fingers. "For that matter, eyewitnesses saw him murder the protesters too. We have phone records proving he was in contact with Porras, who already confessed and who gave up Fred as part of the conspiracy. And, it should be noted, confessed to his role in Harper's murder."

"It's enough for a warrant, but it won't be enough for a jury." Wragge sighed. "Everyone in this room knows he's guilty, so don't give me that look, Gomes."

Luis hadn't realized he was glaring, but he guessed he was angry enough to look hostile. He got himself under control as quickly as he could. "Sorry. Much as I hate to admit it, you may be right. He's an older guy and living the way he has makes him look even older. His lawyer will trot him out and make him look downright grandfatherly for the jury. We have to nail this down so tight even Mother Teresa couldn't wiggle out of it."

Borchard nodded. "The warrant gives us the ability to find the gun, assuming he kept it. There's no reason to suppose he wouldn't have. Bullets taken from the protesters appear to have been fired from a standard-issue Boston Police Department Glock, which weren't compared to anyone's gun at the time. It wasn't exactly a secret that they were shot by cops, and there wasn't the political will to press charges."

"We'll do that now. And if we can confirm

it's the same gun that killed Harper, then we're home free." Fontana cracked his knuckles.

"Are we certain that Fred Carey was allowed to keep his service weapon when he retired?" Holcombe tapped her finger on the desk. "I don't want us pinning this whole case on something we can't prove."

"It's documented in his file, Patricia has a picture of him receiving it as a gift, and all four of the Carey children have confirmed it." Luis left out the part where one of Donovan's siblings, a brother named Tony, informed Luis that Fred should use it to shoot him in the head. Apparently, not all the Carey children took Patricia and Donovan's side.

"Excellent. We'll get the search warrant and go forward. Unfortunately, the search warrant ensures he knows we're coming for him, but he has to have at least suspected. He wouldn't have come to bother Donovan otherwise." Holcombe broke up the meeting, and Luis headed for the exit.

Kevin followed. "What's on your mind?" He kept his voice low as they returned to their desks. "You look like a man on a mission."

"Sorry. I'm just frustrated, I guess." He took a deep breath and tried to calm himself.

Kevin drew his brows together. "Well, Luis, I mean, you have to understand why we have the legal process we do. I definitely don't want his lawyer to be able to come back and give any nonsense about his due process rights being violated or anything like that."

Luis could see it all stretching out in front of him. Fred lurking around their house, taking potshots whenever he wanted. Donovan having to leave the force because of some scheme of Fred's. "That'd be rich, coming from him. Yeah, I know we have to be sure. Not just sure, but by the book on everything."

Kevin's voice dropped even further. "That means no 'confidential informants,' Luis."

Luis didn't have words for a response, so he just trusted the look on his face to do the work for him. "As it happens, I do have a handful of said informants who would love to encounter our suspect on a dark night downtown. I'm just having trouble thinking of a good reason to get him down there."

Kevin gaped at him. "You'd seriously take him there to let . . . them . . . hurt him?" Then, after a second, "Would it work?"

"I don't see why not. And, yes. If I thought he could walk, I'd definitely let the ghosts finish him off. They seem to have a problem with state-sponsored violence. Go figure." He shrugged. "It probably makes me a terrible person, but it's Donovan. This guy has been targeting Donovan for a year. I'm not sure what he'll do next, and all because he sees Donovan as disobedient. I have to keep him safe."

Kevin looked away for a second, and then he shrugged. "I guess I can't think of a good reason why you shouldn't. It seems wrong, but this is a guy who set up a whole scheme to frame his kid for mass murder. He's capable of anything."

"Hopefully, it won't come to that." A plan was taking shape in the back of Luis' head though.

It would be wrong, and equally important, he didn't know if he'd be successful. He got to work strengthening the cases against both Porras and Fred until well past dark, and then he went down to his car.

He didn't take much with him, just a folder with a photo from the case file in it and a bottle of rum in a price range that qualified as decent.

His conscience did fight him, just a bit. Due process existed for a reason, and Luis believed in it with his entire heart, mind, and soul. The problem was, Fred had already perverted the concept of due process when he set Donovan up for murder. He'd violated Harper's rights. He'd violated the rights of the protesters he'd killed. He would do it again and again, and he'd manipulate the system to get out of paying the price for his crimes if there was even the slightest chance he could get away with it.

Luis had an obligation to keep it from happening again.

He believed in due process, but he couldn't let Fred hurt Donovan.

Downtown Boston was still alive with people by the time he got there, both living and dead. He greeted the ghosts of the 1919 Police Strike riot (and dropped off Groat's rum), a few smallpox victims, and avoided a few living drunks stumbling toward the red line of the Freedom Trail. He had someplace to be, and while people would still be around, they weren't going to be paying too much attention to him.

He slipped into the Granary Burying Ground and let himself open up, just a little. The hair on the back of his arms stood up as a familiar stink filled the air. Even the best, most innocent ghosts reeked of decay. They couldn't help it. They were, after all, dead.

Crispus Attucks stood before him, his massacred companions arrayed behind him. "I believe we told you not to return unless you had the murderer."

"You did." Luis swallowed. He'd run afoul of angry ghosts before, and had managed to fight them off. He didn't want to fight these dead. They were on the same side. More importantly, he didn't

340

see anything he could use to fight them with. "I want to make absolutely certain we're targeting the right man. The authorities in your time might not have been particular about that sort of thing. Most of us today are trying our best."

One of the companions, the one standing toward the back and left, huffed out a little laugh. "Did that help the men gunned down ten years ago?"

Luis had to grin wryly. "I did say most of us. I've brought a picture of the man we believe did the deed. Witnesses have said it was him, but there was a lot of chaos and violence that day. We're hoping we can get more hard evidence to prove it was him. If we can't arrest him for murder, I'm going to bring him down here and you can take care of him."

The men exchanged glances. "Why not cut out the middleman?" Attucks asked, wrinkling his nose. "A trial will take an eternity and isn't a guarantee. We are certain."

"Because the families of the victims deserve to know. They deserve to see, in public, that someone in law enforcement was willing to act for them. Someone was willing to find the person who killed their mother, father, brothers, and sisters. Someone was willing to say that person's name and charge them with what they did.

"After that, it's up to the jury. And if the jury

is too full of hate or too turned around by fanatical loyalty to the police, then those survivors will still see that we made the effort. And I'll find a way to bring him here. But first, let's give the courts a chance to work, so the survivors get the chance your families never did."

The ghosts' posture shifted. They straightened up, looking at each other. The darkness around them seemed to lighten slightly, and then Attucks spoke again. "You've made some . . . interesting points. If he should pass by here, however, we'll still take him."

Luis grinned. "I wouldn't dream of talking you out of it." He opened the folder and pulled out the photo. "Is this the man you saw?"

Attucks curled his lip. The darkness returned as the ghosts reached for the photo.

"Aye, that's the man," rumbled one of the other Boston Massacre victims. "To be sure, I saw him shoot two men in the back with my own eyes. The smile on his face was repulsive. I think he took a carnal pleasure from the act."

Luis shuddered and let the ghosts pass the photo around. "It wouldn't surprise me."

"The first one he killed was a woman." Attucks turned his head. "She put herself in between him and a young man, and he shot her. She was a threat to no one."

"She was a threat to his sense of superiority." Luis shrugged. "Guys like him don't find anything more threatening than that." He took the photo back. "Thank you all very much. We're getting a search warrant now. We've got enough to arrest him for a different crime, but what we want to do is get him for this killing. We can't let men like him walk the streets, let alone with a gun."

"Get him your way, lawman." Attucks shook his hand. "Or we'll get him ours."

Luis gritted his teeth against the chill, thanked his hosts again, and headed home.

When he got there, Donovan greeted him with a kiss and a seared-salmon salad. "Kevin stopped by," he told him. "He said you had an alternative plan in case Fred somehow managed to skate on the whole murder thing."

Luis froze. "That's . . . one way of putting it." He put his fork down. "I'm sorry. I shouldn't . . . it's not something I should have done without discussing with you first. But you're my top priority, Donovan. I have to keep you safe."

Donovan tilted his head to the side, like he was thinking about something. "On the one hand, I'm a grown-ass man. On the other hand, I'm a grown-ass man and it's nice to have someone in my life who loves me enough to do whatever it takes to keep me safe. And I'd do the same for him. Am I correct in assuming this 'alternative plan' involves people who aren't exactly breathing air anymore?"

Luis blushed. "For what it's worth, they'd have taken him out on their own if he'd ever walked past the Granary again."

"Fair enough. It's not even really your fault then." Donovan laughed. "I'm not mad." He picked up his fork and toyed with it. "I mean, yes, he's my father, and I should have feelings about that. But he's also done some awful, terrible things. He needs to pay for what he's done. What he did to me is bad. He murdered five people and left their families waiting and in pain for ten years. He murdered someone who was cooperating with him. He threatened people into doing his dirty work for him. He's done so much to set law enforcement back, I don't know how long it'll take to recover. I'd rather have him pay publicly, with a trial and everything, but it'll be enough just to have him off the streets."

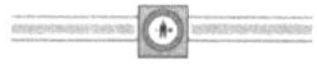

Donovan had thought he'd feel great at this point. He'd been exonerated, Fred was running scared, and Luis had found a bunch of ghosts willing to help him from beyond the grave. The problem was, he still didn't feel any better. He still had that awful, itching ache underneath his skin. Nothing was resolved yet, and everything could still come crashing down at any moment.

After all, he'd thought he was home free, and then Fred had gone and made a public, and humiliating, accusation. Who knew what he'd try now that the feds were going to search his house? Hell, who knew what Orlov had up his sleeve? He was seeped in this mess from the beginning.

Maybe Donovan should be more concerned about what Luis had planned. It was underhanded as hell, and oh yeah, it was a plan to murder Donovan's own father in a way that couldn't ever be traced back to him or Donovan. As plots went, it was devious. What would happen if that mind was to turn against Donovan?

At the same time, this was Luis. Donovan only had Luis' word that the ghosts were already out to get Fred when he showed up, but his word counted for a lot. Luis had shown, time and time again, just how far he'd go to protect Donovan. Their relationship had been rocky sometimes, but Luis loved him.

They took a little time the next day, which was a Saturday, to go visit Patricia. Luis got twitchy, the way he always did until an arrest was made, but Donovan put his foot down. Luis was not to harm himself for Donovan.

He'd done as much as he could, and Patricia was at least peripherally involved with the case. It was right and appropriate for them to visit, and for Luis to spend a little time enjoying human contact in a way that did not involve any murder at all.

Luis just laughed when Donovan told him that, and put on those jeans that made his ass look amazing, and they went to Patricia's.

Alicia was there too, with her son, Nick, and Donovan knew he'd only have half of Luis' attention for the rest of the day. Nick adored Luis and just about monopolized him every time he saw him. Luis didn't quite understand it, but he got a kick out of Nicky's hero worship and liked having someone to talk about soccer with. It worked out and gave Nicky the father figure he needed, leaving Donovan some alone time with his mother and cousin.

"You know, back when Luis first showed up again, I thought he and Nicky would get along like a house on fire." Patricia brought them all drinks as they sat out on the back deck and watched Luis and Nicky run around the yard. "I wanted to set him up with you, Alicia, at least in part because of that." She laughed and shook her head at the memory. "Obviously, I was in the dark about a few things, but it's all worked out in the end."

Alicia smirked and shook her head as Nicky

took a tumble. "That boy gets so many grass stains. It has all worked out, I'll say that much. So how's the whole investigation going, Donovan? Are they close to an arrest? I got a call from Uncle Fred last night. I think he was fishing for information. Lord knows, he hasn't tried to talk since that whole thing last fall."

Donovan blushed. He didn't want to think about his behavior last fall, when Fred had played him like a cheap piano. "I can't really say because I'm not a fed, but they have enough for a search warrant."

"Good. I hope they nail him to a fucking wall." Patricia sipped from her lemonade. When her niece and son gave her shocked looks, she affected an angelic posture. "What? It's true. He brought the whole department into disrepute, tried to frame my son for murder, and apparently, committed mass murder. Yes, I was in love with him once, but the best part of him was in the children he gave me." She sniffed. "The rest of him is quite frankly trash."

Donovan put his arm around her shoulders and squeezed. Before he could say anything though, the fire alarm in the house rang out in its hateful, obnoxious horn.

Donovan jumped up, gun already drawn. He wasn't the only one. Patricia and Alicia each had their service weapons in hand beside him, and Luis had Nicky on the ground in the rhododendrons, hunched over him with his gun drawn.

Donovan opened the door carefully. There was no way this was a natural fire. The wiring in here was top-notch, and Patricia hadn't been cooking. Whoever had set the fire might still be inside.

Patricia swatted his arm. "Put that away," she hissed. "You're still suspended." She stepped into the house, eyes sweeping the kitchen. The kitchen itself was unharmed, but Donovan could see smoke billowing in from the parlor. It matched the stink of burning carpet and drapes. "Call 9-1-1 and grab the fire extinguisher."

Donovan's cheeks blazed. He was supposed to be the hero, to do the takedown. Then he remembered who'd put those kinds of thoughts in his head and did as he was told. Alicia was on SWAT, for fuck's sake. She'd take someone down just as well as he could if not better.

He called to report the fire, giving the dispatcher the address and describing what little information he had so far. The fire extinguisher was near the refrigerator, so he was able to grab it and put the phone on speaker as he went in to douse the flames.

"We'll need the arson inspector," he told the dispatcher, watching the flames die in a shower of white foam. "This was absolutely deliberate."

"Sir, there's no way to be sure of that."

"Ma'am, I'm a state police detective, and I've seen firebombings before. The screen in the window to the parlor was cut. I can see the bottle fragments. It ain't rocket science. But they'll figure it out once they get here. Anyway, the flames are out. Captain Carey is checking the house right now."

He heard sirens screaming up the street, and knew they'd have company soon. Whether that company would be helpful or not remained to be seen.

The first to arrive was a fire truck. While police and fire had a kind of friendly rivalry most of the time, they were all business now.

Patricia greeted them upon arrival, showing her badge and shaking their hands. "My son was able to put the fire out, thank God, but this was clearly deliberate."

The chief of the crew on that particular truck didn't have to do much investigating to agree with her. "I'm no arson investigator, but it doesn't take much, ma'am. I'll let them know to send someone to certify it. They'll probably send investigators—"

Luis strode into the room with Nicky, just as

police from Boston walked in. He flashed his credentials and shook hands with the uniformed Boston cops—then gave a sheepish grin when he recognized Steve Wong. "Hey." He ran his hand through his hair. "Fancy meeting you here."

"Yeah, well, I jumped on it when I recognized Captain Carey's address." Wong grimaced. "I wanted to make sure everything was okay. Which—obviously it isn't given that I can see someone firebombed your house, ma'am."

Patricia scowled. "I don't think we have to look far to come up with a suspect."

Luis pulled out a phone and sent a text. "I've just called Maxwell in. I let SSA Holcombe and the rest of the team know as well. I don't want to be *that agent* who swoops in and steals an investigation or screws with jurisdiction. There's just more than a little bit of reasonable suspicion that this incident is related to our ongoing investigation."

Steve snorted. "Sounds like a problem for the brass to argue about. It's not like your guys are going to screw up chain of custody. We'll just hang out here and wait for someone to come and deal with the evidence, right?"

"Sounds good to me."

Nicky looked up at Luis. Donovan didn't think he'd ever seen his idol act in his professional capacity. "Wait—was a bad guy trying to hurt Auntie Patricia?"

Luis got down to his level. "It does look that way, Nick. But you know what? Your aunt is an amazing lady. So is your mom, and so is your Uncle Donovan. They did exactly what they're supposed to do, and they put the fire out and got help. Know what that means?"

Donovan bit the inside of his cheek. He knew Luis was trying to keep the kid from panicking, but he was also teaching Nicky to keep *himself* from panicking.

"No." Nicky squirmed for a second. "It means they're superheroes?"

"Well, yeah. I think so. But it also means the bad guy who did this isn't as smart as he thinks he is. Now—don't touch anything, but look around here and tell me what you see."

Nicky frowned and peered intently at the burned spot and then at the area around it. "Well, it looks like he cut the window open. The screen, I mean. And then he threw some glass bottles, which will make Aunt Patricia mad because she's always worried we're going to break glass and make the new baby hurt himself.

"And he cut himself too—look, there's blood on the windowsill, and on the screen."

Luis ruffled Nicky's hair. "Awesomesauce,

Nicky. You did a great job. I hadn't even noticed that."

Nicky preened. "I'm going to be an FBI guy, just like you!"

"Maybe you will. Hey, do you want to hang out and see how my friend Maxwell collects the evidence?"

"Yeah!" Nicky, who'd openly referred to police work as "boring" to the despair of the whole Kennedy family, clapped his hands and cheered.

Patricia shook her head and smiled, despite the situation. "That man's a keeper."

Donovan's heart swelled as he and the rest of his relatives went back out into the yard to await the FBI's evidence response team. "He's definitely a keeper. Fortunately, he seems to think I'm a keeper too."

"Of course he does! I raised you." Patricia took his arm and stood with him in the sunshine.

Luis followed him out. "Donovan, can I talk to you for a second?"

Luis led him off to a corner of the yard a little way away from the rest of the family. It counted as out of earshot, if they kept their voices down. "What's up?" Donovan frowned at Luis. "Did you see something weird?"

Luis sighed, slumping his shoulders. "No. I just—I wanted to give you the option to call things off."

Donovan stared at him. "I must have inhaled too much smoke. I know I didn't hear what I thought I just heard."

Luis made a strange, impatient little sound in the back of his throat. "Donovan, I love you. It's my job to keep you safe, remember? Are we just going to pretend your father didn't try to frame you for murder and now just try to firebomb your mother's house, all because of your relationship with me? If you want to lighten your load, it's okay. I won't be mad or hold it against you. I don't expect anyone to risk not just their own lives but the lives of their families for me."

Donovan stepped forward and caught Luis in the tightest embrace he could. "Luis, you are the love of my life. You're my family. I'm not letting anyone get between you and me. For one thing, it's possible the firebomber is someone on Fred's side, like Orlov. Hell, it could be Tony. He was always a little shit.

"For another, I love you too much to back away. We're not going to let him break us up. It's that simple. I'm not letting him part us again, just because I'm a stubborn son of a gun and I'd stay with you just out of spite if nothing else. And there's plenty else."

Luis gave him a shy little smile. "As long as

you're sure. Informed consent and all."

Donovan kissed him, not caring who could see. "I'm sure. Now go catch my father and throw him in prison where he belongs."

CHAPTER EIGHTEEN

Luis looked up as Holcombe approached his desk. As always, her face remained impassive, but her eyes had a twinkle in them her aura of professionalism just couldn't suppress. "Agent Gomes, Fred Carey is here to see you. He's also here to file a formal complaint of harassment."

"Is he now?" Luis pushed his laptop away and stood up. "I'm happy to go discuss things with him."

"Why don't Kevin and I join you? And why don't we discuss this in one of those fun rooms where everything gets recorded? You know, just for posterity's sake?" She flourished the folder she was holding. "As it happens, Maxwell was kind enough to rush the ballistics report for me. I truly do appreciate his diligence."

"He's a good man." Luis grinned and followed his supervisor to one of the interrogation rooms. He didn't miss Kevin's smirk before he took up the rear.

Just as Luis expected, Fred was angry when he was shown into the room. He didn't need to speak for Luis to know that. His skin was red, a vein stood out enough he wondered if Fred might need medical attention, and he vibrated with the rage in his soul.

"You had people searching my house? My home? How dare you? How fucking dare you?" Fred poked Luis in the chest. "I'm going to have your badge and gun for this. Don't think I won't, you fucking Brazilian ape. You may have used some kind of voodoo to get my son wrapped around your finger, but it's not going to work on me. I've got you dead to rights. I'm going to skin you alive."

Holcombe cleared her throat. "Mr. Carey, you are aware that everything in these rooms is recorded?"

"The hell do I care?" He raked Holcombe over with his eyes. "It's true. This little bitch thinks he can get away with tossing my house because he's in the FBI. That's abuse of authority if I've ever seen it. Who the fuck are you, anyway?"

Holcombe gestured to a chair. "I'm Supervisory Special Agent Holcombe. I'm Agent Gomes' supervisor. You did come in to file a formal complaint, yes? I would be the person to receive that complaint. Please, sit down."

Fred stopped in his tracks and shuffled over to the chair. The vein in his head didn't recede one bit, but some of the color did. Luis wasn't surprised. "They're letting girls supervise in the FBI now? Since when? They certainly weren't doing that in J. Edgar's day, let me tell you."

"No, they weren't. Of course, Director Hoover had issues of his own that also weren't allowed in his day. Let's discuss the nature of your complaint against Agent Gomes, shall we?" She picked up the folder and pretended to look through it.

Luis watched Fred closely. Fred was a professional, or had been at one point. He had to know what she was doing was a ruse. He still seemed to be mollified somewhat by the gesture.

"They ransacked my fucking house! They even went through my safe and took my guns—even my service weapon."

"Mmm. I see here that they had a warrant to do so."

"A fake one. I know a fake warrant when I see one. I mean, seriously, there was no probable cause to seek a warrant to search my home. It's bullshit. He knows it, and I know it. It's entirely retaliatory. He's got my son under some kind of spell, and he's pissed that I'm getting Donnie back from under him."

"Actually, Mr. Carey, I sought the warrant." Holcombe gave him a little smile. "I sought the warrant after you violated the restraining order against you, went to your son Donovan's home, and admitted on camera to being part of a conspiracy to frame him for the murder of five protesters during a riot ten years ago."

Fred's face drained of all color.

He rallied though. "Look. I know good and well that it's illegal to record someone in Massachusetts without their knowledge."

"There's a security system. Anyone stepping onto the property is notified of the recording via signage." Kevin cleared his throat. "You walked into that one. Literally."

Fred opened and closed his mouth several times, like a fish stuck on concrete. "This is entrapment!"

"No, Fred." Luis spoke to his nemesis for the first time during their encounter. "You've made the choices for yourself, every time, with your eyes wide-open."

"It's true." Holcombe nodded. "Your intention today was likely to bluster and bombast your way out of whatever they found when they searched your residence, before test results could come back. Your problem right now is that test results are already back. When you served, you had to share the crime lab with the entire state, and your cases just didn't get priority. We don't have that problem here. This case is highly visible, and the higher-ups in Washington want it cleared for a wide variety of reasons."

Sweat broke out on Fred's bald head. "That warrant was illegal! It's only because of bias against me that you searched my house at all."

"No, actually. It's because you spoke out on camera and then because your partner in crime, Detective Porras, isn't the world's most loyal man." Kevin cracked his knuckles. "If you think the search warrant was illegally obtained, you can take it up with the judge, but take it from me—we were very careful about our case."

"This is some bullshit. You're going to take the word of a dirty cop? It's never going to fly with a jury. I promise you that." Fred laughed. It sounded hollow to Luis' ears, but he supposed it would.

"Well, this is why we searched instead of arrested." Luis turned his head to look at Holcombe. He hadn't seen the evidence yet. Surely, she had it.

Holcombe pulled out a piece of paper. "We have the ballistics report on the bullet removed from Jason Harper's head. It's a match to your service weapon, which you were gifted when you retired."

Fred waved a hand. "Stolen. Tragic, I know. I miss that gun."

"It was found in your gun safe." Holcombe rolled her eyes.

"A miracle—or a frame-up. You feds will always pull some shady shit to set a guy up."

Luis accepted the report from Holcombe. He didn't find any surprises in it, but that may have been because he believed the survivors from the original protest and he had the dead to confirm. "Here's the thing, Fred." He closed the file and looked Fred in the eye. "I've been curious about something. Framing Donovan for a ten-year-old murder—it's out of character for you. I get that it's about power and control—you want to force Donovan to leave me, make him go back into the closet, whatever. I even believe that's part of your motivation.

"It's still not something that you'd do. You're not the kind of guy who'd just sit there, nursing your rage until the right opportunity to frame someone came along. Not that you're stupid, not at all. Far from it. You're just ... well, your temper is more explosive. You get mad at something, you do something about it, and then you move forward."

Fred shrugged, but he didn't look Luis in the

eye. "I ain't admitting I even set him up because I didn't."

"Caught on camera, Fred." Kevin shook his head. "I'm just saying."

Luis chuckled but recovered his aplomb quickly. "The problem is, the murders at the riot shouldn't have been on your radar at all. Let's face it, they're not even something you're likely to object to."

"First off, they're not murders. Christ, you make it sound like someone went hunting for people in the crowd." Fred rolled his eyes. "It was a fucking riot, dumbass. That's how it works. Rioters riot, cops shoot them, life goes on."

Kevin scratched his chin. "Yeah, I hear you. Except, well, there were witnesses. Folks who survived, who've painted a pretty clear picture of what happened that day, and from what they tell us, someone *did* go hunting. It was a peaceful protest until a cop opened fire."

Just like that, Fred's scarlet color returned. He jumped to his feet and pointed his stubby finger right at Kevin. "Those bastards threw a bottle of piss right at me! You can't tell me it was a fucking peaceful protest when they chucked a bottle of piss at me!"

Holcombe just raised an eyebrow. "Hm. Last time I checked, urine wasn't deadly.

Repulsive, yes. Deadly, no. It certainly doesn't authorize deadly force and especially not against people who can't be proven to have thrown the bottle.

"And you, absolutely, are the one who shot those protesters. The bullets recovered from their bodies have been in storage these ten years. They were a match to the one that killed Jason Harper. They were fired from your service weapon, Mr. Carey."

Fred sat back down. "Every one of those shootings was justified, and you know it."

Luis met his eyes. "You wouldn't have tried to frame Donovan for those murders if they weren't on your mind. You knew the anniversary was going to bring the murders back into the public eye, and you knew no one was going to believe your story about those shootings being justified. Either you knew, or you suspected, that witnesses would come forward now who would not have been heard then. You needed someone to take the fall and who better than the prodigal son?"

Fury rose inside Luis. This disgusting creature had tried to frame Donovan for his own monstrous crime, for no reason other than his own need to control.

"Stupid kid needs to do what he's told. And you just need to go the fuck away." Fred sneered at

Luis. "Go ahead. Arrest me for those shootings. No one's going to believe a cop would just start shooting people at random. With Donnie, you'd have had a case. A young cop, first riot, panic sets in. Sad, not really a crime and look at all the good he's done since then, right? You're seriously going to sit down in front of a jury and tell them a decorated cop with a spotless record went on a killing spree because he was mad someone chucked a bottle of piss at him?"

"I do believe that's exactly what we're going to do. And we're going to trot out plenty of witnesses to prove it. And plenty of evidence." Holcombe leaned forward, just a little. "Which do you think a jury will be more likely to believe—that a father will go for an elaborate setup to frame his son for murder just to teach him a lesson, but will somehow have had his service weapon stolen *and then returned to his own gun safe,* or that a father will set up his estranged son for a murder he himself committed? I know which scenario is more plausible, even without having to see the ballistic evidence."

Fred tried to stare her down but ultimately failed. "I think I'd better get a lawyer."

Holcombe glanced at Luis. It was time.

"You certainly have that right, but you'll be calling him from Nashua Street." Luis pulled out his cuffs and stood up. "You have the right to remain silent. Anything you say can and will be used against you in a court of law."

Kevin finished reading Fred his rights, and Luis got the cuffs on him and patted him down. He didn't find anything dangerous, but he'd have been surprised if he had. They didn't let civilians come into this building armed, after all.

The familiar surge of victory at the close of a case was there, but it had to fight for space with Luis' anger. Getting justice for those protesters and their families was a powerful feeling, and while Luis loved his work, he rarely got to feel as if he was quite such a part of a historic moment. At the same time, Fred could never repay what he'd done to Donovan.

Was it wrong for Luis to think of that now? He didn't know. Right now, all he knew was he had a partner to get back to.

Donovan got the text from Luis just as he was getting dinner ready. There were no words, just an image of Fred being led into Central Processing with his hands cuffed behind him. All Donovan could do was sit back and laugh. Fred looked like a lobster, red with rage and probably about ready to pinch someone too.

Donovan finished fixing dinner, and he gave Tria a few extra treats too. She'd been a great little companion through this whole thing. She deserved to share in his joy.

Once he'd finished plating dinner, he closed the curtains. Then he got rid of his clothes. He was going to show his appreciation, damn it, and that was all there was to it.

Luis must have broken several laws on his way back to Burlington from Nashua Street, because he walked in the door almost before Donovan had finished disrobing. Donovan could hear him downstairs, talking to Tria like she was a human.

"Hi, sweetie. How was your day? Did you catch some good sun spots? Did you take good care of Donovan today? I know you've been doing a good job of that. You want to sit on my shoulder? That's fine."

Donovan grinned and headed down the stairs. "She did, in fact, do a fantastic job of taking care of me today. Not as good a job as you did, from the looks of the text you sent."

Luis stared, and Tria batted at his nose. "Um. Yeah. Text. What?"

Donovan laughed. "Cat got your tongue?"

"Dude, all the blood in my brain just went south for the winter like a duck, okay? You can't expect me to put words together when you come down those stairs looking like that." Luis took a few steps forward.

Tria leaped down onto the couch, and Luis closed the distance to kneel on the stairs in front of Donovan.

He looked up at Donovan with his big brown eyes, shining with need and desire and everything else a man could feel, and spoke two words. "Let me?"

Donovan ran a hand through Luis' curly hair. "The whole point of all of this was supposed to be me doing something for you." He smiled. Who wouldn't smile with Luis looking up at him like that, like he was the whole world?

"You are. Believe me, you are." He rubbed his cheek on Donovan's bare inner thigh, stubble giving just enough sensation to make him hiss. "Please."

Donovan laughed a little. "I'm sure as hell not going to tell you no. Yes. Definitely."

Luis wrapped his lips around Donovan's swollen cock and swallowed him down. He didn't take his eyes from Donovan's; he just put his hands on Donovan's thighs and went for it. Usually, Luis would work up to something like this. Apparently, today, he was out of patience.

Donovan gripped the railing with one hand just to keep himself steady. His cock was suddenly engulfed in heat, tight friction and a determined rhythm set entirely by Luis. The rest of the world faded away. All he could see, feel, or hear was the man below him, working away as if his life depended on it.

He didn't last long. No one would have, not with Luis doing his best to make him erupt like Mount Vesuvius. He spilled, white-hot, down Luis' throat, and Luis took every last drop.

Donovan lost himself for a minute. When he came back to himself, he was seated on a stair.

Luis was still in his suit, although his dress pants had a telltale stain in the front. "You doing okay?" he asked, a huge grin on his face.

He looked more relaxed than Donovan had seen him since this whole thing had started. His voice had a little bit of a rasp, but Donovan had no doubts about why.

Donovan huffed out a little laugh and made sure Luis knew he was giving a hard look at his pants. "You got off just from that?"

"Hell yeah, I did." Luis got up and offered Donovan a hand. "I should go get changed."

"Meh. I mean, I'm sure those will get uncomfortable, but clothes are for the weak. Let's have dinner, and then maybe we can go for round two." Donovan followed Luis up to the bedroom.

Luis didn't hesitate to free himself of the shackles of clothing, but it didn't surprise Donovan. Donovan was usually the one who insisted on clothes just in case someone stopped by. Luis was the one who typically lacked shame. Today was no exception, and he quite happily flopped down onto the bed for a little rest time before they went back downstairs for dinner. Donovan joined him.

It occurred to Donovan as he reheated their food that he should probably feel something about his father being arrested, and by his partner. He didn't. Maybe it would sink in later. Maybe he'd wake up a few weeks from now and it would hit him like a ton of bricks. For now though, all he could think about was freedom.

True, nothing had been announced yet. Luis had apparently come straight home from Nashua Street. Donovan didn't know what was going on with Orlov, and he wouldn't feel comfortable going back to work until the situation with Internal Affairs was handled. Still, the biggest danger was out of the way.

His phone rang during dinner, with an incoming call from his mother. She was beyond furious, and she told him to put it on speaker so she didn't have to repeat herself.

"Can you believe that son of a bitch had the temerity to call *me* from prison?" If Patricia could have stabbed with the tone of her voice alone, Fred would have been dead in jail a long time ago. "He gets one phone call, and he uses it to call me. Me! He tried to claim I owed him. I hung up on him, like any sensible person. Hope he likes the public defender because I'm sure as hell not finding a lawyer for him."

Luis shook his head. "I guess it makes sense. He's in a scary situation, so he's returning to his older behavior patterns. It was a successful strategy for him during the times when he was happier, so he's reverting. Still—if there was ever a time when he should seriously be learning, this is it."

"I hope he rots in there. I hope someone sets his bunk on fire. I hope they put him in general population and tell everyone he's a retired dirty cop."

Donovan winced. His mom was one vindictive woman when she put her mind to it. "Yikes."

"Well, they're not putting either him or Porras in general population until after they're formally found guilty and sentenced." Luis sipped from his water. "But once that happens, I wouldn't be surprised to find you get your wish. How are people in Boston PD taking it?"

Patricia sighed. "One or two of them are calling it a setup, but they haven't seen the evidence. Once my place got firebombed, he lost most of his support. It's one thing when people thought rioters got shot in the heat of a riot, when things got out of hand. When *that* happened, people got a little more uptight. And now, well— the FBI isn't going to arrest a retired cop for something that happened ten years ago if it was just a mistake. Everyone knows that."

"Thanks, ma'am."

"Don't you ma'am me, Luis. You can just call me Patricia. You know better. Anyway, there are some real die-hards, but for the most part, people have come around. I'm a little more concerned about the state troopers, but you'd have to talk to Alicia about them."

"We'll do that, Mom." Donovan grinned over at Luis. "Probably tomorrow though. It's been a bit of a week, and right now, I'm kind of just wanting to hang out with Luis and process everything."

"Of course. I just wanted to let you know what an ass your father still is." Patricia hung up.

Donovan laughed, and Luis joined in after half a second. "Do you think she realized we're sitting here nude?" Luis hated to think of Patricia stuck with that image.

Donovan shuddered away from the thought. "I don't think she'd have reacted nearly as well. She's gotten over herself about me being gay and us being together. No parent wants to think about their kid having sex, even in his midthirties. That's just wrong." He laughed.

Then he sobered. "About what she said . . ."

"What, about the troopers?" Luis toyed with his water glass. "Holcombe and the people above her have been handling the discussions with them. My part of the case has been focused on the riots and how you were framed."

"Isn't Orlov part of that though?"

"He is and he isn't. You're part of the case against him just as he was part of the case against you might be a better way to frame it." Luis looked up at the ceiling. "I'm not sure how far it goes, to be perfectly honest with you. He's had his hand in a lot of pies, which is one of the reasons it's a whole separate investigation. I'm being kept separate from that investigation specifically because you were targeted, and it was a big deal for me to be part of this one.

"That said, a lot of state troopers have lost their jobs and their reputations because of Orlov. I'm not a hundred percent sure what he gets out of that, not without a deeper investigation. It could be a sense of power or control. He's not getting paid, I can tell you that much. Maybe he's just doing it because he's an incompetent investigator and he needs some way to pad his solve list, I don't know."

Donovan pursed his lips. "Unfortunately, I can't go back to work until the whole thing with Orlov and Internal Affairs is handled."

"I honestly don't know what's going to happen there. State police brass are going to find out you've been exonerated sooner or later. I mean, Boston PD already knows, Patricia just told us. And we'll probably do a formal announcement tomorrow, both of the arrest and clearing you. It's going to put a pretty big spotlight on the state troopers and some of what's been going on there."

"That's exactly what they didn't want." Donovan cringed away from the thought, remembering the talk with Power's boss.

"Funny how that works. The things we least want becoming public have a way of getting out into the light." Luis gave a nasty little grin. "I don't know if everything is going to be the same. In a lot of ways, I hope it isn't. They were willing to hang you out there, knowing you're innocent, just to avoid looking bad. That's unacceptable."

Donovan stared at Luis, and then he reached out and took Luis' hand across the dinner table. "You're going to make this some kind of crusade, aren't you?"

"Hell yeah, I am. I can pretend it's for noble reasons or whatever, because what they're doing endangers law enforcement everywhere and blah blah blah. It's true, but that's not why I'm doing it. I'm doing it because they threatened *you*, and I love you. It's that simple. It just happens to be the right thing to do."

Donovan gave Luis' hand a squeeze. "What the hell did I ever do to deserve this kind of love in my life?"

Luis grinned and squeezed back. "I don't know. Breathed?"

Donovan laughed.

CHAPTER NINETEEN

Luis headed back downtown under cover of darkness. He brought Donovan with him tonight, since the investigation was over now and he could get away with it. Donovan wasn't sure he wanted to be part of this aspect of the investigation, but he also wasn't okay with sending Luis into a haunted graveyard in a haunted city alone.

They walked along the red line of the Freedom Trail, dodging drunks and tourists.

"So the victims of the Boston Massacre are still just . . . hanging around?" Donovan looked around at the mixture of colonial and modern buildings. "Isn't that . . . I don't know, isn't that kind of a long time for innocent people to stick around? I know your buddy Lightfoot is still here, but he's kind of—well, he's got a kind of spotty record."

"He's a serial killer, Donovan." Luis grinned and opted not to tell him Lightfoot was walking behind him, leering at just about everyone he passed. "It's okay to say it."

"Okay. He's a serial killer. I can see why he's stuck here."

"I'm not stuck." Lightfoot put a hand on his chest, looking almost elegant. "I choose to be here. Who else would keep your arse on your side of the veil, hm?"

Luis fought back a snicker. "He's here by choice, actually. It might be the same situation for the folks in the Granary, although they might be held back by a different issue as well."

"Aye, now ye're talking sense." Lightfoot sloshed his gin around.

Encouraged, Luis continued. "They seem to have a real issue with state-sponsored violence. They remember the police strike in 1919, and not kindly—"

Donovan frowned and stepped around a confused teenager, possibly a college student. "Wait, they can't be mad at the cops for that one; it was the police who were the victims."

"The State still killed them." Luis eyed a woman, probably residual energy, running past with her dress on fire. The dress looked like something from the nineteenth century—Luis wasn't an expert, but if he had to guess, he'd put it there. "That's the point. And they saw Fred murder the protesters. I want them to know we made the arrest."

Luis couldn't quite put a finger on why he needed to update the five men in the Granary. He didn't report to the dead. It wasn't in his job description. At the same time, they'd provided him with information and he'd struck an agreement with them. It was important to him that they know this agent of the State, at least, was a man of his word.

They entered the graveyard without trouble. Technically, the historical burying ground was closed for the night, but Lightfoot hadn't ever been troubled by laws before. Locks hadn't exactly been a barrier either, and now, they were less. Donovan shoved his hands into his pockets and glanced furtively around as he shuffled along the brick paths, but Luis had gotten used to this by now. Even the smell only stood out a little bit.

"We'll have ye acting like a proper medium in no time." Lightfoot clapped him on the back. "Go on, call your mates."

Luis didn't need to call them. They seemed to sense his presence and appeared before him. Donovan, as usual, couldn't see them. He could smell them though and took a few steps backward.

"Well? You have news?" Crispus Attucks raised his eyebrow at Luis. "And who might your friends be?"

Luis had always wondered if ghosts from different eras could sense each other. He guessed he had his answer now. "I'd like you to meet my friend Captain Lightfoot, and the other gentleman is my partner, Detective Donovan Carey. He's the one the killer tried to blame for the murders."

Attucks approached and poked at Donovan.

Donovan jumped when the spectral finger jabbed into his ribs. "What the fuck?"

Attucks cackled at Donovan's reaction. "I see. He's perceptive, even if he isn't gifted enough to see us. He was there, although not close enough to have killed people. He helped people instead. He's a good man."

"He is." Luis found himself softening as he thought about Donovan. "He's the best."

"And he's why you sought out the killer."

Luis shook his head. "Hunting killers is my job. I'm not sure if I would have agreed to bring the killer to you if the trial went bad if it weren't for Donovan, but I'll hunt down killers from any background. I don't care if they're police, paupers, or kings."

Attucks tilted his head and gazed at Luis for a moment. "I believe you," he said after a moment. "And the murderer. He's been caught?"

"Yes. We made the arrest. His attorney took a look at the evidence against him and is strongly advising him to plead guilty."

"And they'll hang him." Attucks beamed.

"Er, no." Luis scratched behind his ear. "This is Massachusetts—"

"It's what the Common is *for*." This came from one of Attucks' companions.

"Aye." Lightfoot gestured to the rope around his own neck. "But times have changed and they no longer practice hanging in this state. Trust me, it was a shock to me system too. But they'll lock him away for a good long time, and at his age, it's as good as death. He'll never breathe free air again, and that's the honest truth."

Luis wondered if he should point out that some of the charges against Fred were in fact federal. He didn't think it would be helpful, and explaining the modern legal system to six dead men in the dark just didn't seem like his idea of a great time. "I wanted to thank you again for your help and to introduce you to the man you helped save. Is there anything I can bring you or offer you?"

The five men exchanged glances. "You've already helped us. All we've wanted, for centuries, was to stop what happened to us from happening to other people." This was from a different companion of Attucks' than the one who'd previously spoken.

"You gave us what we wanted." Attucks glanced back at his companions and then to Luis. "I thought once we had that, we might be able to leave this place."

"Why can't you?" The thought sprang from Luis' mind to his lips, bypassing any filters that would normally have caught it.

"The cemetery is surrounded by iron fencing. It doesn't bother me, but I'm a little different. Most spirits are bound by iron. It's why people used iron for boneyards in the first place." Lightfoot nudged Luis and reached out to the others. "Take my hand. If you want to leave, or even to move on, come with me." He winked and disappeared.

Luis looked outside of the Granary and found all six ghosts on the sidewalk in front of the graveyard. Three of the victims of the Boston Massacre smiled and turned into balls of bright light before disappearing.

A murmur went up among the small crowd of tourists and drunks who'd seen the phenomenon. It certainly hadn't been subtle.

"Time to go," Donovan told Luis.

"Yeah. Let's get out of here." Luis took Donovan's hand and fled the cemetery, taking back streets and alleys until he got them back to the car undetected.

Donovan was laughing when they strapped themselves into their seats. "Who knew you'd have such a good grasp of back-alley Boston?" He was beautiful. He'd always been beautiful, but it had been a long time since Luis had seen him freed from care like this. Maybe it hadn't been that long—maybe it just felt like it.

He leaned over the center console and claimed Donovan's mouth with a kiss. It wasn't the best kiss, not with the gearshift poking him in the side, but it was a kiss all the same. "I'm so in love with you," he said, and started the car.

Donovan was still grinning, but he stared at Luis as he drove. "What brought that on?"

"I just wanted to make sure you knew." He laughed. "And yeah, that was fun."

Donovan spread out a little. "Did Fred's lawyer really tell him to plead guilty?"

"Oh yeah." Luis scoffed. "The evidence is just too strong against him, you know? The dead told us where to look, but come on, what kind of cop doesn't know enough to get rid of the evidence?"

Donovan blew a raspberry. "We never meet the smart criminals, do we?" Then he sighed. "He never expected to get caught, and come on. It was his service weapon. When he did the crime, he couldn't get rid of it, and then after he retired, there was no way he was going to let go of it. We get those things the day we start at the academy, and we never part with them."

"He's lucky he's not getting a needle. That gun should have earned him a date with a very permanent punishment. I don't necessarily have an opinion one way or another when it comes to capital punishment, but mass murder, then murder to *cover up* the mass murder, then obstructing a federal investigation—I mean, there's a very real probability he'd be facing the death penalty here, and that gun is the strongest piece of physical evidence we have." Luis shook his head. "I know he's not stupid, but this—this is so arrogant it just jumps right into stupidity. It could have gotten him killed."

Donovan blanched. "You think so?"

"Yeah. I do." He glanced at Donovan. When he'd had doubts about being able to get Fred indicted for the protesters' murders, Donovan had been okay with Luis letting the ghosts get Fred out of the way. Now, the possibility of Fred being put to death for his crimes seemed to throw Donovan for a loop.

Luis spared a moment of gratitude for his foresight in not just letting the Boston Massacre victims do what they wanted.

Donovan rallied beside him. "So, what

happens now?"

"Well, hopefully, Fred and Porras both plead guilty, and we can all move on. The brass is moving forward with their investigation into Internal Affairs at the state troopers. After that, I'm not sure. I mean, you get your job back because there's no goddamn reason you should have been suspended to begin with. Hopefully, in that respect, at least we can get back to normal."

"You know what's getting to me?" Donovan thumped his head against the headrest. "Well, there are a couple of things bugging me right now, but the biggest thing is how none of this would have happened if it weren't for all these activists making goddamn sure we're held accountable for the things we do. I don't mean the shit with me and Fred. I mean finding out that Fred murdered five people in cold blood. He'd have gotten away with it, but then the activists all over the country made enough noise to make *this anniversary* important.

"And then he decided he needed to do something to cover it up. He panicked, so he did this, which is the only thing that led to the crime being investigated in the first place. And they put you on the case for ridiculous tokenism reasons, which sucks, but you're also the best there is. Fred basically dug his own grave here."

Luis ran his tongue against his teeth. "Yeah.

You're right. I want to think we'd have done something about the murders even without pressure from the community, but we'd have had to be invited and we wouldn't have been if Fred hadn't panicked and tried to frame you. And he panicked because of pressure from that community."

"Exactly." Donovan shook his head. "We *really* need to send Dwayne a fruit basket."

Luis grinned so wide it hurt. They'd come a long way since last fall. "Let's get on that. He's a good guy. I hope he finds someone who's good for him someday."

"Yeah?"

"Yeah. I hope he's as happy as I am, because I've got to say—this is pretty goddamn awesome." He took Donovan's hand and held it all the way home.

Donovan had become fond of Dwayne during this whole miserable ordeal, but the words coming out of his mouth had catapulted him back from *friend* to *Luis' ex* in no time at all. "Excuse me? I know the words coming out of your mouth were in English, but they can't have meant what I think they meant."

Luis struggled, and failed, to hide a smile.

"It's pretty simple, Donovan." Dwayne's voice was calm and smooth, almost good-natured. Like he hadn't just suggested the most ridiculous thing ever heard in human history. "There's a guy here from one of the biggest cable news stations in the country. They want to interview you, and I think it's a good idea."

Donovan considered throwing things but settled on a slow blink. "Still doesn't compute."

"Look, you're not going to be alone." Luis covered Donovan's hand with his own. "I've gotten clearance from Quantico to do the conference with you. The thing is, the state troopers are going to be having their own press conference, putting their own spin on what happened. It's wonderful that we got the real killer. Now we have an opportunity to set the record straight and counteract some of the damage they did to you specifically."

"Exactly." Dwayne nodded, eyes wide and earnest. "Plus, it will give you the chance to show that there are good cops who are willing and ready to stand up to the bad ones. Don't think of it as being just about you. Think of it as being about helping your whole profession."

Donovan pursed his lips and glared at Dwayne. "Goddamn it."

Dwayne's grin lit up the room. "So we can

go down to the church?"

Right, the church down in Mattapan. "Yeah, sure. Let's do it." Donovan rubbed at his face. "It's not like I can say no to that, can I?"

He and Luis got dressed in more professional clothes, and then all three of them piled into Donovan's car for the ride down to the little Pentecostal church. The film crew had set up in the basement, with some people from the community still there too. Apparently, they'd been interviewed for the segment as well. Donovan wondered how much of their testimony would be edited out.

The reporter introduced himself. Donovan had seen him a few times, on the rare occasions he watched the news. His name was Alistair, he was young, and he would probably go far in the business.

"Detective Carey, Agent Gomes, thank you for coming down. I'm glad you were able to join us on such short notice."

A crew member with an impressive beard quickly clipped microphones to both men. Someone had warned him to approach from the front, so neither Donovan nor Luis thought he was going for his gun. Smart work.

Luis smiled, slick and professional. "We like to be as transparent as possible at the FBI. I know that's not the reputation we have, but it's the truth. We're happy to provide information whenever we can."

Donovan almost believed it.

Alistair guided them to a set of chairs surrounded by powerful lights, and the interview began. "So, Detective, you were actually present at the riot?"

Donovan cleared his throat. "Can we maybe refer to it as a protest?" He squirmed a little in his chair. "I've been calling it a riot too, for ten years, but back then, I didn't know what any of it was really about. I went where I was told to go, I tried to keep people as safe as I could, and I didn't think too hard about what had happened farther up the trail until it came around to bite me. I figured— most of us probably figured—it was probably someone who panicked, which is bad but it's logic you can follow.

"It wasn't a riot. It was a protest. It was a *planned* protest, with permits and everything. There were police out there because city leaders were able to plan in advance, thanks to the permitting process. This wasn't a bunch of people coming together at random looking to loot and destroy. This was an organized, peaceful protest of people who were legitimately upset about an awful act of violence." Donovan wiped his palms on his pants.

Alistair nodded, but Donovan knew he did that a lot. He might agree. He might think Donovan had lost every last one of his marbles. There was no way to tell.

"And you were there in a professional capacity. We've had several people say you helped keep them from getting trampled. That makes you a hero."

Donovan shook his head. "No. I mean, yeah, I pulled people out of the crowd when it was clear they were hurt, but that's literally what I was getting paid to do. It would have been heroic to push for more of an investigation, but I didn't think to do that at the time. I regret that now."

"Even though your father would have been caught up then instead of now."

Donovan couldn't stop the dark chuckle. "Hindsight is always twenty-twenty, isn't it? Yes, even though I'd have lost nine somewhat-decent years with my father."

Alistair smiled gently. "And that's kind of the meat of the story, isn't it? The protests and the murders are one story. The frame-up is another."

Donovan's left leg bounced up and down. Maybe he should have talked to Father Geoffrey about this before he agreed to anything. He hadn't had time to process any of this. It had only been a couple of days since Fred's arrest, after all.

"I guess, yeah. It's . . . it's a thing. I'm still kind of working through it. From an enforcement perspective though, it all comes down to the same thing. Luis and I were just talking about this the other day."

"What's that?" Alistair leaned forward, just a little bit.

"Well, we'd never have found out who the killer was if Fred hadn't panicked. Him panicking made him decide to try to frame me, which led to the FBI investigation. The FBI didn't just shelve it, they assigned it to Luis, who has a great record of tracking down some absolutely terrifying killers and would be like a dog with a bone."

Alistair cleared his throat and glanced over at Luis. "Was there any concern over conflict of interest? There must have been. The accusations were against not just your partner but the man you actually live with."

Luis nodded, still cool and professional. "We did have some discussions about that, both at the local level and with more senior people at the Department of Justice. I did ask to be recused for precisely that reason. It was decided that I would continue to work the case but with a great deal of input and confirmation, to avoid even unconscious bias. For what it's worth, Detective Carey and I were not dating at the time of the protest."

Alistair chuckled. "I'm not sure of the extent to which that will matter. When did you start to suspect Fred Carey? Was it obvious immediately?"

Luis shook his head. "No, not at all. It took time, and even then, I wanted to confirm with some other people that my suspicions were valid. It's not a secret that Fred and I were never in each other's fan club, but there's a line between sniping at each other from a distance and actually arresting your partner's father for murder. Believe me when I tell you, *no one* wants to be that guy."

Donovan grimaced. Luis must have tied himself up in knots about that.

"Now, Detective, do you think your father tried to frame you as a crime of opportunity? Or do you think it was more of a calculated effort on his part?"

Donovan paused before answering. "Saying 'both' isn't going to be helpful here, is it?" He sighed and groped for the words he needed. "Fred and I were estranged and had been ever since I came out. I don't think he plotted to frame me for this from the time of the protest. I think when he panicked about the anniversary, he needed someone to pin the shootings on, and I was convenient. He wouldn't have done it to one of my siblings, but I was fair game.

"That said, it was a pretty elaborate plot. He

had to bring a bunch of other people into it. He had plenty of opportunities to say, 'Hold up, this is pretty wrong, in fact, it's the opposite of what I'm supposed to do as a cop.' So—It was definitely a calculated effort, but he did it because he felt he had to, not because he was sitting around looking to get revenge and this was the best plan he could find."

Donovan bit the inside of his cheek. He'd wanted to give credit to the protesters across the country who'd created Fred's panic in the first place, but they'd gotten sidetracked. Thankfully, Luis was right here and on the same page.

"We can't emphasize enough that Fred got caught because he panicked. He panicked because individuals and groups across the country have been working hard for a long time to make it clear that police violence against civilians isn't okay. Sometimes, things happen in the course of the job, and I think most people understand that, but the job isn't the free pass it used to be. Sometimes, it feels like your voice isn't being heard or that all your hard work isn't going anywhere.

"If *you* hadn't made Fred panic, he wouldn't have made the choices he did, which led to a deeper investigation. *You* led to the killer being taken off the streets. *You* also instigated a much deeper investigation into practices at other agencies. *You* held people accountable, whether you're in Saint

Louis, Baltimore, California, Arizona, New York, or Boston. It was you."

Donovan smiled and relaxed. "Thanks, Luis. I also need to thank Dr. Dwayne Mason. He was instrumental in helping to bring the community together and get justice for the people Fred killed. It's not something either of us could have done, I don't think. Dwayne has a long history of fighting for what's right. I'm glad I had the chance to work with him."

Alistair grinned. The facade of the cool newscaster was broken. All that was left was a young guy admiring someone else's work. "You totally did that on purpose, didn't you? I was going for the family drama angle, and you totally went for nobility and purpose."

Both Luis and Donovan laughed, and Donovan held his head up. "I'm not going to pretend I'm not more comfortable giving the credit where it's due. I'm serious. I hadn't put a whole lot of thought into who killed those protesters before now. I thought it was sad, but I didn't think a lot could be done about it. Now, I know better. It's been a big learning experience for me, and while it was pretty terrible to go through at the time, I think it was valuable experience.

"You know what else I learned? When the accusation came out, most of my colleagues in the department were disgusted. They wanted nothing to do with a killer cop. It hurt like hell to know they thought I was capable of something like that, but I'm glad to know they'd shun someone who'd do something so awful."

"That is good to know." Alistair shook his hand. "Thanks to both of you for coming in and speaking with me, seriously. I know you've been busy catching a killer and saving Donovan's career, but this story's been closely followed all over the country. Hearing from both of you will fill in so many of the blanks for people. I admit some people at the network wanted to get at more of the family drama behind it, but what you actually told us is arguably more crucial information. Thank you again."

"Glad to do it." And Donovan found he was. "I was nervous at first, but it gave us a chance to say thank you. Thanks for giving us the opportunity."

CHAPTER TWENTY

Luis crept up the shaky stairs in the dark. He knew Camila was downstairs, listening. He'd rather do this while she was out. He didn't want her to get hurt if things went seriously sideways, and he didn't want her to know if he screwed things up either. It was still the work week though, and he hadn't been able to justify sneaking down to the ancient triple-decker before now.

The whole top floor reeked of rot, so Luis didn't have to worry about whether or not Jason Harper would show. There was one worry down. He wasn't sure he hadn't substituted it for a bigger worry, but he'd cross that bridge when he came to it.

"Jason, it's me. Luis." He kept his voice soft, both because he knew he didn't have to shout and because he didn't want to have to take a deep enough breath to yell. It was all he could do to avoid gagging as it was. "Let's talk."

The form of Jason Harper coalesced in front

of him. He looked worse than he had the last time Luis had seen him. A mouse climbed up his exposed ribs, and that wasn't good. "What?" Harper screamed the word, rattling windows and making the lights flicker.

Luis sighed. He'd heard about angry ghosts like this. Kids' stories were full of them. He'd met plenty of angry ghosts, but their anger was more specific. Jason was just angry. It made him dangerous.

"There's no need to shout, Jason. I'm right here. The neighbors tell me you've been making things difficult for them."

"So?" Jason tried to shove Luis.

Luis had expected the gesture and pushed back with his mind. For Jason, it would have been like shoving a brick wall.

Lightfoot had taught him the technique, after Luis explained his plan. He didn't want to hurt Jason. He suspected, after reading Jason's file, he'd been hurt enough. Luis didn't want to get hurt either. Hopefully, this would work for everyone.

"So, what do you think happens to you if you burn the house down?"

Jason sneered. "At least I'll get to fucking leave! I haven't been able to get out of this apartment since I died! This is bullshit! It's like having an ankle monitor while your body decays around you.

Luis nodded slowly. "As near as I can tell—and I'm still pretty new at this, so bear with me—the way your body presents after death is representative of your mental state."

Jason stared.

"You're losing it. It's making you lash out, and it's also the reason you feel and look like you're falling apart. You need to move on. You're a danger to yourself and others."

Jason roared again. "I just told you I can't leave!"

Luis shrugged. "I might have a couple of ideas about that. Do you want to try them?"

"I thought you said you were new at this." Jason's tone had turned sullen, but at least he'd stopped shouting.

"I'm new to the whole ghost thing. I'm not new to how people work. It's my whole thing. And ghosts are just people, really. You're dead people, but you're people. I think part of what I need to do, if I'm going to help people in your situation, is go with what I know."

"You don't know shit about me. You're just some cop." Jason waved a hand and lost a finger.

Luis gestured toward the TV and gaming console. Jason curled his lip but went to sit down.

"You've been in the criminal justice system

since you were what, ten? I'm in the FBI, Jason. There's not much I can't find out." Luis turned on the console, sat on the couch beside the festering ghost, and picked up a controller. "Plus, we have some things in common."

"I ain't got shit in common with you."

"I lost my mom when I was eight." Luis kept his eyes on the screen as it warmed up. "Yours disappeared when you were ten. You didn't know this, no one managed to pass the information along to you when you were in juvenile detention, but she was found dead in Rhode Island two years later. She didn't leave you. She was murdered. I'm sorry to be the bearer of bad news, but that's something else we have in common."

Jason froze in place. Luis didn't want to get too hopeful, but some of the more grotesque aspects of Jason's torso seemed to heal. At least Luis couldn't see the mouse anymore.

"She didn't just run off with some guy?"

Luis shook his head. "No. She loved you. She had your school picture in a locket on her body when she was found. You were deeply loved, Jason."

"I started stealing after she—well, after she got killed, I guess. I needed food." Jason clicked over to a game. Luis didn't recognize it. He wasn't a big gamer. It didn't look like one Alicia would

398

ever let Nicky play though. "It kind of kept on going from there, I guess."

"You grew up pretty fast from that point on. It's not an excuse. You did some pretty crappy things. But your dad was a criminal too. It was kind of the family business, right?" Luis forced himself not to roll his eyes. He seemed to be assigned to play a character in some kind of shoot-'em-up game. Fabulous. He hated shooter video games, but this wasn't about him.

"Yeah. It was what it was. I didn't think there was anything else out there for me."

"There were opportunities and possibilities, but you'd have needed help to see them. You were a kid. Your dad probably meant well, but he didn't have much to go on. I did reach out to him. Yesterday, I mean. He's in the infirmary at Walpole."

"He got picked up for dealing a couple of years ago." Jason shook his head. "It was one of those things. I mean, yeah, he's been dealing a long time. Ain't like he ever got rich from it."

"That's the truth." Luis nodded. "He loves you too. He says he knows he was hard on you sometimes. He says he tried to give you the skills you'd need on the street. He didn't see a big life outside of what he knew or, I guess, not a lot of opportunity. Which is sad, but I think he was providing for you in the only way he knew how."

"Sure. Whatever." Jason glared. "I should've gotten to be a kid a little longer, maybe. I don't know. Maybe I'd have liked to do a sport or something. Maybe I'd have been good at art."

"Notes from your teachers suggest you had a gift for math. None of them seem to have shared that with you or done much to encourage you to pursue math. The thing with cases like this, for me, is that I have a great privilege. It's very easy for me to look back over the decades and say, 'Here's where an intervention could have changed things. Here's where pushing him just a little more toward this gifted program might have kept him from going to jail later on.' What I'm not able to see is what that other person was dealing with that day. Maybe on the day the teacher could have made the recommendation her mother'd just had a stroke, her kid dragged home a friend who couldn't find his mom, and she had to fill out paperwork to support suspicion of abuse. She might not have had the bandwidth. Yeah, making that recommendation would have changed things, but it was the last thing on her mind because of all this other stuff."

Jason bowed his head. "And not because I just wasn't worth it." A few more pieces of flesh seemed to pull themselves over his skeleton. Even the stink dissipated, just a little.

"Exactly. Don't get me wrong, I'm not condoning some of the choices you made."

"What, like lying on your boyfriend?" Jason curled his lip.

"Actually, I don't care about that."

Jason dropped his controller. "What?"

"I did at first, don't get me wrong. The guy's own father told you he'd shoot you if you didn't. You're not going to go playing hero for some guy you don't know." He cleared his throat and handed Jason his controller. "The day you were killed, we were on our way down here to check on you. Not to hurt you, not to arrest you, but to warn you and make sure you were okay. It was too late."

Jason shook his head. "I don't know, man. I really don't. I just—cops don't show up to check on guys like me. I'm not worth their time, unless they want something."

"That's true for some." Luis wasn't going to lie to him. "But for others, we legitimately want to help. Yes, guys like you. Sometimes, the same cop could go one way or the other, depending on the day." Luis laughed. "I'm not going to pretend I'm above it either."

"You really think I could've been somebody?" Jason's voice sounded smaller, even younger.

"I think you *are* somebody. You're somebody now, you were somebody in life. You did things that weren't so great. You also gave me information that led to a mass murderer being sent to prison. I'm sure you've done some other good things in your life."

"We found a little kid." Jason seemed to shrink as he sat beside Luis, de-aging as he played the video game. "He was, like, three. I think he wandered off from his mom or something, in the park. We stayed with him for, like, eight hours. I sent my buddy out for some juice and one of those crackers-and-cheese things they sell in the supermarket, we kept that little guy happy until his mom found him." He looked over at Luis, somehow fifteen again. "You know the pigs would've arrested her and put him in the system."

Luis nodded. They probably would have. "That's a pretty damn good thing you did."

"I bought her groceries too one time." He blushed. He was probably thirteen now. "I stayed in touch. She didn't want me around anymore after my next arrest though."

"It happens. You respected that, right?"

"Yeah." He was ten now. "I did some bad things, I know."

"You did. But you paid for them. It's okay to go now."

Luis was ready for the bright glow. He wasn't ready for the clatter of the controller as it fell to the floor.

Donovan had gotten the notification—formal, written notification, none of this untraceable phone call stuff for the Massachusetts State Police—to report back to work for "assignment." He wasn't sure how he felt about it. On the one hand, sitting around the house playing happy housewife was starting to chafe something fierce.

On the other hand, Donovan already had an assignment. He'd *earned* that detective badge. He'd earned that day shift slot. He'd worked goddamned hard; he'd done nothing wrong. He shouldn't have to report for *assignment*. He should be able to just get back to work.

Luis glanced at the notification and set his jaw. "Want me to sic Kevin on this? I think he's technically a lawyer. Or I can ask Dwayne for a recommendation. He knows a few who would probably take this on for free."

Donovan shuddered at the thought of bringing in an activist lawyer to take on an internal police matter. The union might have his back if he at least showed up and found out what the assignment was. They'd hang him out to dry again, if he even thought of bringing one of the "enemy" lawyers in. "Let's leave that as a last resort."

So in the end, he dressed and went to Framingham the same way he usually would, before any of this mess had started, and alone. His stomach tied itself into knots all the way down, but he ignored it. His stomach had tied itself in knots on the day of the protests ten years ago, but that hadn't stopped him from helping people. He could function without it, if he had to.

Hey, look at that! This old dog might have learned a new trick after all. He'd learned and grown from this wretched experience. He huffed out a little laugh and accelerated, just a bit.

Of course he had to sign in because he didn't have his badge or access pass. It was one more humiliation at his father's hands, but he could bear it. He had to sign in, but Fred was sitting in a cell waiting for sentencing and was heading for someplace where humiliation was routine. Donovan would get over this.

Lt. Power appeared. He looked grim as ever, but he smiled broadly when he saw Donovan. "It's good to see you home, son." He wrapped an arm around Donovan's shoulder and guided him into the building. "I don't know if you're aware, if you've stayed in touch with anyone over the past

404

week or so, but there've been a few changes."

Donovan raised his eyebrows. Lt. Power wasn't guiding him toward Major Crimes. He was guiding him toward the area where the brass sat. "No, I've been a bit of a pariah. What's going on?" Did this have something to do with reporting for *assignment*? Was Major Crimes being dissolved?

Power led him toward a conference room. "I thought maybe one of your FBI friends would have told you something. You know, under the circumstances."

"They've kept Luis very sealed off from anything to do with investigating the state police, for obvious reasons." Donovan cleared his throat. "What's going on, sir?"

Power opened the conference room door. The room was filled with state trooper brass, people so highly placed Donovan didn't even recognize them. He did know one of them—his cousin Alicia, who wasn't brass but was there anyway.

Major Wilson, from Human Resources, rose. "Good morning. Thank you for joining us. As you're aware, the past few weeks have been fraught here at headquarters. Recent events have proven that the state police have some issues that we need to work out. Several people have been relieved of their duties, effective immediately."

Power gestured to an empty seat beside Alicia. Donovan hadn't seen her in her dress uniform before, only in SWAT gear or street clothes.

Another commander, one in full uniform whose insignia showed him to be a lieutenant colonel, cleared his throat and grimaced. "What has happened with regard to the accusations against you has led to a certain amount of introspection here. Having the FBI open up civil rights and corruption investigations against us didn't help."

"They did that on their own, sir." Donovan might be getting fired, but he wasn't going to go without speaking up for himself.

"And it's a good thing they did. It's uncomfortable. It should be. We've gotten . . . maybe complacent. We didn't want to get rocked by yet another scandal, but it seems like maybe we should have been concerned with why we're getting hit by so many. What is it about our culture that is causing so many people associated with our agency to think they can get away with shady, unethical behavior?" The lieutenant colonel put his fingers into a steeple position in front of his face.

"The detective captain in charge of Internal Affairs has been discharged. Detective Captain Power has agreed to take on the position, with the provision that we understand he will cooperate fully with the FBI investigation and he will pull people in from other departments to replace anyone he sees fit.

"This leaves us with a dilemma. We have an opening at the top of Major Crimes. In theory, we should post the position and leave it open to competition. Under the circumstances, however, we feel the department needs someone at its head whose ethics and whose record are unquestionable and who already knows the department."

"You, Detective, already fit that description." Power put a hand on Donovan's shoulder. "In addition to your incredible track record, what you just endured means you've been vetted far more thoroughly than anyone else in the department. We need that right now. We need you right now. And there's no one else I'd want to see sitting behind my desk."

Donovan's head spun. He didn't think he was ready to take on the responsibility of running the department. Then again, did anyone? "Are you sure about this, sir?" If he focused on Power, he didn't have to think about all the brass watching. "Are you sure I'm ready?"

"Sure as I've ever been. There'll be an adjustment period, but I know damn well you'll work your ass off to succeed. It's not like I'm going anywhere. I'll be right here to guide you in terms of the administrative stuff that comes with the job." Power stared into Donovan's eyes.

"Then I'll do it, sir."

Alicia passed him his gun and badge, which had been stored in a box. "You're going to have to dust off your dress uniform, cuz." She winked. "Management has to go to a lot more functions than staff."

"Congratulations, Lieutenant Carey, and welcome home."

ALSO BY J. V. SPEYER

Hollywood Lighting
Faith
See Ya, Space Cowboy
Under His Skin
Rites of Spring
All This Could Be Yours
Nine Cocktails
Building Up To Love
Absolution
Paper Hearts
Snowed In – Ross and Ashton
Professional Courtesy
Hunter
Whirlwind
Carriage House
The Dented Crown
Starlit
Midnight

ABOUT THE AUTHOR

J. V. Speyer has lived in upstate New York and rural Catalonia before making the greater Boston, Massachusetts, area her permanent home. She has worked in archaeology, security, accountancy, finance, and nonprofit management. She currently lives just south of Boston in a house old enough to remember when her town was a tavern community with a farming problem.

J. V. finds most of her inspiration from music. Her tastes run the gamut from traditional to industrial and back again. When not writing, she can usually be found enjoying a baseball game or avoiding direct sunlight. She's learning to crochet so she can make blankets to fortify herself against the cold.

J. V. can be found at www.jvspeyer.com, on Twitter or Instagram at @JVSpeyer, or on Facebook at https://www.facebook.com/JVSpeyerAuthor. You can get exclusive updates, cocktail recipes, and other notes here: http://eepurl.com/dtlwBH